Following Me

K.A. LINDE

DIAMOND GIRLS SERIES

Rock Hard • *A Girl's Best Friend*

In the Rough • *Shine Bright* • *Under Pressure*

PARANORMAL ROMANCE

BLOOD TYPE SERIES

Blood Type

Blood Match

Blood Cure

YOUNG ADULT FANTASY

ASCENSION SERIES

The Affiliate

The Bound

The Consort

The Society

The Domina

in the least likely of

you won't know how

...out. It's like

you. foll...

how hope blo...

likely of circumstance

CHAPTER ONE

Chicago Bound

DEVON SAWYER SKIPPED to the next song on her iPod and adjusted the small earbuds to fit more comfortably. She bobbed her head to the '90s punk rock blasting through her headphones, her blonde hair falling around her face. She was thankful that no one else was clued in to her choice of music. She wanted to listen to something that felt comfortable to her, and her older brother's music always did the trick.

The train rattled along on its course. It had pulled out of the countryside and moved into the suburbs until it would finally reach the heart of Chicago. During the six-hour train ride from St. Louis into the city, Devon couldn't quit biting her nails. They weren't particularly long to start out with, but they were quickly turning into stubs.

Her feet tapped softly against the carpeted floor as she stared out the closed window at the passing flatlands and cornfields prominent in the Midwest. Since stepping onto the first train with nothing more than her purse and carry-on suitcase, she hadn't paid much attention to anything. Although she was still focused on the end of term and her immediate departure, she couldn't stop thinking about the one thing she didn't want to think about.

But she had made her decision. For better or for worse, she had left St. Louis.

"Next stop, Chicago Union Station," the conductor called over the intercom.

Devon popped up from her daydream. One of her earbuds fell out as she straightened in her seat. She looked down at the open notebook sitting in her lap. Words filled the pages, but she couldn't remember writing them down. Reading the first few lines only intensified her despair, and she decided not to continue with the rest at the moment.

A stewardess walked through the cabin, smiling at the passengers as she stamped their tickets. Devon had the last seat on the train, and the woman was fast approaching her. She averted her eyes, hoping the woman would just leave her be. The last thing she wanted was to talk to a peppy stewardess.

Devon was out of luck.

"Miss," the stewardess said, leaning into her chair.

Devon ignored her.

"Miss. Excuse me, miss?"

Devon pulled out the other earbud, shut her notebook, and turned to face the woman. "Yes?"

"Did you want anything else from the cart before we enter the station?"

"No, thank you," Devon answered.

"Here, let me stamp your ticket," she said, reaching out her hand.

Devon bent down to retrieve her bag, and then she began rifling through it to locate the ticket.

"So, why are you traveling to Chicago?" the woman asked, making polite conversation.

"Just meeting a friend," Devon said.

"That sounds fun," she said.

When Devon glanced up at her, the woman gave her an even bigger smile.

"How long are you staying?"

"Uh..." Devon murmured, trailing off as if looking into her bag distracted her. "As long as I want, I guess. Haven't really thought that far."

"Wow! You're just picking up and going?" the stewardess asked, surprised.

"It's my summer break, and I have some friends in the city,"

Devon told her, not sure why she felt like she had to justify it.

"Neat. Are you at a school in St. Louis then?"

She finally located her ticket and handed it to the woman. Devon was ready for the woman to leave. "Yep. Washington University."

"That's a great school! My son always wanted to go there, but we just couldn't afford a private school, you know?" She placed a stamp on the ticket and returned it to Devon.

"Sure," Devon said, not really understanding.

Her parents had told her she could go to whatever school she wanted. They were songwriters in Nashville, and business was good. Devon had wanted to start over and move far away from the South into a new city. Her parents would have preferred an Ivy League education if she were going to leave, but Devon hadn't gotten into the Big Three.

Wash U was close enough to Ivy anyway. Plus, as soon as she had stepped onto campus, she had fallen in love with the school. Everything from the brick castle-like edifices to the large open grounds to the people she had met on her tour had pulled her in completely. She had spent the last three years there, and now, she didn't know if she would ever go back.

Swallowing down the lump in her throat, Devon reminded herself that she had made the right decision by leaving. She had to get away. She just needed to keep telling herself that.

The train began to slow as high-rises flew past the surrounding windows.

"That's my cue!" The stewardess jumped up. "Have a fun trip in Chicago," she called before bustling about through the cabin.

Devon stood and collected her bags. The passengers were cast into darkness as they rolled into Chicago Union Station. As the train rattled to a stop on the tracks, she pushed her way through the crowd. She was more than ready to be off the train. A man swung his bag backward, catching her in the ribs, and she grunted.

"Sorry," the guy muttered, not even glancing at her.

Devon knew she was on the shorter side, but she wished people would be more considerate. She pushed past him and got off the train, struggling to bring air back into her lungs.

As the crowd headed for the exit, people jostled her on all sides. Relieved to be out of the fray, Devon lugged her bag with effort into the train station. It was white marble in every direction with a high-arch glass ceiling, enormous pillar entranceways, and benched seating. Standing there to admire it all, Devon thought it was beautiful.

She had only been to Chicago once with her parents during her junior year of high school. They'd had some kind of music appearance, and she had spent most of her time in the hotel room while her younger sister had followed her parents around the event. The record label her parents worked for had put them up in a suite, and in no particular order, Devon had alternated between the Jacuzzi tub, pool table, and minibar. She had regretted not getting to see much more of the city.

She craned her neck, looking around the giant room for her

friend. Hadley was supposed to be picking her up. Devon wasn't about to try to traverse the subway or L all by herself.

She turned around and nearly ran smack dab into someone.

"Sorry," she muttered, moving around the stranger.

Then, she found Hadley standing there. She was staring down at her cell phone, ignoring the masses swarming around her.

"Hadley!" Devon called. "Hadley Bishop!"

Hadley turned around and rushed toward Devon. "Hey," she cried, throwing her arms around Devon. "So glad you made it. I just couldn't believe it when you called and said you were coming to the city!" Hadley released her and took a step back.

"I know. I'm so last minute," Devon said.

"Oh, whatever," Hadley said shoving her phone into her front pocket. "You know you always have a place with me."

"Thanks," Devon said appreciatively.

"Need help with anything?" Hadley asked, looking Devon up and down to see if she had other stuff with her.

"Nope. Just this." Devon motioned to her oversized purse and suitcase.

"All righty! This way then," Hadley told her, motioning back toward the trains.

Devon followed with a smile plastered on her face. She had missed her friend more than life itself. Hadley had graduated from Wash U in December, leaving Devon without a roommate for the spring semester. Hadley always did exactly what she wanted. For instance, she had graduated early, moved to Chicago, and accepted a job at a high-end marketing firm. It was just something Devon would have never thought to do. In fact, this whole trip was something that Hadley, not Devon, would do.

Thankfully, Hadley knew her way around the metro. They took a seat on the train, and Devon angled her body to face her friend. She had forgotten how much they looked alike.

Devon's parents had always said that she looked like country music royalty. She didn't know if it was because she had a small, curvy body that looked great on camera or because her mother had started bleaching her naturally light brown hair in middle school. Magnifying the country music image, her parents had dressed her in cowboy boots and a hat, had her belt out every song on the radio, and paraded her around to every music venue they could get her into. Since leaving for St. Louis, she had resisted all of these things except for her blonde hair. She hadn't been able to get rid of the blonde.

Hadley was taller than Devon by a couple of inches. They had the same blonde hair. Though Devon had seen Hadley change it to black, brown, red, and every color in between in the two and a half years they had lived together. They used to have similar styles, but now Hadley was moving toward business professional, and Devon was stuck in her jeans, even in the summer heat. It made Devon wish she had packed some dresses.

"So," Hadley began, "are you hungry?" She crossed her right leg over her left, crinkling her grey pantsuit.

She looked positively radiant. Devon wasn't sure she had ever seen Hadley quite like this.

"Yes, I am," Devon said staring at her friend. "There's something different about you. I can't put my finger on it."

"I moved in with someone!" Hadley squeaked, unable to hold in her excitement.

"Already?" Devon asked, her mouth falling open. "You've only been here for six months!"

"I know! It's so new and so fresh, and I probably shouldn't, but I did. I just had to! Wait until you meet him. You'll see he's perfect!" Hadley gushed.

Devon tried to keep her smile as natural as possible. She had hoped that they would spend time together, just the two of them, like old times. Not that she wasn't happy for her friend. She was. It would just be different.

"Congrats. I'm so happy for you," Devon told her. "That must be why you're practically glowing."

"You have no idea, Dev. You'll get to meet him tonight. Can't wait!"

The L slowed down and Hadley stood, indicating that this was their stop. Devon stared down the stairs, cursing the person who had decided escalators weren't needed in this town. Flying down the stairs in front of Devon, Hadley seemed to forget her earlier offer of assistance. Devon grumbled under her breath as she hauled her bag to the ground level.

"We're going to go this restaurant that I love. It's kind of a you-have-to-know-it type of place. I think you'll like it. It's right around the block, so let's eat first, and then we'll take your stuff to my place," Hadley said, walking into traffic without a backward glance.

She's going to kill herself, Devon thought. She waited for traffic to stop before following Hadley.

"What is this place?" Devon asked when she finally caught up. As she rolled her suitcase behind her, it made clicking sounds every time it hit a bump in the sidewalk.

"Just a restaurant. Nothing fancy, but my friend Brennan works there as a bartender. It's the place right now if you know what I mean," she said.

Hadley turned down an alleyway and then immediately walked into a restaurant. Devon hadn't even seen the door. She read the sign, Jenn's Restaurant, over the door and went inside.

Hadley was right about the restaurant. It wasn't anything fancy, but the place was slammed. It was on the smaller side, and all the tables and booths were full of young professionals still in their suits after leaving work. Although some had stripped down to their button-up shirts, Devon felt woefully underdressed even if the atmosphere was welcoming.

As Hadley veered through the crowd, people on all sides called out hellos to her. She elbowed a couple out of the way and took the last two remaining seats in front of the bar.

"You're popular," Devon muttered, plopping down in the seat next to her.

Hadley had always been popular though. She radiated energy, and people seemed to gravitate toward her spontaneous personality. Hadley always seemed to be going, going, going and waiting for life to catch up with her. Devon had missed Hadley's fast-paced mindset.

Hadley just shrugged with a confident smile on her face. "Ay! Walker!" she called, leaning over the edge of the bar. When he didn't immediately respond she called out again, "Brennan!"

The bartender turned in their direction and shot Hadley an exasperated expression. He was good-looking in the she-shouldn't-go-anywhere-near-that kind of way. He had devious eyes and a knowing smile that made Devon wonder what secrets he had tucked up his sleeves. He wore a barback uniform of black slacks and a white button-up rolled up to his elbows with a towel slung over his shoulder. His brown hair was styled in a way that made it appear he hadn't spent any time on it.

"Gimme me a minute, Hadley. I'm with a customer," Brennan called.

"What do I look like?" she asked with a sassy smile.

"An annoyance," he said loud enough for everyone to hear.

While the other customers snickered like this interaction was commonplace, Devon was having a hard time peeling her eyes off of the bartender.

He definitely has bad news written all over his pretty face, she thought

Hadley huffed but slumped back into her seat with a roll of her eyes. "He's always like this. You can't get his attention even when it's not this busy."

Devon nodded, feeling completely out of her depth in the big city.

A couple minutes later, Brennan walked over to them and rested his forearms on the front of the bar. He cocked a smile like he owned the place. "The usual?"

"Yeah." As Brennan began pouring her drink, Hadley continued, "This is my friend Devon. She's here visiting on her summer break."

"Hey," he said, tipping his head at her while he mixed the drinks. "I'm Brennan."

"Hey," Devon murmured back, meeting his gaze.

"Where ya from?" He slid Hadley's drink toward her and began making another.

"Well, I go to Wash U in St. Louis, but my parents live in Nashville," she told him.

He slid a mostly clear drink across the bar to her. Devon cautiously picked it up.

"You don't seem much like a Southern belle to me," he observed.

"You'd be surprised," Hadley butted in. "Her parents work in the country music industry. She's a Southern belle through and through."

"Huh," he said as if contemplating this information.

Then, he just shrugged his shoulders like he had come to a conclusion. Devon wondered what it was.

"Well, you two having dinner?"

"Yeah," Hadley told him. "I'll have the chicken, and she's going to want the shrimp."

Devon glanced over at her in frustration. They hadn't even

looked at a menu.

"I promise you'll like it, Dev. Don't worry!"

Brennan nodded and then left to go put in their orders. Devon noticed he wasn't bad to look at from the backside either.

"I'm so glad you're here," Hadley cried, throwing her arms around Devon. "I have so much to show you. How long can I keep you?"

"Oh," Devon began, not yet figuring out how to have this conversation, "only for a week or so probably."

"Well, when is your return ticket?" Hadley asked.

"I didn't get one," Devon said.

It was totally something Devon would have never done. She always came with a plan, but this hadn't been planned. She had decided she was leaving, and then she had left. She had needed to get away and leave the life that was haunting her, destroying her. It hadn't been an easy decision.

But she couldn't tell Hadley any of that. Devon was so happy to see her friend, and maybe all she needed was a week or so for things to get better. She couldn't run away from her life forever even if she wanted to.

"Whoa!" Hadley cried, putting her hand on Devon's forehead. "You're turning into me. How is Reid taking all of this?"

"Oh, Reid's fine," Devon told her. "He's, you know, perfect."

Hadley gagged. "If that boy could get any more perfect, I'd fall dead."

Devon offered a stilted laugh. "Yeah, me too."

"I'm just surprised he didn't bring his ass with you. You two were connected at the hip last year."

"Well, he's spending a lot of time at home in Kansas City. Plus, he has to start applying to med schools this year. I know he wants to go to Wash U since his dad is a legacy. It's one of the best in the country, but he's also applying elsewhere," Devon informed her, feeling like she'd had this conversation too many times already.

"That just means I get you all to myself," Hadley said, grabbing Devon's arm and pulling her close. "Lucky me."

"Yep. Lucky you," Devon responded, wincing.

CHAPTER 2
Home Sweet Home

Devon stared at the impossibly tall, circular buildings where Hadley lived. She said the complex was called Marina City. All Devon knew was that it was way nicer than any place she expected to live in after graduation. The two buildings boasted the House of Blues, a full-scale hotel, and a working marina where people could dock their boats. It was all a bit overwhelming.

"Come on," Hadley laughed at Devon while dragging her through the residential entranceway toward the elevator.

They took the elevator up to the forty-third floor where it

deposited them on a rounded track leading to Hadley's apartment. She jiggled the key into place and stepped inside. Following close behind, Devon took in the small apartment.

It wasn't much bigger than her apartment in St. Louis, and based on the location, Devon was pretty sure it cost triple what she was paying. The layout resembled a slice of a pie, with hallways on each side of the entrance leading into bedrooms, a small kitchen off to the right, and an L-shaped living room with a conjoined dining room. The best part was obviously the view through the floor-to-ceiling glass wall that led out onto the balcony, overlooking Michigan Avenue, Grant Park, the Chicago River, and beyond to Lake Michigan.

Being the Windy City and all, Devon briefly wondered how cold it got up here in the winter. She was cold enough in St. Louis without being forty-three floors high.

"Make yourself at home. Garrett won't be back for another hour or so. I hate how late he works, but at least it's not the night shift. I hate when he has to work the night shift." Hadley tossed her bag onto the couch and turned to face Devon. "We have an extra bedroom if you go through the door on the left. You can put your things in there."

"Thanks," Devon said, walking into the guest bedroom. She placed her bag at the foot of the queen-size bed and stared around the room.

Devon could tell that Hadley had decorated this room. It didn't look like anything a guy would have put together. Long white panel curtains hung from the glass wall, which opened to its own balcony. The bed had a pretty patterned quilt on it with a couple of matching pillows. A dark wooden five-drawer dresser sat against another wall, and large paintings of flowered landscapes were displayed around the room.

Walking toward the balcony, she flipped the lock, slid back the door, and walked out onto the platform. It was really a very pretty view. So much to see and so little time, Devon thought.

She pulled out her phone from her pocket to check her email. She immediately deleted a newsletter from Wash U along with a series of spam emails. As her finger lingered over the next one, she bit her bottom lip, indecision creasing her forehead. She really wanted to read it, but she couldn't do it.

Not having the courage to just delete the email, she moved it to a separate folder. Out of sight, out of mind.

Just as she was scrolling to the next email, her phone lit up. She stared down at the screen, letting it ring a few more times, before steeling herself and answering.

"Hey, Mama," Devon said.

"Hey, Dixie!" her mom cheerfully called into the phone.

"Mom," Devon complained, "it's just Devon now."

"You'll always be my Dixie girl," her mother drawled.

Devon was pretty sure she would never convince her mother otherwise. "I know, but can't you just give it a try? You named me after all."

"Why do you have to be so difficult? Dustin and Dani don't

seem to have your propensities."

"You must have screwed me up real good," Devon joked.

"Always have to blame me," her mother said.

"It's not like it's Dad's fault."

"Oh, shush! You know I just miss you," her mom said, tears spilling into her voice.

"Miss you, too, Mom," Devon said softly.

"When are you coming home? Reid can't steal you for the entire summer. Your father and I have a big event in July, and we'd really like you to come. I know you'll want to bring him. It's so close to your birthday, and we'd like to celebrate with you, honey."

"I don't know, Mom," Devon answered uncertainly.

She had already told her mom that she was going to stay in St. Louis for the summer. This was already the second or third attempt to get her to come home. Devon hadn't been able to tell her mom that she had left. Her mom wouldn't understand her reasoning.

"Oh, come on, Dixie...Devon," her mother quickly corrected. "I'm only asking for a bit of time. You've been away for so long, and I haven't heard from you as much lately."

"I know. I've just been so busy."

"I know you are, honey, and I'm so proud of you. I just feel like we haven't talked as much this year. Are you sure everything is okay?" her mother pleaded.

"Yeah, Mama. Everything is fine," Devon lied, taking in a deep breath.

She didn't want her mother to pry. She was hitting too close to home, and Devon couldn't talk about it.

"All right," her mom said. "Well, think about July. We're going to New York, and I know how much you love the big city. I'll take you to see shows on Broadway, and we can go shopping, have cocktails at fancy parties—"

"That all sounds great, Mom," Devon told her wistfully. "I just don't think I'll be able to make it."

"You can bring Reid with you if you want, dear," her mother said, offering a plea bargain.

"Thanks, but I don't think he'll be interested. He's taking the MCAT and applying to med school. You know how important that is to him."

"I know, but…" she began, clearly biting her tongue.

"But what?" Devon couldn't stop herself from asking.

"I think you spend too much time with that boy, that's all," her mom responded quietly.

"I'll be fine. Don't worry so much."

Her mom sighed. "Well, think about New York. I miss you, and I know it would mean a lot to your father to have you there."

"All right, I'll think about it, but I'm not making any promises. I have to go though. Love you," Devon said.

"Love you, too."

Devon quickly ended the call. She buried her head in her hands and took a few steadying breaths, trying to remind herself over and over that she was doing the right thing. Lying to her mom was the hardest thing in the world to do, but she couldn't be in St. Louis.

She wished that she could really talk to her mom. She wasn't wrong when she had said that Devon had stopped talking to her. If only things were the way they had been when she was younger, when she had told her mother everything. But things had changed so much since then.

Stuffing her phone into the pocket of her pants, she left the balcony and walked back into the living room.

"Sorry about that. My mom called," Devon told Hadley.

Hadley was stretched out across the couch, watching Millionaire Matchmaker on the mounted television. She had a proclivity for bad reality shows and Lifetime movies. Devon had never understood her obsession, but Hadley had often referred to it as her only flaw.

"Shhh! Patti is about to bitch out the girls. It's the best part." Hadley's eyes were glued to the television.

Devon laughed and shook her head. At least some things hadn't changed. Taking a seat next to her friend, Devon watched the woman on TV work her magic. She was pretty sure they had already seen this episode.

Devon easily fell back into the simplicity of living with Hadley. They had always been easy living mates. She couldn't even remember if they had argued over anything more than whose turn it was to empty the dishwasher. Devon had taken a chance her freshman year and allowed Housing to choose her roommate. She had won the jackpot. Even though Hadley had been a sophomore, they had gotten along perfectly.

The year before, Hadley had had a terrible experience with a roommate that she knew from home. After that, she had decided to live in the dorms again and chance fate with a stranger. They had stayed in the same room the next year as well. It had helped that the dorm had been renovated the summer before to an apartment-style layout with small bedrooms, a communal living room, and a kitchen with granite countertops and stainless steel appliances.

Last year, they had opted to move into an off-campus apartment. When they had made the decision, Devon hadn't thought that Hadley would be graduating early. After Hadley had moved out, Devon had spent all her time with Reid. Even with him there though, the apartment had felt empty without Hadley.

"Where are your cups?" Devon asked, standing during a commercial break.

Hadley pulled out her phone and immediately started texting. "Second cabinet on the left from the refrigerator."

"Thanks."

Devon walked into the kitchen and filled a glass full of ice water. As she took a sip, her phone beeped three consecutive times in her pocket. She pulled out her phone and flipped through the texts. They were all from Reid, wishing her a safe trip and telling her how much he would miss her while she was gone.

Her heart skipped a beat as she read the last one.

Come home to me quickly, Dev. I'm too busy to fly to Paris, but I already miss you. I miss you so much.

She swallowed back the emotions rushing through her as she

cradled the glass of water to her chest. She had told him that her family had planned a trip to Paris for the summer. The lies were piling on top of her, and not for the first or last time, she regretted her decision.

At that moment, the front door opened, causing Devon to jump out of her self-pity.

"Hey, baby!" a guy called, walking through the door.

Peering through the kitchen door, Devon watched as he lifted Hadley right off the couch and into his arms. Hadley giggled like mad as she threw her arms around his neck while her legs wrapped around his waist. He pulled back long enough to deeply and thoroughly kiss her on the mouth. Feeling intrusive, Devon stepped back into the kitchen to give them some privacy.

"Put me down. Put me down. You have to meet Devon!" Hadley cried.

Devon heard a few thuds that sounded like Hadley was playfully hitting Garrett.

"Is she here already?" he asked.

"Yeah. Hey, Dev. Come meet Garrett!" Hadley called.

Devon took a deep breath, preparing herself for the utter cuteness that always came from the honeymoon stage of a new relationship. She waved awkwardly as she entered the living room. "Hey."

"Garrett, baby, this is my bestie, Devon Sawyer," Hadley said. "Dev, this is my boyfriend, Garrett Jones."

"Hey, Devon. So nice to finally meet you," Garrett said, striding forward with his hand extended.

Devon politely placed her hand in his and shook.

"I've heard so much about you," he said.

"I've heard a lot about you, too." Which was true. Hadley hadn't shut up about him at lunch, not that Devon was complaining. She would rather talk about anything but herself.

"Don't believe a word she says. She thinks I'm a nice guy," he said with a wink in Hadley's direction.

"You are a nice guy!" Hadley said, rolling her eyes and walking over to them.

"Kiss of death, babe. Kiss of death," he said, wrapping an arm around her waist and pulling her in close.

Yes, that looks like the kiss of death, Devon thought.

"So, how long are you here for?" Garrett asked, directing his attention back to Devon.

"Uh…probably just a week," she said, finding his wide brown eyes unnerving.

"Well, glad to have you. I brought home a couple bottles of wine from the cellar," he said, gesturing to the side table where he had deposited a bag.

"I didn't know you were going to see your dad," Hadley said, her voice strained.

"He asked to see me after work. Told me to tell you hello. I think he wants us over for dinner sometime this week."

"Oh, well that sounds nice," Hadley responded flatly.

Devon would be sure to ask her about that later. She hadn't

mentioned anything about Garrett's parents, and she knew Hadley too well. There was definitely something off in her voice.

"I'm going to go pop open a bottle. You ladies get back to your Millionaire Matchmaker. I'm cooking dinner tonight since I'm actually home at a decent hour, and then we're going out to celebrate Devon's arrival." He picked up the bag from the table and pulled out a bottle. "Red okay with you, Dev?"

He's already using my nickname like he knows me. How the hell does Hadley always get this lucky? Devon wondered.

"Red is perfect," she answered.

When he left for the kitchen, Hadley grabbed her arm, pulling her close on the couch. "Isn't he incredible?" Hadley swooned.

"He might be too good. He brought home wine, and he's making dinner? Is this guy for real?" Devon asked, nudging Hadley in the ribs.

"Totally for real, and he's been like this for the past five months," she said, sighing contentedly. "It's like hitting a gold mine as far as boyfriends go."

Devon couldn't agree more. Her friend seemed truly, very happy with Garrett, and Garrett seemed to adore her. Any man who greeted a woman by picking her up and kissing her senseless was all right on Devon's list.

Plus, he was pretty easy on the eyes. He was tall, really tall, which was nice since Hadley was on the taller side. He had broad shoulders, a friendly smile, and the cutest dimples. His brown hair was short but styled professionally. He'd had on a black suit when he walked in, but he had since changed into dark jeans and a green button-up rolled up to his elbows to cook in. He seemed comfortable in his skin and in his affection toward Hadley. Devon liked that about him.

***

THE TRIO SPENT the evening lost in debates about which match was going to be successful on Millionaire Matchmaker while downing glass after glass of the expensive red wine Garrett had brought back with him. To accompany the wine, dinner consisted of a perfectly cooked chicken marsala with spaghetti and garlic bread. As they laughed and joked during the meal, Devon felt the tension and anxiety of the last semester melt away from her.

Each day had been a battle to keep going, and in this moment, she felt lucky because she was here with her friend. She had made it through the day.

CHAPTER 3

The Bean Thing

DEVON TURNED THE corner, looking over her shoulder. As she wound through unfamiliar streets, she was surprised to find each one deserted. Where are all the people?

She was still walking, but her pace was rapidly increasing. She hated being lost, especially at night. She remembered a similar experience she'd had in a new city. The driving directions had been all wrong, and her GPS hadn't directed her properly. She had freaked out and pulled over to figure out where she was supposed to be going. The overpowering feeling of utter insecurity and danger had made her stomach tighten and tense.

She hadn't been in real danger, but it sure had felt like it.

And it felt like it now.

Devon swallowed hard, pushing her blonde hair off her face, as she walked faster and faster, hoping to find something that would trigger a memory of some sort. She tried to recall where she was or what she was doing, but it just wouldn't come to her. Panic rose in her chest, causing her heart to flutter faster, as sweat began to bead on the back of her neck.

She glanced over her shoulder again, feeling eyes on the back of her head, but no one was there. She was all alone. How could she be all alone? Surely, someone else had to be around.

Against her better judgment, Devon went up to the first building and tried the door. It didn't budge. She did the same to the next door and the next one after that, but they were all locked up tight. She pushed her shoulder against another door to no avail. She wasn't in some crime show. There was no way she would try to kick her way through a door. The longer she stood and tried to find a way into a building, the more she felt like someone was watching her, stalking her movements. As she banged on a door, her throat seized, keeping her from screaming for help.

Someone please answer the door! she screamed in her head.

No one came to the door. Nothing moved, not even the wind.

Tears welled in her eyes as desperation kindled in her gut. She moved on from the doors, knowing she was having no luck here.

Her walk turned into a jog, and the sounds of footsteps behind her fueled her on to a full run.

The only problem was she didn't have a clue where she was going. She knew she could run for only so long before exhaustion overtook her. How long did she have before they caught up to her?

Keeping up her fast pace was tiring, and she felt herself slowing, but she could tell from the patter of feet behind her that her pursuer was catching up to her. Tears streamed openly down her face, and she did nothing to stop them. She had a terrible, terrible feeling about this.

When she turned a corner, she saw a light on in the building directly in front of her. Angling straight for it, she gained a burst of speed. It felt like she was running toward the light at the end of the tunnel.

Devon yanked at the front door, and it mercifully opened. She didn't wait to see if the person behind her was still following her. When she stepped inside, light streamed in all around her, and loud party music filled the room. People were dancing in every inch of space, but no one stopped to look at her.

As she closed the door behind her, the lights dimmed, and flashes of color bounced off the walls. She reached for the first person she could, but he brushed her off. Every person she tried to speak with after that ignored her completely. It was like she wasn't even there. Pushing her way through the room, her head was spinning as the volume of the music seemed to increase tenfold.

What is happening to me? she thought.

Then, she felt the eyes on the back of her head again. She turned around in a circle, looking for the source, but she found only a sea of other people. If she had thought she hated feeling isolated in a deserted city, then she hated being invisible in a sea of people even more.

She pushed people out of the way, shoving them like they were rag dolls, until her arms were screaming in pain at her. She couldn't move fast enough. Her feet were giving out, and her arms were failing her. She couldn't escape.

When Devon looked back to see if the person was still pursuing her, she saw a single figure walking directly toward her, but the person was indistinguishable from the dark surroundings. Turning around, she rushed forward with one last bit of effort. She propelled herself through a set of double doors, stepping into a stark white bedroom that blinded her.

Just when she reached the other side, she felt a person grab a hold of her arm.

***

DEVON AWOKE WITH a start, gasping for breath. Her hands clenched into the quilt, her chest heaved up and down, and her body racked with tremors. A cold sweat had drenched through her thin T-shirt, and she shook as the chilly air sank into her skin.

Where the hell was she?

Anxiously, she looked around the dark room, searching the

unfamiliar space. Whose bed was she in? And why didn't she recognize this place at all?

Taking a deep breath, she tried to return to reality. She took another breath, calming her still racing heart, and it came back to her. St. Louis. The train. Hadley. She was staying at Hadley's place with Hadley's boyfriend. They'd had dinner and wine. They had gone out drinking afterward, and she had fallen into bed drunk.

Her stomach grumbled angrily at the memory, and her head throbbed against her scalp. Great. Hangover.

Her eyes roamed to the red-numbered alarm clock on the dresser.

Six thirty in the morning.

Devon still had two or three hours left before she had to get up. She sank back into the comforter, feeling completely emotionally drained.

It was just a dream. Just a dream. She had to keep telling herself that over and over again. No one was after her. No one was following her.

Just a dream.

***

Devon jumped in the shower a few hours later. No matter how hard she had tried, she hadn't been able to fall back asleep. The haunting memory of someone chasing her through the streets had stayed with her. She had emptied the contents of her stomach in the bathroom twice since waking. She was dead tired, and she just wanted to crawl back into bed and crash, but she knew she wouldn't be able to shut off her brain. As soon as she had tried, everything had rushed back to her all over again.

She changed into a pair of light jeans and blue tank top, pulled her hair up into a ponytail, and then covered the dark circles under her eyes like an expert. Her head was still aching, despite taking 1,000 milligrams of Tylenol earlier. She knew she needed to eat, but the thought of food sent her stomach into a fit.

Finally feeling human enough to leave the bedroom, she edged out into the kitchen. She poured herself a glass of water and slowly sipped it.

"Good morning!" Garrett called cheerfully, walking into the kitchen.

Devon jumped and immediately regretted it. "Is it?"

"Well, probably not for you. I heard you getting sick earlier. Feeling any better?" He opened the refrigerator door.

"No," she said, shaking her head. "How are you so cheerful?"

"Product of working nights, I guess. When I get a good night's sleep, I'm a much happier person."

"Right." She took another tentative sip of her drink.

"Are you going to be able to go sightseeing today?" he asked, pulling out a full banquet of food.

The night before, they had agreed that Garrett would take her around the city while Hadley had to work. Devon really wanted the chance to be a tourist while she was here, but she knew that she wouldn't get to see everything if she waited for Hadley to get home.

"Not sure," she said, walking into the living room. She sat on the couch and put her head between her knees. Seeing that much food was making her want to run to the bathroom again.

"Well, I'll whip you up something that will make you feel better, and we can get going."

"You really don't have to show me around…or make me food," she groaned.

"Just some toast. Drink up that water. It'll help," Garrett said, popping some bread into the toaster.

"Okay," she muttered.

She drank as much as she could manage. He brought her a plate with plain toast and replaced her glass of water with another full one. She took it without comment and tried to choke down the food. It did help some, but she wasn't a hundred percent better yet. Garrett had created an elaborate breakfast plate for himself, and he ate it all in the same amount of time it took for her to finish her toast.

She tried standing again. The headache was finally dissipating, and her stomach was feeling only partly queasy. She could make it through another day.

"You ready?" he asked, coming back for her plate.

"I think so."

"Great. We better get going then. Hadley gets off at three thirty today, so we have a good five hours to try to get in the best tourist traps out here before I have to go to work," Garrett told her.

"Perfect. If I can make it five hours, it'll be a miracle," Devon said. She was happy that she had a tour guide even though Hadley was at work.

Garrett shook his head at her as he stuffed his wallet into his back pocket. "Come on. It'll be good for you to get some fresh air."

Devon grumbled something incoherent before standing. She grabbed her purse from the table and followed Garrett to the elevator. Riding the elevator might have been the worst part of the morning. Garrett rested a hand on her back as he warily watched her. She was pretty sure he was expecting her to burst any second, and she felt like she might.

When they finally reached the bottom of the huge complex, Devon uneasily walked out of the elevator.

"Let's never do that again," she murmured, clutching her stomach with one hand.

"I've got bad news for you."

Devon glared up at him.

"Well, at least you won't have to take the elevator for a few more hours," Garrett offered.

"I don't even want to think about it."

"So, what did you want to see?" He stood at the entrance, debating which direction to walk in.

"Everything," Devon said with a shrug.

"I don't think we can see everything by three o'clock."

"The bean thing then," Devon told him.

"The bean thing?" He looked at her skeptically.

"Yeah, isn't that what it's called? I don't know. I've never been there before," she stated defensively.

"Come on. You'll figure it out," he said, walking toward the river.

She started after him, walking past the House of Blues and onto the State Street Bridge that crossed the Chicago River.

"What did I do wrong?" she asked, staring out across the water.

"Well, it's not the bean thing," he said, shaking his head. "It's the Cloud Gate, and we call it The Bean, just The Bean."

Devon rolled her eyes. She hadn't thought she was that far off.

"It's in Millennium Park, not too far from here."

He strode purposefully across the bridge. Devon stopped for a second to take a picture. She knew she couldn't post it anywhere online or send it to her mom like she normally would. No one really knew where she was, so it would totally blow her cover if she started posting pictures of Chicago. But she wanted memories of where she had been even if they were just for her.

"While we're playing tourist, I should let you know that directly ahead of us is the famous Chicago Theatre," Garrett said, pointing out the giant red Chicago sign.

Devon snapped a photo because…hey, why not?

They continued through the busy streets, and despite having to avoid other tourists admiring the pretty buildings, walking seemed to help her stomach. She still wasn't prepared for food, but the fresh air was breezy, and Devon found that moving was helpful.

Garrett directed her down a side street and pointed out the glass exterior to the Joffrey Ballet. Looking several stories up, she watched the dancers jumping about as they passed by the building. They exited the cross street onto Michigan Avenue, and Millennium Park stood across from them. Garrett showed her the way to The Bean, and she saw clusters of people were already surrounding the massive mirror sculpture.

From the perfect location, Devon could see the entire Chicago skyline in the reflection of the structure. She crossed her arms and stared up at it, wondering what she would see if she saw her own reflection. Would she see herself rounded and distorted like the city line was in some places or would she appear whole and perfect?

A part of her hoped to see herself rounded and distorted like she felt, but as she approached, she saw her reflection was like any other mirror—a lie.

"Want me to take your picture?" Garrett offered.

Breaking her out of her silent reverie, she shook her head. "No, thanks."

She didn't want any pictures of her by The Bean. It reflected the skyline, and that itself was the masterpiece. Her image would only obscure the view.

"Are you sure?" he asked, extending his hand for her iPhone.

Devon pulled it out of his reach. "No, really, I don't want to be in any pictures."

"Come on, everyone wants their picture taken with The Bean. I even have Bean pictures. Don't you want to show your friends or post it on Facebook?" Garrett asked with a smile though it was clear he wasn't really joking.

"I appreciate it, but no pictures for me. I'm not on Facebook anymore, so I don't have anywhere to upload them," she told him, tucking her phone into her pocket.

"How do you survive? Hadley lives on there. Half the time, I can't even reach her through her Facebook daze."

Devon shrugged. She'd had to shut it down, at least temporarily. If she were to check in, it could show her location, and she didn't want to accidentally make a mistake. It wasn't like she could rig Facebook into saying she was in both Paris and St. Louis at the same time. She was no genius with computers, and even if she were, she was pretty sure it was illegal.

"I'm living in the present," she told Garrett, which was true. She didn't even want to think about the past.

"It's the best place to live." Garrett just stared at her with the same curious expression on his face.

The whole conversation had triggered something within her. She felt like if she didn't get her feelings out right then and there, she would lose it. Digging into her purse, Devon pulled out her notebook. She grabbed her favorite pen, stalked over to a park bench, and immediately started writing down bits and pieces of whatever came to her mind.

Garrett followed and sat down next to her, peering over her shoulder. "What are you writing?"

Moving the notebook out of his view, she murmured, "Nothing."

"Looks like something. I don't know many people who carry

notebooks around with them."

"Me neither." She continued to jot down ideas as they flowed through her.

"Is it like a journal?" he asked, trying to read what she was writing.

She scooted down the bench. "Just give me a second."

She wrote one last line and then shut the notebook. Garrett was staring at her intently, and she made a point of not looking at him.

"So, not to pry or anything," he said, obviously prying, "but who just whips out a book in public and starts writing?"

He laughed at her, and she couldn't hold it in as she laughed softly with him. He had a point.

"I can't help it sometimes. The words are just there." She stuffed the notebook back into her bag and stood.

"Are you going to tell me what you wrote?"

"Nope," Devon said, turning away from The Bean.

"Is it like a journal or a diary? Is that why I can't read it?"

"No. I don't talk about my writing. Sorry," she said. "Is that a garden? Can we walk through?"

"Sure," Garrett said, "but don't think you can change the subject so easily."

"It's not a big deal. Just forget about it." She walked briskly in the direction of the garden.

She hated when people asked questions about her writing. It was deeply personal. She kind of hated herself for the compulsive habit, but she had been doing it since she was a kid. She was good at it, but she didn't share well with others.

"It's kind of a big deal to you, isn't it?" Garrett asked as they walked into the garden.

"Not really," she said, biting her lip.

"Then, you can tell me about it," he said smoothly.

Devon stopped and shook her head. She knew he was just being nice, but he was meddling into things she didn't want him near. She needed to change the course of the conversation. Any question he asked about her was going to be one question too many.

Bending down, she took a series of photos of a purple flower in bloom. It was better than answering Garrett's questions. He might be trying to get to know her, but she wasn't ready to open up to anyone anytime soon.

"Hey, sorry," he muttered.

She glanced up at him as his hand brushed through his dark brown hair. He actually looked sheepish.

"I didn't mean to get in your business. I didn't know it would be so private."

Devon slowly stood. "It's all right. Don't worry about it."

"Afraid your writing sucks? I know that's why I don't show anyone anything I've ever written," he told her.

"No, it's not that," she said. Writing came very natural to her. "I just don't like to show people."

"I hope you're not an English major or anything. It would be pretty bad if you never showed your professors your work,"

Garrett said with a smile.

"Oh god, no! I'm a social work major." Devon walked next to him as they left the gardens and headed toward the lakefront.

"Social work?" he asked, wrinkling his nose. "What do you want to do work with inner-city kids in gangs or handle abuse cases? Either sounds awful."

Devon swallowed hard and bit down on her lip until it hurt. "No," she answered sharply.

Everyone always looked down on social work as if it wasn't a legitimate degree, but Wash U had the number one program in the country. Social work majors dealt with all sorts of issues, and were very prominent in the lobbying world. A friend of hers was currently working on protection of women's rights in D.C., and she didn't have any complaints about her social work background.

"Social work benefits a normal productive life span. Just because you were raised with a well-to-do family does not mean that the rest of society is so fortunate. People should receive the same care and help," Devon answered vehemently. "Besides, social work can be used everywhere—government, counseling, nursing homes, community planning. I could go on and on."

"I do believe you could," Garrett said with a smile. "Didn't mean to come off as condescending."

"We can't all be business majors," Devon said curtly.

"Sounds like you really want to be, too."

"Is that sarcasm?" she asked.

"I would never be sarcastic."

Devon rolled her eyes as the traffic light changed. They walked across the street and down a set of stairs to the lake. The water was choppy from the wind and the boats out in the harbor. Off in the distance, the Navy Pier looked crowded, and the Ferris wheel turned slowly, stopping every few feet to let passengers on and off. Runners crisscrossed the path, and a couple was rollerblading hand-in-hand. It was a rather picturesque day.

"Stay here a minute," Garrett said before rushing away.

Devon sighed and pulled out her notebook again. Now that he was gone, she reread what she had written by The Bean. She studied the words and the tone that they had taken. Everything seemed to drift back to the moment that had pushed her over the edge.

Thumbing back to the day after it had happened, she saw the faint bumps in the paper that signified where her teardrops had fallen onto the page. They marred half the page, and as she skimmed the words, she felt a lump form in her throat. The memories and emotions were as all too much. Why was she actively reliving it? She couldn't seem to get away, and half the time, she didn't think she wanted to.

She took a few minutes to compose herself before Garrett returned.

Carrying two Popsicles, he smiled brightly at her. "Hope you like strawberry because I'm taking the blueberry-lime," he said, offering her the red Popsicle.

"My favorite," Devon told him with a big smile. *He got us popsicles? Cute.* "What's this for?"

"I thought it would be easy on your stomach," he said, shrugging. "One of my favorite pastimes. I used to come here a lot when I was younger with my parents. We'd eat Popsicles and sit on the edge of the water. So…sit."

Devon smiled even bigger. She was glad that Garrett was talking about himself and not her for a change. She sat next to him on the ledge and dangled her feet toward the water, enjoying the beginning of summer.

The beginning of a new life.

CHAPTER 4

Square

GARRETT DROPPED DEVON at Jenn's Restaurant to wait for Hadley to get off work. He was working the night shift and needed to get ready, but he felt bad about leaving Devon alone in the apartment on such a nice day. He had given her his spare key in case she decided to go to the apartment. She didn't intend to though. Devon figured she would wait until Hadley got off work, and then they could head back together. She didn't feel comfortable being at their apartment all by herself. She was just a guest.

Her stomach grumbled, reminding her that she had only eaten

a piece of toast and a Popsicle all day. She and Garrett had walked for hours. He was a great tour guide, giving her more information about buildings and events than she likely ever needed to know. Garrett had lived in Chicago nearly his whole life, and he had only left for the four years of college. Devon hadn't been surprised to find out he had gone to George Washington in D.C. Although he had money written all over him, surprisingly, he seemed down-to-earth. She wished that combination happened more often.

Jenn's wasn't as busy as it had been the last time Devon had walked inside. Everyone must have still been working at this early hour. She suspected it would start to get crowded closer to five o'clock.

Hadley had a pretty sweet set-up at her job. She always got off work early on Fridays. Plus, she didn't have to go in at all on the weekends. Hadley had said she would be happy to show Devon around the parts of the city that Garrett had missed during the morning shift. Devon hadn't decided what she wanted to do, but she knew she would think of something in the meantime.

Sitting down in the same stool as she had the day before, Devon leaned her elbows heavily on the countertop and waited for someone to materialize. She noticed a waitress helping a customer in a booth against the wall. The woman looked like she had been working there since the place had opened forty years earlier. Yet, she still wore the same uniform as the younger waitresses—a short black skirt, a white top unbuttoned to reveal cleavage, white tube socks, and tennis shoes. She couldn't be the only one working, right?

The woman scooped up the menus from the other customers

and then walked toward the back door. Looking over at Devon, she smiled with a sincerity she likely didn't feel. "Someone will be right with you, hon."

She walked through the swinging door into the kitchen. Devon wondered if she was now yelling at someone to do his job. It was what she probably would have done when she had worked at a restaurant. At least, she would have grumbled to herself about how she was the only one working.

During the previous summers, Devon had worked part-time as a waitress to earn a little extra cash. She always had something she wanted to spend her money on, and she felt bad asking her parents for anything more than they had given her. They were already paying for her education and room and board, so she didn't feel like she could ask for more.

A minute later, a disgruntled man walked out of the back room, yelling something at the waitress behind him. Devon had been right. When he turned around, Devon smiled, realizing it was Brennan. She was happy to see a familiar face in a sea of the unfamiliar. Chicago was a huge step for her, and she had a lot of adjusting to do.

"You been helped?" Brennan moved bottles around, barely glancing up at her.

"No, I haven't," Devon told him, waiting for him to recognize her.

"What'll you have?" He ran a towel under the faucet and then mopped under the drip mat.

"I don't know. I haven't seen a menu." She pulled out her pen from her back pocket and absentmindedly flipped it between her fingers.

He grabbed a menu for her and slapped it down on the counter. He walked away without even asking her for her drink order. Hadley had been right; getting Brennan's attention was hard even when the restaurant was empty.

She watched him for a second, knowing that he wasn't paying any attention to her. He was bobbing his head, his dark hair moving effortlessly. It wasn't styled like it had been yesterday. Today, it looked more like he had just rolled out of bed, but in a good way. He was humming something to his own tune, but Devon couldn't make out the song.

She knew that she shouldn't be watching him like this. It was rude, and surely he would notice, which would be truly embarrassing. She was just having a hard time pulling her eyes away.

It was strange to say the least. He was the kind of guy her sister, Dani, would fall all over herself for. She would flaunt herself in front of him until he noticed her, and in Dani's case, it didn't take very much time for guys to notice her. Her mother had joked about Devon being the difficult one, but that was only because she had boycotted cowboy boots and her Dixie nickname, but Dani was the one her mother needed to worry about. Dani still traipsed about in too short sundresses, and she had earned the name Pearl from half the guys in school for good reason. It was slightly disturbing since she was only seventeen and a senior in high school. Devon was terrified of her going off to college, especially since she had chosen a big state school.

Devon wasn't the one to get caught up in a guy's appearance, especially with Reid back in St. Louis. No, she didn't even want to think about St. Louis right now. Brennan was nice to look at, that was all.

Brennan turned around then and looked right at her. Her cheeks instantly colored when he caught her staring. He didn't do anything more than smirk before she buried herself in the menu she hadn't yet touched.

Devon felt his eyes linger on her, and the feeling wouldn't leave. She wasn't used to being under scrutiny. She pondered whether he had felt her eyes staring so heavily, if it had been that obvious. She glanced back up when her cheeks weren't flaming hot.

Brennan smiled at her, walked back over, and leaned both of his elbows on the bar like he had done yesterday. "You want something to drink?"

"Just water, please," Devon said, averting her eyes.

Brennan poured her drink and handed it over. "Were you here yesterday?" he asked, returning to his position.

"Yeah." Devon nodded. She folded her menu, removing her diversion. "I was here with Hadley."

"I knew you looked familiar. You're the little Southern belle."

"Devon," she corrected.

"Right. How'd you end up with a friend like Hadley?" he asked.

"What does that mean?" Was he insulting her roommate of two-and-a-half years?

"Don't take this the wrong way, but you're a square, and she colors outside of the lines."

Incredulously, Devon looked up at him. "How could I not take that the wrong way?"

"Because I told you in advance not to," Brennan said, shrugging.

"Telling me in advance implies that I'm going to take it the wrong way. It totally negates everything you say after that," she told him, narrowing her eyes.

"It's too early to be negating this and implying that. I'm a bartender. Order a shot," Brennan said.

He didn't back away as she glared at him.

"I think you can imply and negate with the rest of us." Devon flipped her pen between her fingers faster.

"Can and will are different things," he said, stepping back. He walked over to the bar, pulled out two shot glasses, and filled them with tequila. After he passed one over to her, he set a napkin on the countertop and placed two limes on it. "You keep flipping your pen like that, you're going to cause a nervous breakdown. Now, drink up."

Devon sighed. This was a bad idea, especially after last night. But the shot didn't feel like it came with a choice. Rather, it felt like a challenge.

"Salt?" she asked. If she was going to do it, she was going to do it right.

Brennan placed the salt on the counter. She licked the skin in between her thumb and forefinger and held her hand out to him. He smirked at her, and then without any further prompting, he poured some salt onto the spot. He did the same to himself.

"Are we toasting to anything?" Devon asked because she couldn't help herself.

"Nope," Brennan said, picking up his shot.

She did the same, clinked her glass against his, and then tipped back the tequila. Devon gagged as the burning liquid rushed down her throat. She reached for the lime and sucked on it until the fire cooled.

Brennan chuckled softly as he tossed his lime and cleaned up the shots. "Now, what do you want to eat?"

Devon flipped her pen around. When she realized she was doing it again, she placed the pen on the counter. "I'm not picky. Anything without mayo. Whatever you like."

"Huh," he said, taking her menu.

"What?" She licked her lips and eyed him apprehensively.

"Nothing."

"Okay."

What was his angle? She couldn't figure it out. That was the second time he had seemed to assess her in some way that she couldn't figure out.

Brennan walked back into the kitchen. When he didn't reappear, she wondered what he was doing back there. Was he goofing off with the waitress? It didn't seem likely. It wasn't that she expected him to stay out here and talk to her or anything. She had hated forced conversations with her customers, but she hadn't thought their conversation was forced.

Shrugging, she pulled out her notebook and flipped it open to the page she had been working on when she'd been at The Bean with Garrett. It had flowed so easily then. She wished writing was always like that. Sometimes, it felt like she was trying to force her way out of quicksand.

As much as writing was a release, she kind of hated it. She felt like she relied on it to express herself. When she thought about it, she figured it kept her voice subdued. She didn't need to yell or scream or cry out at anyone when she could do all that on paper. She could pour every emotion onto paper until she felt like she was bleeding. It wasn't enough. It was never enough, but it helped. It helped keep her walls up.

More than anything, she wished she didn't have the same skill as her parents. Because when the words flowed out of her, they weren't a perfect flowing script, a well-crafted novel, or even something as simple as a journal. They were lyrics. All of her writing came out in the form of a song. What made it even worse was that she could never, would never sing. She didn't like other people to hear her voice because she felt like it was just too personal, so she would never sing her own stuff.

How could she sing between the tears?

Mulling over the words in her notebook, she rearranged the lines that formed the chorus. She could imagine someone great singing her songs with smooth perfect vocals that rose and fell in time with the music, but she didn't think she could ever follow through. Hearing her pain all over the radio wasn't exactly her style.

A few minutes later, Brennan walked out and placed her food in front of her. It was just a burger. She was surprised. She had thought he would have come out with something creative.

"Best thing on the menu," he told her, refilling her water.

She hadn't even noticed that she had drained it. She guessed the hangover had dehydrated her more than she knew.

"Thanks." Devon added ketchup to the burger and then dug in. "Wow! This is great!" She had never been a burger fan, but this was outstanding.

Brennan nodded his head, like he knew she would like it, as he leaned back against the bar. "How long are you in town for?"

"Just the week," she said before taking another bite of her burger.

"Gonna be hanging out at my bar while you're here?"

Devon looked up at him, trying to figure him out. Did he want her there or was he hoping she wouldn't be there? Or was he simply making conversation? "Probably," she answered.

"All right."

"Why?" she asked curiously.

"Didn't know how much tequila I should keep in stock," he said without even cracking a smile.

Devon, however, laughed at him. She preferred his humor to him assessing her. "I'd keep it handy."

"I'm thinking I'm going to have to."

"You think you're going to have to do what?" Hadley walked up behind them, intercepting the end of the conversation.

"Hadley!" Devon turned around to greet her friend with a smile.

"Hey, good to see Brennan is taking care of you for me. I see he's feeding you the burger," she said with a shake of her head. "He thinks it's the best thing on the menu. He's wrong. It's the chicken."

"Hadley, always so opinionated," Brennan said, straightening as she approached. He started pouring her a drink.

"Is it really opinion when it's obviously fact?" Hadley asked, taking the seat next to Devon.

"She thinks all of her opinions are facts," Brennan told Devon, pushing the drink toward Hadley.

"Aren't they?" Devon asked with a smirk.

"Oh, so you're on her side then?"

"Was there ever a doubt?" Hadley asked.

"I tend to doubt everything."

"And I tend to disagree with everything you doubt," Hadley told him with a shrug.

"Just drink up and stop disagreeing with me," he said with a smile.

Hadley shrugged again, sipped on her drink, and turned to face Devon. "So, how was your day? Did Garrett show you around the city?"

"Yeah. We had a great time before he had to go to work. The city is beautiful. Why haven't I been here before?" Devon asked.

"I don't know. It's not like I haven't asked you to visit."

"Just had that little thing called school," Devon told her.

"School. Psh! Who needs that?" Hadley's lips quirked up. She glanced down at Devon's notebook and tapped it twice. "You still writing?"

"I haven't changed that much since you left," Devon said.

"Can I read your latest?" Hadley reached for the notebook with a knowing smile.

"No," Devon responded quickly, pulling the notebook off the bar and stuffing it back into her bag. She picked up the pen again and began flipping it between her fingers absentmindedly.

Hadley laughed and shook her head. "You really haven't changed. You should let more people read your songs. They're really good, Dev."

Devon blushed and looked back down at her food. She didn't want to have this conversation, especially not in public. She had too many emotions locked in her notebook. There was no way she was just going to open it up.

"Brennan could even play guitar for your lyrics," Hadley offered without Brennan's approval.

"What's that?" he asked, leaning forward.

Hadley glanced at Devon as if asking for permission to continue. Devon rolled her eyes, knowing she didn't have much choice now that Hadley had already started.

"You play guitar?" Devon asked, being quicker on the draw.

Brennan seemed artsy enough, but she wasn't sure if he actually fit the bill. She had grown up around musicians, and while he seemed to have the whole desperate bartending routine down, there seemed to be something more to him. Her distaste for her own lyrics bled over to people who thought they could play instruments. She was too accustomed to how musicians acted and how they thought they ruled the world. They weren't exactly her speed.

"Devon writes lyrics," Hadley interrupted.

"Yeah, I play," he said, locking eyes with Devon. "You write? I wouldn't have pegged you."

"A little," she said with a shrug. She liked proving his judgments wrong. "I wouldn't have pegged you as a musician."

"I'm a struggling musician."

"What are you doing in Chicago if you're a musician?"

"I said I was struggling."

"And by struggling, you mean you have no talent?" Devon asked arching an eyebrow.

"I have talent," he said, off hand like it didn't matter what she thought. It likely didn't. "I just find I should spend more time on my bartending talent while I continue to fail the entrance exams to get into med school."

Devon swallowed, her mind immediately going to Reid. She felt really bad that she hadn't told him the truth. He was going through such a hard time, applying to medical school himself, and she had just left him to go through it alone.

Maybe she should call him.

No.

She couldn't do that without telling him that she had lied, without telling him that she wasn't in Paris for the summer. Then, she would have to go back to St. Louis, and she just wasn't ready for that.

"He has talent," Hadley said as if it were the most painful thing for her to admit. "I've heard him play. Do you have an open mic gig this week? We could stop by."

"Nah," Brennan said, shaking his head as a large group walked into the bar. "I don't have anything for a couple weeks."

"Bummer," Hadley muttered. "They're so much fun. We'll have to take you up to the bar at the John Hancock building before you leave. That will be fun. I was up there once. It was snowing on the ninety-ninth floor, but it wasn't even raining on the bottom floor. When are you off, Brennan? You could come with?"

"You want me to go to an overpriced bar over a thousand feet off the ground when I work at a bar?" he asked.

"Yep!" Hadley said with a big smile.

"I have Monday off, but I'm busy. What about next Sunday?"

"Are you going to be here next Sunday?" Hadley asked Devon.

"Uh…yeah. Next Sunday works for me."

"Great! Next Sunday it is then," Hadley said. "It can be Devon's going-away party."

"Yeah," Devon said dejectedly.

She didn't want to spend only one week in the city. She would need to find a place to stay for the rest of the summer or else she would have to fess up to Reid and her family sooner rather than later.

And that was something she just couldn't do.

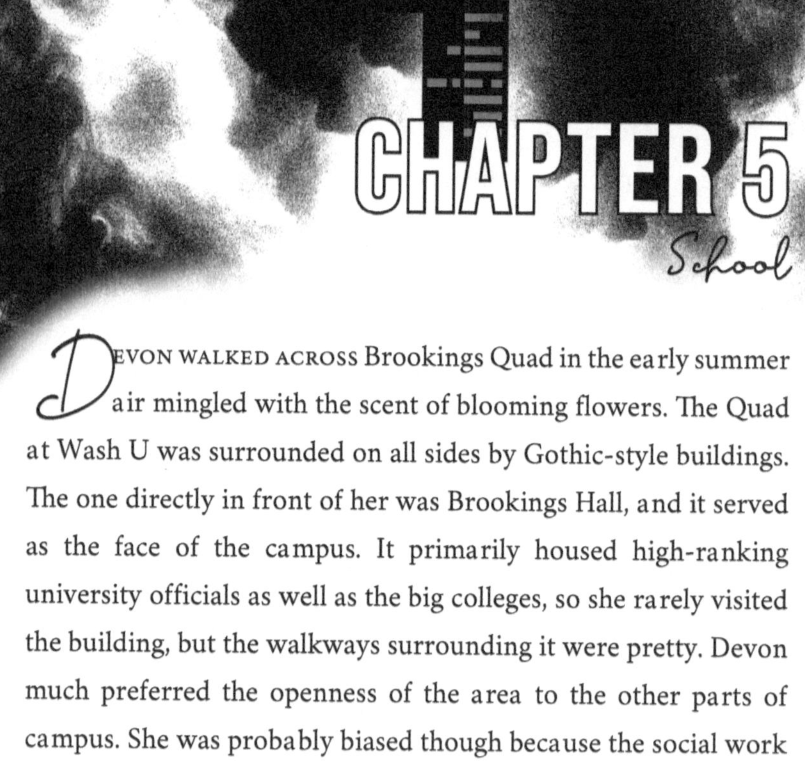

DEVON WALKED ACROSS Brookings Quad in the early summer air mingled with the scent of blooming flowers. The Quad at Wash U was surrounded on all sides by Gothic-style buildings. The one directly in front of her was Brookings Hall, and it served as the face of the campus. It primarily housed high-ranking university officials as well as the big colleges, so she rarely visited the building, but the walkways surrounding it were pretty. Devon much preferred the openness of the area to the other parts of campus. She was probably biased though because the social work building, Brown Hall, was right next door to Brookings.

Devon would have taken the shortcut to Brown Hall, but the weather was so nice that she wanted to delay the inevitable. She nearly reached the archway through Brookings when she felt eyes on her back.

Strange. She hadn't remembered seeing anyone else on the Quad.

It was such a beautiful day that she thought others would be out there studying, tanning, goofing off, and generally, enjoying the sunshine. But it was the summer session, and few people remained on campus, so it wasn't all that surprising.

Trying to push away the nagging feeling that someone was watching her, Devon quickened her pace and walked through the archway. She didn't like being in there anymore than she liked being out in the open on the Quad, but at least in the Quad, she could see whoever was following behind her. It wasn't likely that whoever the person was would do anything in the middle of the day at the heart of campus.

But the archway at Brookings was different. While it was still a very public place, connecting the Quad and Hoyt Drive, it bottlenecked through the corridor. She felt suddenly trapped even though it wasn't a far distance. The hair on the back of her neck stood on end, and the blood coursed through her body. She could feel her pulse beating rapidly in each of her fingers, and she swallowed back the cotton balls lodged in her throat.

Devon glanced back over her shoulder, her blonde hair spinning out around her face, as she hoped to catch a glimpse of the person behind her. But no one was there. She didn't even hear footsteps or anything. Yet, she couldn't shake the feeling. Whoever was following her was rather adept at not being seen. The only way she would see the person was when he wanted to be seen, and that unnerved her even more.

Dashing through the archway, Devon crossed to the other side, unharmed. Her eyes shifted left and right, looking for anyone waiting to ambush her on the other side. No one was there. In fact, no one was anywhere.

There were no cars on the usually busy Hoyt Drive or Brookings Drive, which led into campus. Cars sat idly by in parking spaces along the road, but she couldn't see anyone in them. Even on the best day, incoming freshmen flocked the school to make their final decisions about enrollment. Despite her annoyance with them, Devon wanted to know where they were.

She didn't have more time to think about it. Someone was tailing her and almost instinctively, she knew he was getting closer. Without a backward glance, she barreled down the stairs leading to the street. Devon had walked up and down the soft sloping and seemingly endless staircase more times than she could count, but today, the descent felt excruciatingly long.

Finally reaching the sidewalk on Hoyt, she immediately turned right toward Brown Hall. She had a strong desire to be inside a familiar environment. Plus, she knew the entire faculty, and someone had to be there. Professor Turner was there every day. She had spent countless hours in his office going over assignments and catching up. She never had to make appointments since he was always just there. If no one else were on campus, he would still be there in his loosened tie staring at his Mac. She could get to him. She could make it.

It wasn't a long walk. It was literally right around the corner. Why hadn't she taken the shortcut through Busch Hall? All she would have had to do was taken a right before the Quad, walk straight through the Humanities department, and Brown would be standing right in front of her. Instead, Devon had wanted to enjoy the weather, but she wasn't enjoying the weather right now.

She jogged up the sidewalk, feeling eyes on her from every direction. She felt completely ambushed. They were coming for her. They were closing in. They would get her.

No. She had to be strong and push herself harder. Someone would be inside Brown Hall. If not Professor Turner, then another professor or even a student would have to be there. Devon would make this work. She had to.

Reaching the double doors, she wrenched one open as fast as she could and rushed inside. It smelled exactly as it always had, like too many cleaning supplies had been used to mask the dusty smell of the old building. She padded down the familiar hallways, navigating the corridors like an expert. Professor Turner's office was on the fourth floor of the building. She knew it was a bad move to run all the way up the stairs. She would be trapping herself in the stairwell, but she didn't have another choice.

Jerking the door open, she took the stairs two at a time. Her breathing was ragged by the time she reached the top floor, but at least she didn't feel eyes on her now. Her pursuer must not have known where she went.

Cautiously, she strode down the corridor, searching for Professor Turner's office. Halfway down the hall, she heard a door click. Her heart leapt out of her chest, she spun around to see if someone was behind her, but no one was there. Although she didn't get that nagging feeling in the pit of her stomach, telling her someone was watching, she felt like she was in the wrong place, like she had made the wrong move. She felt as if she had accidentally placed her guarding Bishop in front of her opponent's Queen.

Having no other choice, she moved in front of Professor Turner's office and knocked softly. "Professor," she whispered, "are you in there?"

No response.

"Professor, it's urgent! I know it's not during school hours, but I must speak with you. There are things I need to tell you."

Still no response.

"Professor! Someone is following me!" She knocked again, anxious to get out of the open hallway and into the safety of his office.

Yet, no response came.

Devon swallowed back her rising anxiety, and she did what she never would have normally done. She reached out her hand for the door handle, knowing that it wasn't smart, knowing that it would lead to her downfall, but she had to get away. Whoever was chasing her was forcing her hand.

She twisted the knob and slowly eased it open to a seemingly empty room.

"Professor," she murmured softly, glancing around.

"Devon," someone called out.

But she didn't know who it was or even where the voice came from.

Just then, a hand clamped down on her wrist.

"DEVON. DEVON," SOMEONE called out to her, shaking her shoulder.

Gasping in air, her eyes shot open, and she stared up at Hadley. She couldn't breathe, and her heart was racing. No matter what she did, she just kept sucking in dry dead air.

"Hey, it's all right. It's just me," Hadley said, rubbing her shoulder reassuringly. "Are you okay?"

Devon tried to get herself under control, but she was having considerable trouble. Her skin was cold and sticky, and her shirt was soaked through. She pulled in a shuddering breath, and her chest expanded appreciatively as oxygen filled her lungs. She slowly released the air. The movements became easier with time. As she brushed her fingertips under her eyes, she felt her eyelashes were wet.

God, can you cry in your sleep? she wondered.

"Seriously, Devon, you look like a ghost. Do you need me to get you something?" Hadley asked with concern written across her pretty face.

Devon ran a hand back through her matted blonde hair. Great, she would have to take another shower. "Yeah, I'm all right," she whispered, her voice strained.

"You sure?" Hadley asked, her eyes wide. "I'm going to get you some water. Be right back."

Hadley disappeared, and Devon was grateful. She was grateful for the silence and the light that streamed in through the window, signifying it was still daytime. Her bottom lip quivered as she scooted up against the headboard, letting the chills work their way out of her body.

She had been having nightmares all week, the most vivid ones she had ever had in her entire life. Every morning, she had woken up more exhausted than when she had went to bed, like she had been running a marathon instead of sleeping for eight hours. She felt beyond dehydrated, and her head constantly ached.

Devon had taken to napping during the day, so she could sleep less at night to avoid dreaming. Until today, the nightmares had never come for her while she was napping.

Hadley reappeared in the doorway with a glass of water. She carefully handed it to Devon, looking really freaked out. Devon felt bad about the whole situation. She took a few sips of the water, feeling the ice-cold liquid slide down her throat and coat her stomach.

"Sooo…are you okay?" Hadley asked, repeating her question.

"Yeah, I'm fine," Devon said reflexively.

"Bad dream?" Hadley asked, clearly not buying her statement.

"I don't know. I don't remember," Devon lied. She couldn't tell

Hadley what she had been seeing day in and day out; that would only raise questions. Devon didn't know what all the dreams were about, but she had a clue. And if she had a clue, Hadley could fathom a guess as well.

Hadley gave her a perplexed look. With a sigh, she nodded. "All right. If you don't want to talk about it, that's fine. I've just never seen you like this. You've never had nightmares before, did you?"

What could Devon say? Hadley had lived with her for two-and-a-half years, and Hadley knew her like no one else. Devon could only hold up pretenses for so long.

"No," Devon finally answered. "I didn't have them before. They're new."

"When did they start?" Hadley asked like an overindulgent parent.

"I don't know," Devon said, looking down. She knew perfectly well when they had started, but she wasn't about to spill.

"Well, I hope they stop. It's not healthy," Hadley said, standing. She seemed resigned to let Devon off the hook.

"I hope they stop, too," Devon agreed with a tentative smile.

"We're leaving for the party soon. I was about to get dressed. See you in a bit." Hadley walked out of the room, leaving Devon in peace.

Devon sighed, sitting back against the headboard. She closed her eyes, submitting to the darkness. How could this keep happening? When she had left, she thought the dreams would go away. She had hoped that maybe she made the right decision, so they would stop entirely. Instead, they had done the opposite.

Peeling her eyes open, she finished off the rest of the water

Hadley had given her and walked into the bathroom. She stripped off her clothes, tossing them into a basket next to the toilet, and then she turned on the shower as hot as it would go. She ran a brush through her tangled hair until it was free of knots as the room thickened with steam. All she wanted to do was scald away the memories of someone's eyes on her, the desperation of the chase, and the nauseating feel of the person's grip on her arm.

She stepped into the water, hissing as it touched her skin. The water felt like needles piercing through her skin wherever it touched her. It hurt. She couldn't deny that it hurt, but the pain felt like home. And so, instead of turning down the heat, she succumbed to it.

Her hair soaked through as she finally edged her body back into the blistering water. Closing her eyes, she let the water slowly rake over her face, rush down her front, and pool at her feet. At least in here, she only felt the pain from the water. A pain she could endure.

Devon turned, facing the stream of water. She pressed her forehead against the cool ceramic shower wall, and she let the water flow down her back as rivulets from her wet hair ran over her chest. She sighed and allowed her mind to forget.

Her hand trailed down her front to the heat between her legs. She tentatively brushed her fingers up against herself, testing to see how sensitive the heated water made her. Her body jerked lightly at the touch...even more sensitive than she would have thought. It was a welcome touch. Her body hadn't had any release in a long time…too long.

Devon bit her lip as she slid her finger across the wet surface, spreading and delving in. Her mind raced as her finger came out slick and ready. Her body tightened fractionally as she moved across the soft area, one digit slipping in and out teasingly.

Her breathing slowed, and her core pulsed as she thought about someone gripping her in all the right ways. Her mind traveled to a distant place, far away from the life she was living.

He grabbed both of her arms and pushed her onto the bed, spreading her legs wide for his enjoyment. She smiled up at him, waiting for him to take her. She wanted him. God, she wanted him. Her body heated as he slid his pants to the ground and pushed his way inside.

Devon came in a sputter as the memories and her fingers pushed her over the edge. Her knees weakened, and she hunched over in the shower, panting.

CHAPTER 6
Signature Room at the 95th

SOME HOURS LATER, Devon was standing at the base of the John Hancock Center, one of the tallest buildings in the world, in downtown Chicago. Looking straight up the glass structure made her stomach flip-flop. The wind was particularly vicious in the Windy City, and Devon was pretty sure the building was visibly swaying.

"You want me to go up there?" Devon asked Hadley and Garrett incredulously.

"It'll be fun," Hadley told her reassuringly.

Not that Devon had ever had a particular fear of heights, but tempting fate didn't seem like fun by any stretch of the imagination. Her face must have shown her disbelief because Hadley wound her arm around Devon's, pulling her toward the entrance.

"Come on, Dev," Garrett said, taking the lead. "You'll like the bar, and you can't even tell it's swaying when you're up there."

Devon's face paled.

"Garrett!" Hadley said, swatting at him.

He chuckled and ducked away from her.

"I want you to have a good time, and you've never been here. I mean, when are you going to be in Chicago again?" Hadley asked her.

Devon bit her lip and diverted her eyes, avoiding the question. She still needed to figure out how to have that conversation with Hadley.

"Plus, I've been working so much this week, and we haven't really spent much time together. Come hang out with me like old times," Hadley pleaded, widening her eyes.

"I want to hang out with you. I'd just prefer to do it somewhere...I can't die," Devon said, looking back up at the building.

"You won't die!" Hadley rolled her eyes. "Garrett and I will be there to take care of you in case you feel like you might die. Plus, Brennan will be there, too, I think...if we can pin him down to anything. I mean, you like Brennan, right?"

Devon swallowed. "Yeah, he's all right," she said dismissively.

She had spent the last week in Jenn's Restaurant, eating burgers and occasionally taking shots of tequila. Brennan had been there every day, except Monday, just like he had said. He had usually left her in peace while she went through pictures on her phone or scribbled away in her notebook. Sometimes, he had come over to talk to her, but only when it had seemed she was deepest in thought over something else. She had the hardest time pinning down what it was about him that she liked so much.

"Well, see, this will be perfect. The building has been standing since the '60s. I don't think we'll have a problem tonight," Hadley told her, shoving her inside.

Garrett veered them toward the elevators, and they waited a couple minutes for it to reach their floor.

How long do I have to be in that thing? Devon wondered.

When the elevator doors finally opened, they rushed inside. Devon looked around skeptically while Hadley pressed the button for the 95th floor. The elevator shot up like a bullet, leaving Devon's stomach floors below them. Her ears popped uncomfortably as she tried to ignore the headache that was a constant on her temples since she had awoken from her nightmare.

She closed her eyes, feeling the pressure all around her as the elevator ascended, and then it slowed, coming to a gradual stop before pinging open on their floor. Devon tentatively walked out into the Signature Room at the 95th, the John Hancock Center bar and restaurant. She half expected the ground to shake beneath her, but it was completely solid, no swaying or anything. She felt better about that at least.

The room was open and spacious. A long bar took up the far wall, and black tables and chairs were already crowded. The real view lay beyond the bar itself. Floor-to-ceiling glass walls showed off a spectacular view of Chicago and Lake Michigan as far as the eye could see.

Garrett gestured to the right, claiming it had the better view, and they nudged through a small crowd to gain seats near the window. Devon walked right up to the glass and stared out at the city lit up a thousand feet below her. She drank in the sight, wanting to remember what it felt like to be on top of the world.

Devon pulled out her phone and snapped a few shots, wishing she had something better to take pictures with. Her camera phone just wasn't doing the view justice, but then again, maybe nothing ever could.

"Want me to take a picture of you?" Garrett offered, standing next to her.

Devon shook her head. "No, thanks. The view is good enough."

"You have something against getting your picture taken?" He crossed his arms, turning his attention away from the window to her.

"No, I just don't need my face plastered in front of something so exquisite. How could I ever measure up?" She gave him a soft smile.

Garrett had been unconditionally kind since she had arrived. He had allowed her to stay in the guest bedroom of his apartment for an entire week. He had taken care of her when she had been sick, and he had shown her around the city. They had gotten lunch a few times before he had to go to work. One night, she had fallen asleep while watching reruns of Whose Line Is It Anyway? After he had gotten home late from work, Garrett had woken her up and ushered her into bed. They had repeated their excursion to the park complete with Popsicles another time when Hadley had been working. Devon found that even though she hadn't spoken to Garrett about why she had left, he had pried open her shell, and she was able to relax around him. She knew why Hadley liked him so much.

"I think this blonde runs a little too deep," Garrett said, deflecting the question.

"How original. A blonde joke," Devon responded, rolling her eyes.

"I doubt you have one picture of yourself in Chicago. How will anyone believe you were actually here?" Garrett asked.

I hope no one ever does, she thought.

Devon just shrugged. She couldn't tell him that.

"Have it your way. What do you want to drink? I'm going to the bar," he told her with a smile.

"Gin and tonic would be great. Do you need some cash?" she asked, reaching into her purse.

"On me." He held up his hands to show he wouldn't accept any money from her.

"Thanks, Garrett," Devon said sincerely.

Where did Hadley find this guy?

With a heavy sigh, Devon watched him walk away. She wished she could tell someone what she was going through. But how could anyone understand? Hadley would have a field day, and Devon wasn't ready for that kind of freak out. She didn't really know Garrett, so he wasn't an option. She knew she should try to talk to her mom, but Devon had been avoiding her calls all week, hoping her mom would get the hint.

Each time Devon really thought about it, she felt sick to her stomach. *How can I tell anyone if I can't even decide whether or not I made the right decision?*

"I can't believe it's already been a week," Hadley said, coming to stand next to Devon. "Where does the time go?"

"Well, you have a job," Devon said.

"Ugh, don't remind me," Hadley said dramatically.

"You love your job."

"Yeah, well, it's still a job," she said with a shrug.

"Garrett's pretty great," Devon said, changing the subject.

"Dev, he's more than pretty great. He's like so freaking amazing. And let me just tell you," Hadley said, angling her body to look directly at Devon, "he's beyond impressive." She raised her eyebrows and smirked.

Devon laughed at Hadley attempt at being discreet. It was so unlike her friend.

"Plus, seriously, he's an animal in bed. I just…I'm blown away," Hadley told her.

Now, that sounded more like her.

"You know the kind of luck I had in college."

"Oh, yes, poor little Hadley always had to date the hottest guys on campus."

"But they all had small dicks, and I had to teach them how to use it," Hadley complained.

"What about Jason?" Devon asked. "You never complained about him."

Hadley glanced away with a big goofy grin on her face. "I forgot about Jason. But it doesn't matte; Garrett is better than them all! I can't get over how good the sex is."

"Good," Devon said, looking back out across the Chicago skyline. She didn't want to have this conversation. Not only did she not want to think about Garrett and Hadley going at it like animals, Devon really did not want to think about sex at all. Too many complications there.

"I know we don't spend all that much time together because our work schedules conflict, but our time is well spent," she said with a giggle.

How did the conversation steer in this direction?

"Thanks for making me come up here. It's really great," Devon said, changing the subject once again.

"Oh, I know what's good for you!" Hadley said.

"Is that so?" Devon asked curiously.

"Psh! I've always known better than you."

Devon wanted to ask Hadley what would be good for her. Maybe Hadley knew the answer. But the moment was lost.

"Here you are, ladies," Garrett said, returning with three full glasses in his hands.

Devon accepted her drink out of his hand and smiled. "Thank you."

"No problem," he said with a broad grin as he handed Hadley

some bright blue drink.

Devon took a gulp of her gin and tonic. It was the only way she could drink it. She didn't really like gin, but it gave her the best buzz. She wasn't sure why, but it worked so fast and made her so happy. She would gulp down the taste of pine needles to get to that high any day. Maybe she would eventually learn to like it.

She finished her drink in a hurry, wanting to wash away the memories of her dream along with the thoughts Hadley had forced into her mind. Devon might be a wreck later, but it was supposed to be her going-away party after all. She went to the bar and ordered another. She knew she should take it easy, but she didn't want to.

When she returned, unfamiliar faces had overrun their table, and two other tables had been added to their corner. Hadley waved Devon over and introduced her to the group. They were all Hadley's friends from work, all attached to her husband or fiancé. Devon didn't care to know any of their names. They were here for Hadley anyway.

She took a vacant seat next to Garrett and pretended like she was interested in the conversation. Most of the conversation centered on things Devon didn't think about—weddings, marriage, and babies.

Her mother wanted her baby girl to have a huge Southern wedding on a Nashville plantation covered in lace and lilies and complete with cowboy boots and bow ties. But Devon wouldn't be the one to have that kind of wedding. If her appearance in Chicago was any indication, she certainly wasn't ready for marriage.

"Sorry I'm late," a voice said, breaking into the conversation.

Devon looked up to see Brennan standing near Garrett. He was staring at her, and she smiled at him, happy to know someone else here. He was dressed simply in dark fit jeans and a snug grey T-shirt. He had taken the time to do his hair. It seemed a day off suited him.

"Belle," he said, nodding his head at Devon.

"It's Devon," she reminded him, like she had done all week.

He had taken to shortening Southern belle when he referred to her. She was pretty sure he would do it just because she would correct him about it.

"Hey, man!" Garrett said cheerfully. He stood and shook Brennan's hand. "Good to see you."

"You, too," Brennan replied.

He never had as much enthusiasm as Garrett, but then again, Devon didn't think many people did.

"Take my seat," Garrett offered. "I'm heading to the bar. You want anything?"

"Just a beer," Brennan said.

Garrett nodded and loped off toward the bar. Brennan took his vacant seat between Hadley and Devon. As he sat down, Devon noticed something was off about him. She wasn't sure what it was, but his movements weren't as graceful and his eyes were a bit glazed over. Was he drunk already?

When Brennan turned to look at her, she glanced down at her nails, acting as if she hadn't been staring at him. She had been caught doing that one too many times this week. He just seemed like a puzzle she wanted to put together.

"When do you leave?" Brennan asked directly, still looking at her.

Devon shrugged, glancing up. "Soonish," she said noncommittally.

"Are you going to stop by Jenn's before you head out?"

She tilted her head to assess him. Was he asking her to stop by? She never knew with him. Sometimes, she thought he had liked her presence hanging around the restaurant and bothering him. Other times, he had treated her more like a bug he was trying to swat away. His changing moods kept her wondering about him.

"Probably," she answered.

He nodded and then looked away.

What the hell was that about? she wondered. She really wanted to ask him, but prying into his personal business wasn't a good idea because it was usually reciprocated.

Devon finished her second drink and placed it on the table in front of them. She glanced over at the bar, which was now overly crowded. She decided she didn't want to go over there to wait in line.

"We should have had this party at Jenn's," Devon said, leaning into Brennan when she spoke.

He turned back to face her, and she found they were much closer together than they had been.

"You think?" he asked, cocking an eyebrow.

She glanced down at his lips and then back up before she

scooted a little farther away. He smelled good.

"I, uh…well, at least then I wouldn't have to wait in line," she said, gesturing to the bar.

"But then, I'd be working," he reminded her. "And I kind of like being here."

Devon swallowed and wondered if he meant he liked being here with her. No, that was ridiculous. Although, she liked being here with him right now, but she would never say that.

"Someone has to be working tonight since you're not there, right?" Devon asked, trying to stay on topic.

He was just a lot closer than she should have been comfortable with, but somehow it didn't bother her.

"Yeah, Kami is covering the bar, but she's not that great," Brennan said, looking down into her eyes and smiling.

The air suddenly felt very warm, and her cheeks flushed.

"I'm sure she's fine."

"Anyway, if this was Jenn's, I would feel obligated to make your drinks. Then, I would get stuck behind the bar. So, really, it's better this way," he said, leveling her with his steady gaze.

"It is better this way," she agreed, not able to hold it back. "Otherwise, you would be too busy."

As soon as the words left her mouth, her face colored further, and Brennan smirked. She wondered what he was thinking. Did he think she was being presumptuous? After all, she didn't know if he had a girlfriend, and he didn't know about Reid. But her mind, slightly addled by alcohol, had jumped right through the barriers.

Instead of trying to cover up her embarrassment or decipher him again, she stood quickly. "I'm just, uh…going to go to the restroom," she told Brennan.

A smile crossed his lips as he stared up at her. "All right."

"If anyone asks, that's where I'll be," she said as she backed away.

"All right," he repeated, his smile widening.

Devon darted for the restroom, her face flaming. How was she such a mess? Had she really said that? Honestly, what was wrong with her?

She couldn't remember the last time she'd had a conversation with someone who made her feel like that much of an idiot. Normally, because Reid would always be at her side, she was never put in those kinds of situations. What would Reid think now if he could see her rushing off to the restroom with her face redder than a tomato? She didn't even want to think about it.

Unsurprisingly, there was a line at the women's restroom. Devon stood just outside of the door, waiting for people to file out. After a few women exited, she edged inside and stared at the large window before her eyes. The entire outside wall was glass with quite literally the best view of Chicago she had seen. It was way better than where they were sitting by the bar. Why would this view be hidden in the women's restroom?

Devon walked up to the glass as she waited for the stalls to empty out. Her mind was all over the place, running between her dream, the shower, Brennan's smile, and the sloshy feeling in her brain, and then back around and around again.

Soon, the restroom was quiet, and Devon entered a stall, hoping the room stayed silent. She did her business and thumbed through her phone. She had been glued to it even more so than normal because she couldn't check in with anyone. She had deactivated her Facebook and Twitter accounts, and she had chosen to permanently ignore the incoming emails. Reid had sent another one, asking about her trip, but she would put off a reply as long as possible. She could feign Internet complications or something.

It was a strange feeling to be completely alone in a world of activity. No technological linkages were rooting her to the ground. Thinking about that made her feel even worse, so she stuffed her phone back into her purse, preparing to leave.

Devon heard the restroom door swing open. She slid her shoulder purse over her head as she listened to the girls on the other side of the wall.

"You want to?" one girl asked.

Devon scrunched her brows. She wasn't typically an eavesdropper, but they weren't being secretive.

"Yeah, I only do it every once in a while," a second girl responded.

That sounded even stranger. Devon swung open her stall door and walked over to the sink to wash her hands. The two girls were huddled in the corner with a third girl hidden behind them. Devon washed and dried her hands, and then took one last glance at the odd group of girls loitering in the corner of the restroom.

She watched one girl bend over and sniff loudly, and then she straightened and brushed under her nose. Devon froze. Holy shit! Were they seriously doing cocaine in the restroom? Just out in the open like that?

Devon couldn't believe it. She stayed rooted to the ground, staring in shock at the girls in front of her. Then, she paid more attention, something she hadn't been doing since she had arrived in Chicago. Those girls looked familiar. The two with their backs to her had been sitting with Hadley. They must have worked with her.

As her eyes shifted to the girl hidden behind the other two, she saw a rush of blonde hair nearly the same color as her own. Devon's mouth dropped open. No way!

CHAPTER 7
Highs of Life

EVON STUMBLED OUT of the restroom. Her mouth was hanging on the floor as she rushed away from the scene behind her. What the hell had just happened?

She was more in shock than surprised over the whole thing. It had come out of nowhere. Hadley had always been driven and ambitious, going after the things she wanted with zeal. Couple that with her spontaneity and the enormity of a big city, and Devon was sure recreational drug use was more likely than unlikely. Classmates who grew up here had told her that Chicago in particular was a cesspool for drug use. Young professionals from all over the Midwest would flood the city and get caught up in a lifestyle befitting their wealth. It was a status symbol, a social norm of sorts.

Devon found it disgusting. She knew she wasn't exactly one to talk about being an upstanding member of society, but she had grown up around musicians. Devon knew all about the lifestyle.

How many parties had she come home to where things had gotten out of hand? Her parents didn't have to be in the spotlight, and it still affected them. The industry was out of control, and anyone touched was sucked into it like a tornado. Even Devon, as far on the outskirts as she could get, had smoked pot in high school. She had given it up when she moved out, and she had become more vocal to her parents about her distaste.

But Hadley…

Oh, Hadley.

Hadley had never even smoked pot in college. People had made fun of her for never trying anything. She was so carefree. She had said she didn't need drugs to alter her mood because she was so awesome without them.

Now, she's snorting coke in public?

Devon couldn't fathom it. How had she lost so much of her best friend in just one semester? Then again, who was she to judge? Devon had lost all of herself in that amount of time. Or had it been happening longer, and she had just finally opened her eyes?

She sank down into her chair and stared out across the Chicago skyline. She probably should have left right away. She didn't know how to deal, and the more she thought about it, the more pissed she became. Hadley was just being irresponsible doing that shit somewhere she could get caught. How often was she using? Did Garrett know? Was he also on drugs?

Devon had so many questions. But if she asked Hadley to open up, would Hadley require her to do it in turn?

"Hey, Belle. You all right?" Brennan asked, sliding back into the chair next to her.

"Stop calling me that," she spat.

"Huh," he said.

"Stop that, too!"

"Stop what?" He stared at her blankly.

She looked away. "Oh, nothing."

"You need a shot?" He offered her the tequila in his hand.

"No. Shots don't fix everything," she said, turning to glare at him.

It was enough that her life was a mess. Hadley wasn't supposed to be fucked up, too. Hadley was supposed to be the well-grounded, smart, and successful one. She was supposed to have the world at her feet.

"Suit yourself." Brennan tipped back the drink.

"What's your deal?" she asked, her despair getting the best of her.

Brennan shrugged. "What's your deal?"

He was looking directly into her eyes now. It made her uncomfortable, so she looked away. She really just wanted to say that she had asked first, but in the interest of not sounding like a toddler, she held it back.

"I just don't get you."

"Sorry," he said unapologetically.

Sorry? Like that explains everything away, she thought bitterly.

"Are you always this talkative?" she asked dryly.

"Well, I thought you were quiet," he said with a shrug.

She was certain that he was purposely evading her questions now. Considering how little she was telling anyone, his nonanswers were downright infuriating.

"Whatever," she finally consented. "I think I'm going to leave. I need to talk to Hadley about…some shit, but I think she'll be more articulate tomorrow."

"Why? Is she wasted?" he asked, looking up at Devon where she now stood over him.

Devon sighed in frustration. "You could say that," she huffed.

"Hey," Brennan said, catching Devon's arm before she walked away, "you're not going home alone, are you?"

He slowly stood up, wavering a bit on his feet. If anyone was wasted, it was Brennan. Devon was feeling surprisingly sober after her rendezvous in the restroom.

"Yes," she said, looking down at his arm, "I'm going home alone."

"No way." He shook his head. "The city isn't safe at this hour."

"And you're going to do what?" she asked, looking him up and down. "You can barely walk."

He blinked a few times and then straightened. He was clearly trying to make himself look more stable, but Devon wasn't fooled.

She had been drunk enough before to know that look in his eye was far from sobriety. And she wasn't going to have some drunk guy she had only known for a week help her home. That offer didn't sound like it promised anything but mayhem.

"Seriously, I'll be fine," she told him.

Though, to be honest, the thought of going out in the city by herself was daunting. As it was, her nightmares left her running through unfamiliar dark streets. She didn't want to live her nightmares in real life.

"No, you won't. Not in Chicago, Belle," he said, slurring her nickname.

"Brennan, you're drunk. Pretty much wasted. You're going to be no help on the streets tonight," Devon said.

"Plan on getting on a train tomorrow? Well, you walk around Chicago by yourself, and you won't be," he told her.

Devon swallowed hard. She didn't want to be on a train tomorrow. In fact, she wanted nothing less than to not return to St. Louis. She just hadn't figured out how to stay.

"What do you suggest then?" she demanded, wanting to get out of here.

He smiled lazily. "My place is just around the corner. You can crash there."

Devon flushed. "I think I'll just find a cab or something."

"Hey, guys!" Hadley cried, crashing back into the party. "Let's do some shots!"

"I think I'm going to go back," Devon said, crossing her arms.

"What? No, you just got here, and you're leaving tomorrow," Hadley said.

Devon didn't want to make a scene in the middle of the bar, but she was becoming more and more irritated because Hadley was treating her like an idiot. Devon was far from an idiot.

"I just think it's time to leave," she said.

"Nope, nope," Hadley said, hanging on Devon's arm and leaning on her shoulder. "This is your party. You're staying."

Devon pulled Hadley out of earshot. "It stopped being my party when you and your friends went into the restroom to snort cocaine. Hadley, what the fuck?"

Devon wasn't going to ask. She had never thought that it would happen, but she was worried about her friend. Ironic, to say the least, but the last thing she wanted was for Hadley to get addicted to drugs and give up everything she had been working toward.

Hadley's face paled. "What?"

"You heard me. I was there."

"I didn't—"

"Hadley, please," Devon said, holding up her hand.

"It's only been once or twice, Devon," she said, realizing she wasn't getting out of it.

"I don't care. It's addictive for a reason. It could ruin your life."

"It's not going to ruin my life," Hadley said, rolling her eyes. "We're just having a good time."

"I've heard that before," Devon said.

"So, what? You're leaving because you're judging me and my

friends?" Hadley asked.

Devon watched Hadley's pupils visibly dilate before her eyes. Yeah, as if she hadn't taken cocaine.

"I don't care about your friends. I care about you."

"Well, don't worry about me," Hadley said with a shrug. "Will I see you later at the apartment?"

It was a dismissal. She was riding into her high, and likely, she wouldn't care about much.

"No," Devon said with a shake of her head. "I'm leaving with Brennan."

"Ohhh," Hadley said, raising her eyebrows. "Now, who is the rebel? Does he know about Reid? I say fuck him anyway. Brennan's gorgeous."

Devon rolled her eyes. In the morning, Hadley would realize that Devon wasn't there, and that would do enough to freak her out. She was too far-gone for Devon to reach anything logical.

"Bye, Hadley. Get home safe," Devon said sadly.

Maybe she should have waited with Hadley or should have said something more to get her to go home. Maybe she should have done more in general. But Devon felt completely defeated. If Hadley was this messed up, then what did it say about her?

Devon walked away from Hadley and back to where she had left Brennan.

"I'm going to find Garrett. Just give me a minute, and then we'll go," she told Brennan.

He seemed to find this acceptable. She left him standing there with his arms crossed over his chest. Garrett's bulky form was easy to locate in the crowd. He was talking with the husbands and fiancés of Hadley's friends. Devon couldn't even begin to remember their names.

Garrett smiled as she approached. "Hey, Dev. Are you enjoying your party?"

"I'm getting tired actually," she said, yawning. "Going to call it an early night."

"Oh, all right," he said, sounding a bit disappointed. "Have you told Hadley?"

"Yeah, she's pretty messed up though. Just wanted to make sure you knew to take extra care of her."

"I always do, but thank you. Do you need help getting home? Need me to hail you a cab or anything?"

"No, I'm fine. Brennan is going to help me out," she told him.

Garrett frowned at that. He clearly was more concerned. "I think he's pretty gone, too. Are you sure you don't want me to help?"

She did want his help, but she didn't want to go back to the place he shared with Hadley. She wanted to be angry with Hadley for her stupidity, and she couldn't do that if she were surrounded by her hospitality. She couldn't face Hadley the next morning when she would wake up and go about her life like she wasn't destroying it.

Devon declined his help once more and then left as quickly as she could extract herself. Garrett was too nice, too caring. Devon had never once thought that someone would be too good for Hadley…until this moment.

"I'm ready," she told Brennan when she reached him.

***

IT WAS A chilly night, and Devon hugged herself against the wind as they headed to Brennan's place. He hadn't been lying when he said he lived right around the corner. His apartment was no more than two or three blocks from the John Hancock Center. They took the elevator up to his apartment where it was thankfully warm.

She was surprised by the interior. She knew he probably made good money as a bartender in this part of the city, but she wouldn't have thought his apartment would be so nice. It was a one bedroom with a full kitchen with adjoined dining room, and spacious living room. The apartment was clean with relatively new furniture. It wasn't what she would have considered Brennan to have, being a bachelor and all.

Devon set her purse on a side table. "Nice place."

"Thanks," he said, walking into the kitchen and pulling out a beer. "Want anything?"

"No, thanks. I think I'm done."

"You didn't have much to drink for being so done." He was clearly more comfortable in his own home than at Jenn's or the bar.

"Just a long night is all."

"We left early."

"Yeah. Long in a different way then."

Devon sat down on the sofa and got comfortable amid the throw pillows. Brennan took a seat next to her and flipped on the television.

"You want to talk about it?" he asked, putting on ESPN as background noise.

"No," she said instantly.

"All right."

The conversation ended, and Devon sat there frozen, watching baseball highlights. She felt bad for cutting him off so abruptly. Maybe she was being ridiculous.

"How do you afford this place bartending?" she asked, hoping that the subject was neutral enough.

"Don't like to talk about it." He took a drink from his beer.

"Oh," she breathed.

Brennan finished his beer in silence and then placed the empty bottle on the coffee table. Devon watched as he stood and stretched out his lean muscles. He wasn't overly built, but he was all muscle. He raised his arms over his head, and her eyes darted to his exposed stomach, then quickly away.

He left for a minute and then returned with a bunch of blankets in his arms. He tossed them onto the couch. "You taking the bed, Belle?"

"Couch is good with me," she told him.

"Whatever suits you, suits me," he said. "Here's the remote."

"You can just turn it off. I'm going to pass out," she said, averting her eyes.

He turned to go, but then he seemed to think better of it. He sat down next to her on the couch again. "You going to tell me what's eating at you?" He looked at her more intently than ever before.

She shook her head. "Nothing is."

"You pissed about Hadley?" he asked, hitting on the most superficial problem.

"How did you know?"

"I pay attention."

"So…you know what she's up to?" she asked carefully.

"That she's snorting coke?" he asked. "Yeah, I know about that."

"Does Garrett know?" she asked quickly.

Brennan shook his head. "No way. He thinks she's perfect. Could you imagine if Mr. Perfect found out his Princess was a coke addict?"

"She's an addict?" she squeaked.

"Depends on your definition. She's done it more than a few times."

He was being loose with his words because he was drunk. Devon probably shouldn't have been taking advantage of the situation in his state, but she wanted answers.

"How do you know all about her problem if he doesn't?" Devon asked out of curiosity.

"When you've done shit before, you can see it in a person. Once she found out that I knew, she stopped hiding it around me," he told her honestly.

"You do…coke, too?" she asked, her heart sinking. Was that what was up with him? But didn't it normally make them upbeat or fidgety?

"Nah. Just once and knew it wasn't for me. Mostly weed."

Ah, that explains it, she thought.

"You could use some weed," Brennan told her. "You're too uptight, Belle."

Devon frowned. Typical. "I'm going to pass."

"Suit yourself, but I think you'd like it," he said, turning to face her with a smile.

"I've done it before," she said, not wanting to admit how much she used to smoke. For a long time, she had thought she studied better high. It had become a problem when she was pretty much always studying.

"You?" he asked with raised eyebrows.

"Yeah. Surprised?"

"Wouldn't have pegged you."

"Oh right, square." Devon gestured at herself with her hands.

"I dig square," he told her bluntly.

Oh damn, how messed up is he? Devon wondered.

"Thanks," she whispered, glancing down.

She didn't know how else to deflect the conversation. Brennan was nice…well, kind of, and he was very attractive. She needed to get out of this territory. She was here for a place to crash, and crashing sounded like a good idea right about now.

When Devon felt his hand reach out and touch her cheek, her eyes fluttered up to meet his. Before she had a chance to react, he leaned forward and kissed her lips. Her shock held her at bay. He did nothing more than hold his soft lips against hers. They were foreign and strange yet enticing.

She felt her body respond to his touch. His fingers moved and threaded through her hair, tugging on it slightly in his haste. She had too many thoughts swirling in her head to keep it all straight at once. The most prominent ones were how good this felt, how wrong this felt, and how surprised she was that he was even doing this.

Had he ever given her an indication that he wanted to kiss her before that last comment? She couldn't remember.

She didn't know why, but tears welled in her eyes. They slid easily down her cheeks, mixing salt with the taste of alcohol on his lips.

Brennan pulled back to look at her and she gasped out, "I have a boyfriend."

Brennan dropped his hands into his lap. "Oh."

Devon bit down on her lip as she waited for him to say something more. He just stared at her, his eyes slightly hazy. She wanted him to say something, anything. Was he pissed? Was he shocked? Did he expect something from her?

"Good night then," he said finally as he stood.

She stared up at him, her brow furrowed with trepidation. Was that it? He wasn't mad? He wasn't going to push the topic? Didn't he have more to say?

He made it all the way to his bedroom door before turning back to look at her. He seemed to be waiting for something, but she didn't know what it was.

"Good…good night, Brennan," she told him.

Whatever she was supposed to say…that wasn't it.

He hung his head a little and then nodded. "Have a safe trip tomorrow, Devon."

FOLLOWING ME

As Brennan shut the door behind him, she realized that was the first time he had ever called her by her name.

D EVON WALKED DOWN the dirt lane kicking her cowboy boots against the small rocks in her path. The day was approaching dusk, and the sun was hanging heavy over the horizon, splattering the sky with pink, orange, and yellow. She finger combed her blonde hair down to her waist. She wished she had a hat because her hair was a rat's nest.

She whistled her latest tune recalling the lyrics she had sang for her parents earlier that day. They liked them the song so much that they wanted to send it off to a label. They thought their Dixie girl would be a star. She didn't know about any of that, but she liked writing it all down.

Devon veered off the road, taking a shortcut through an open field. She was thankful for her boots as she trekked through the waist-high grass. It had been a warm day, but the night was rapidly cooling the temperatures. She shouldn't have been surprised in the least, but somehow, she would always forget her cardigan for the walk.

The wind whipped across the grass, tying her hair in knots and matting it to her face. She struggled to keep it away, but there was just too much of it for it to make a difference. While she fought with her hair, her sundress flew up around her stomach. She yanked it back down to cover herself, but she was having little luck. Grumbling in frustration, she cursed the wind for its timing.

She and her brother, Dustin, had taken this shortcut for years. It was only a matter of time before Dani knew about it as well. That thought terrified Devon.

When she crossed the halfway point between the road and the woods, she heard boots crunching against the earth behind her. Rolling her eyes, Devon turned back around.

Dustin better not be trailing me again, she thought.

Her eyes roamed the field, trying to make out if someone was on the road. She couldn't really see anyone, but out here, that didn't mean no one was there. Shaking off the feeling, Devon turned and continued across the open field. She had plans, and getting spooked out in the open wasn't going to stop her.

When her feet hit the tree line, the hair on the back of her neck stood on end. Devon swallowed and looked around, her stomach sinking in apprehension. She felt ridiculous for feeling anxious like this, but her parents had filled her head with stories from the news about girls getting abducted, being sold into prostitution, and then getting killed. Too many stories like that had happened recently. She had always told her mom that she was a worrywart, but now that her nerves were getting to her, Devon was wondering if her mother worried for good reason.

She still didn't see anyone approaching, but she could feel eyes on her. It was an obvious feeling, like the way Matt had stared at her in the back of the classroom. But this was worse.

Hightailing it out of there, Devon broke through the trees onto the narrow trail. It wasn't a long walk from there, but she increased her pace anyway. She had a terrible feeling about all of this. Why hadn't she just stayed home? Why couldn't she listen to anything anyone told her?

She definitely heard footsteps behind her. They weren't exactly close, but they didn't have to be to freak her out. She was alone after all, and all things considered, she was a small person. There was no way she could fend off someone purposefully chasing her. Her only hope would be for her to make it out of the tree line.

Fear pushed at her pores, and she felt panic hitting her like a ton of bricks. What kind of person would chase after her in the middle of the woods? Would she be one of those news stories—pieces of a dead body from a young woman found buried in the woods near her house? Bile rose in her throat, and she swallowed it down. She was only freaking herself out more.

Taking off at a sprint, Devon pushed forward as fast as she could go. She had never been a runner, and the last beer she'd had was sloshing around in her stomach, slowing her down. Why had she done that? If she hadn't, would she be faster? She couldn't think about it.

Her boots slowed her down even more. They weren't meant for running distances. They were meant for horseback riding, and more importantly, they looked good.

Her feet pounded the dirt as she tried to hold her pace. The end of the trail was approaching, but she could feel her pursuer gaining on her. On a straight stretch in the trail, she looked over her shoulder, and her long hair flew out in every direction around her face. She could definitely see a figure, but with a quick look, she couldn't tell who it was or if she even recognized the person.

Hadn't her mother told her that 95 percent of reported cases were people that the victim knew firsthand?

Finally reaching the road, she looked both ways before crossing. She ran straight across the lawn between the double oak trees and up the creaking wooden stairs. She yanked open the screen door and banged on the front door. Devon heard a familiar answering call, and she pushed into the house without another thought.

It was a small run-down one bedroom shack that hadn't been inhabited for as long as Devon had known about it. She had been sneaking away here to have sex with her boyfriend for nearly as long. He should already be here. He would protect her. Would the person following her try to get into the house? It wasn't secure by any means. Her pursuer wouldn't have a hard time breaking in.

Devon slammed the door shut and slid the lock into place, hoping that it would help.

"Mason!" she called out frantically.

No answer.

"Mason!" she yelled again, rushing to the closed bedroom door.

He had knocked back when she came to the door. It was their signal. She hadn't made up the fact that he had knocked back. Where the hell was he?

Devon pushed open the bedroom door and found the room transformed. It was stark white everywhere from the walls to the four-poster bed to the carpet and curtains. The room was unbelievably bright, like she had entered another world.

She looked around, taking a few hesitant steps into the room. When she heard the door close behind her, she jumped and glanced over her shoulder. Her exit had been sealed off, and as far as she could tell, there wasn't another exit.

"Mason?" she whispered, the words lodging in her throat. Her heart hammered in her chest as tears welled in her eyes.

How do I get out of this? she thought.

She felt eyes on her again, and she turned around to meet her pursuer. Before she had a chance to scream, the person grabbed her arm, wrenched it painfully behind her back, and planted her face-first into the mattress.

***

FOLLOWING ME

Devon awoke with a scream erupting out of her throat, the one she hadn't been able to let loose in her dream. She sat straight-up on the couch, her breathing heavy and her skin clammy. Pushing her hands up into her hair, she let the tears fall freely. She cried there helplessly until she had no more tears left, until her eyes were red and puffy, and until her throat was sore.

She moved the covers off her body and pushed herself off the couch, standing up on shaky legs. The door to Brennan's bedroom remained closed. She wondered if he had heard her screams or if he had slept through them. Either way, he hadn't opened the door, making his position very clear.

Stumbling forward into the kitchen, she poured herself a glass of water and downed it. Her clothes were wrinkled, and she didn't even want to think about how rumpled her hair was. Knocking on the bathroom door, she waited for an answer, and when she didn't hear one, she entered.

Her reflection stared back at her from the mirror over the sink, and she tried not to cringe away. She looked like a wreck—pale and gaunt with dark circles under her eyes. At least Brennan hadn't seen her like this. It wouldn't have mattered after what had happened last night, but still, it was better this way.

She scrubbed her face and tied her hair back into a ponytail, trying to make herself look presentable. It wasn't much use, not after crying so hard. She was an ugly crier; she always had been. Now that the blood was rushing back to her face, she was all red and splotchy. At least it would go away eventually.

Bending forward at the waist, she cradled her body against herself and begged and pleaded to whoever would listen for the nightmares to stop. This was the first time she had dreamed of home. It had felt so nice to be back in the Tennessee woods, and then the same thing had happened all over again. How many more times could she be chased? How many more times could she get caught? How many more times before she didn't wake up in time?

Her heart ached for home, and she pulled out her phone. She really wanted to call her mom, but in her condition, her mom would know how messed up she was. Instead, she tried calling Dustin's phone. He had just finished his third year of pharmacy school at the University of Michigan, and he was sticking around Ann Arbor to be close to his girlfriend, Kelly. They were in the same program and had only been dating for one semester.

"Hey, Dev," Dustin said, answering the phone.

"Hey," she said. "How have you been?"

"Better than you, it sounds," he said, knowing as quickly as her mom would that something was wrong.

"Well, I've been better," she admitted honestly.

She had a hard time lying to Dustin. Growing up, he had been her rock. They'd had their differences, but he was her big brother, and he had always been there for her.

"What kind of trouble are you getting in? Does this have anything to do with Mom badgering you about New York?" he asked.

"Has she been doing that to you as well?" Devon asked, thinking about how she had avoided her mom's calls the past week. She would rather talk about New York than her real issues.

"Hounding me like a dog, but she doesn't want me to bring Kelly. Said she wanted it to be a family thing." He sounded irritated.

"She said the same thing to me."

"I wouldn't worry about it, Dev. I don't think I'm going to go, but if you have a better suggestion for your birthday, let me know. I'd rather get wasted in St. Louis with you than spend quality time with the fam."

"Seems a bit unfair to Dani," Devon said.

"Oh no, it doesn't. Mom wants her to bring her boyfriend. Personally, I don't think Mom trusts Dani enough not to sleep with every guy she meets there. But who knows Mom's reasoning?" Dustin told her.

Devon laughed lightly. It felt good to laugh after everything else that had happened. She didn't feel healed, but Dustin certainly had a calming effect upon her.

"I never know her reasoning."

"So, you going to tell me what's wrong?" Dustin asked, changing the topic.

She sighed, wishing she knew how to tell Dustin. The more removed she got from what had happened, the more she wondered if it had happened at all. Maybe she had just blown it out of proportion. Maybe she had simply overreacted, and there was no need for her to run away. Maybe a conversation could have changed it all, and then she wouldn't have had to leave. Maybe she just hadn't tried hard enough.

What if she told him and it all became a reality? Then, she couldn't take it back. It would be out in the open.

"Do you remember when we used to go through that shortcut in the woods off the road that led to the abandoned house?" she asked tentatively.

"Yeah, we used to go there all the time," he said.

"I had a dream about that place, and it really freaked me out," she told him lamely.

"A dream about the old abandoned house? That's random, Dev."

"Yeah," she said softly, "really random. Someone seemed to be chasing me. Seriously, Dustin, it was really scary."

Dustin laughed in a mocking way that Devon had become so accustomed to. "It was just a dream, Dev. I have dreams about zombie attacks and getting chased up trees by a Tyrannosaurus rex. They're pretty scary, too. I wouldn't let these dreams mess you up too badly."

"True," she said disbelievingly.

"Oh, hey, Kelly just woke up. I've gotta run. I'll talk to you later. Let me know about your birthday."

After Dustin hung up, Devon dropped her head in front of the sink. He hadn't given her the opportunity to say anything more. It was reason enough for her to stay silent for a bit longer. She needed to figure out what she was doing and where she was going. She couldn't stay in Chicago because she didn't have the funds to remain, but she couldn't go back. Her life was in limbo as she teetered between staying and leaving. She had a decision to make, and it had to be made today.

Straightening, Devon exited the bathroom, smoothing out her clothes along the way. She didn't know if she should knock on Brennan's bedroom door and say good-bye or not. She nearly did three times, and then she decided against it.

When she reached the front door, she saw a note taped to it.

Went to the gym. Food in the fridge if you're hungry. Just lock the door on your way out. —Brennan

Ugh! How could he even want to go to the gym after the amount of alcohol he had consumed last night? Or was that just a cover so he could leave the house and avoid her?

She shook her head, lost in her own frustration. She grabbed her things, left the apartment, and walked to the nearest train station. She took the train back to Marina City. She wanted the embarrassment of what had happened with Brennan to be as far from her mind as possible.

Instead, Devon focused on something else she couldn't control. She needed to talk to Hadley before she packed up and left. Last night had ended poorly, and Devon didn't want to leave on these terms. Hadley was her best friend. Devon was pissed at her, no doubt, but she didn't want to see Hadley devolve any more. Devon couldn't leave and wonder if her friend was on a further downward spiral than she, herself was.

Lunch? We need to talk, Devon texted Hadley.

Devon received her response as she took the elevator up to the apartment. Fine. Jenn's? Hadley responded

I'll just meet you at that place across from your work. This is going to be quick.

I'm off at noon.

Devon changed into fresh clothes and brushed her teeth. She was glad Garrett wasn't there. She didn't want to face him this morning. He was always so bright and cheerful, and while he did tend to make her feel like a better person, she wasn't ready for that right now. Plus, he might know how pissed she was at Hadley. He might somehow see it, and she wasn't going to be the one to tell him that his girlfriend was a coke addict, at least not until Devon knew if it was necessary.

***

DEVON HOPPED ON another train to Hadley's building. Arriving at the restaurant across the street, she took over a booth in the back. It appeared to be nicer than Jenn's with fancy tablecloths, classical music playing in the background, and expensive artwork hanging on the walls. Devon wasn't a big fan, but it would be better to meet here than somewhere comfortable...somewhere near Brennan.

Hadley walked in, looking worse than Devon had expected. Had she been looking like this all week and Devon just hadn't noticed? Had Devon been so lost in herself that she hadn't seen her own friend's problems? She hadn't seen a lot of Hadley this week because of her job, but Devon didn't think Hadley had seemed that different.

"Hey." Hadley took a seat across from her and opened the menu, not making eye contact.

"Hey," Devon responded.

Hadley clearly wasn't going to throw her a line or anything. She stared stock-still at her menu. Devon was sure Hadley wasn't reading it.

"Hadley, come on," Devon pleaded.

"Don't act like you've been forthright the whole time you've been here," Hadley snapped, still not looking at her.

"Fair," Devon said, trying to bite back her retort. "I'll give you that, but I also wasn't flaunting my problems in everyone's faces in a public place."

Hadley dropped her menu down on the table. "I wasn't flaunting anything, Devon!"

Devon sighed, seeing how this was all going to go. "Fine. You weren't doing that either. I just happened to see it. But how long has this been going on? And how long are you going to keep it up?"

Hadley bit on her lip, her anger slipping slightly. She looked really young in that moment, less than her twenty-two years. "It hasn't been that long."

"How long?" Devon prompted.

"Only a month or two."

Devon's eyebrows rose.

"Okay, two."

"And you're stopping…when?" Devon asked.

Hadley looked away, her blonde hair framing her face. "It's not as often as you think," she said, her wall slamming back up.

Devon swallowed, wanting to take her friend by the shoulders and shake her. It was sad, considering everything she was hiding from Hadley. As much as this mirrored her problems, it was so very different.

"I just want you to take care of yourself."

"I can take care of myself just fine," Hadley snapped.

"I've no doubt," Devon drawled, her Southern accent coming out in full force.

"Don't use that tone with me," Hadley muttered.

"Does Garrett know?" Devon asked. She already knew the answer since Brennan had told her last night, but she wanted to hear Hadley's response. She needed to hear what Hadley would say face-to-face, no hiding.

"Of course, he knows," Hadley said, not meeting her eyes. "Do you think I would be living with him if he didn't know everything about me?"

Devon sat back hard in the booth, staring at her friend. Had Hadley ever purposely lied to her? Had Hadley ever been openly dishonest in any way? Hadley was many things, but a liar? No, she had never been a liar.

And then Devon knew what she had to do...

"I want to stay in Chicago for the summer," Devon told her.

Hadley's eyes shot to Devon's face as she looked at her incredulously. "Well, have a great time," she said sarcastically.

"I'm staying with you and Garrett," Devon told her matter-of-factly.

"What? It's Garrett's apartment. There is no way he is going to let you stay for three more months. Why do you want to stay anyway? Don't you miss your boy toy?"

"Doesn't really matter why I want to stay," Devon said. "I'm staying, and you're going to call and convince Garrett to let me live at the apartment."

"What?" Hadley asked, eyeing Devon like she was insane.

"Otherwise, I'm going to tell him that you're doing coke."

"But he already knows," she spat back as if Devon would believe her.

"Fine," Devon said, pulling out her phone. "Then, I'll just call and talk to him about it."

Hadley openly glared at her. She was clearly waiting for Devon to bluff.

Hadley thought there was no way Devon was going to dial through to his line, no way Devon would actually do it.

Devon's finger was poised over Garrett's number. She was about to push call.

Then, Hadley cried, "Wait! Jesus, Dev. You can stay with us. Of course, you can stay with us. I'll call him right now."

CHAPTER 9
Everything for a Price

GARRETT'S ONLY CONDITION for the summer was that Devon would contribute to the house by paying rent. That left Devon in an awkward position since she didn't have any savings to draw from that her parents didn't actively control. It would look suspicious if she suddenly laid out a grand without telling them. They would wonder if she was the one on drugs.

Devon wouldn't dare ask Hadley to help her with the money situation. Devon didn't want to know how much cash Hadley was shoveling into her new extracurricular activities. Plus, Devon couldn't afford to ask Hadley for more help.

Devon felt bad enough as it was for manipulating Hadley into letting her stay for the summer. She should have just been up-front about it all. If Hadley knew what Devon was going through, then she probably would have been more understanding. Hadley also might have hopped on a train to St. Louis to burn the place down. Devon wasn't really in the right mind-set yet to bare all her secrets, so she had acted impulsively and used Hadley's weaknesses against her. It was low, even with the position Devon was in, but she hadn't seen an alternative. And it had worked.

Now, Devon needed to find a way to pay rent. She knew Marina City wasn't exactly cheap either, and she didn't know how much Garrett was expecting her to pay. It was likely a third, but he hadn't said. He didn't really need the extra money, but Devon was sure he saw it as a compromise for her using the extra space, adding to the utility costs, taking away some of his privacy, and so on.

So, Devon had to immediately start looking for a job. Unless she wanted to sell her body for money, she didn't see an alternative to working during the summer. She couldn't exactly call her parents and ask them to clear the cash.

Her first instinct was to apply at Jenn's Restaurant, but after her last encounter with Brennan, she just couldn't bring herself to go there. Devon hadn't talked to him since she had left his apartment. He had thought she was leaving the city anyway. If she didn't alert him of her presence, then he would never have to know that she was staying. Her life was too complicated as it was without adding a romantic element to her time in the city.

Brennan was dangerous and attractive and caring…and she would have none of it. She had to shut down her brain when her thoughts began to venture in that direction. It would only do more harm than good. Eventually, she would have to return to St. Louis, and she didn't want guilty feelings on her conscience as well.

Without further ado, Devon began walking around the city, filling out applications wherever she could. Not many places were hiring at the moment. So many of them had already filled up their staff for the summer tourist season. The places that had signs up in the windows were looking for more experience or offering low wages or not hiring immediately. Anything that could possibly get in the way did.

Devon returned home empty handed and plopped down on the couch in the living room, propping up her feet on the coffee table. She was exhausted from another day of searching for jobs. It seemed like a futile mission. She was convinced she would never find anything in time to pay rent at the end of the month. She had already been scouting for two weeks, and the month was dwindling away. After three unsuccessful interviews out of at least a hundred applications, Devon was spent. She didn't know what else to do. If she couldn't get a job, she couldn't stay, which meant she had bullied her best friend at a time when she needed her the most for nothing.

She pulled up Netflix on the PlayStation and started flipping through the catalog of TV shows. She had never been a big TV fan before, but this was also one of the first times in her life she didn't have anything to do. Hadley was always at work, and when Garrett was here during the day, he would usually be locked away in his bedroom.

Deciding on the first season of Heroes, Devon kept her phone close by just in case someone decided they wanted to give her a job, and then she vegged out. After she made it all the way through episode two, Garrett made an appearance outside of his bedroom.

"What's up, Dev?" He pulled out a snack from the fridge and then took a seat next to her.

"Just praying that someone calls me for a job," she said, turning on episode three. Then, thinking better of it, she offered Garrett the remote. "Do you want to watch something?"

"No, Heroes is fine. Just so you know, the first season is addictive, but the other ones suck. You should probably stop now," he said.

Devon just shrugged, not having anything better to do. "I think I'll let myself get sucked in."

She swallowed hard, hearing herself say that out loud. Wasn't that always her problem? She always let herself just get sucked in to things, and then she couldn't or wouldn't want to find a way out. Even now that she was out of it, she couldn't believe it had all happened the way it had. She sometimes wondered if Chicago was the dream, and her dreams were reality.

"So, the job search isn't going so well?" Garrett asked, offering her a carrot from his plate.

"Ugh," she grumbled, tossing her head back. "It's the worst

possible thing ever. Why do businesses even advertise that they're hiring if they're not actually hiring? Or better yet, if they already have someone else in mind, why do they waste your time by setting up an interview with you? It's total bullshit."

"That's the worst. What kind of jobs are you looking into?" he asked sympathetically.

"Everything. Anything. I've scoured the newspapers, craigslist, and all over the fucking Internet. I've walked up and down the streets, checking for new signs. I think I'm pretty familiar with the landscape now," she said, half-joking. "There's just nothing out there. Most places aren't likely to hire someone they don't know who doesn't have a degree. Even a lot of the serving jobs…well, most are full, but they want someone who will be here after the summer. And when they see that I went to Wash U, they don't believe me when I say I'm not going back to St. Louis for school."

Devon wasn't sure where it had all come from. During the last two weeks, she had been so frustrated from trying to a find a job and having no one to talk to. Hadley was avoiding her as much as she could, Garrett was mostly absent, and Brennan was completely out of the picture. It was nice to just talk to someone.

Garrett pursed his lips. He seemed to be contemplating her scenario before speaking. She didn't know what he was going to say about it, but it couldn't be worse than what Hadley would likely say.

"I mean, I hate to say it, but it has only been two weeks," he looked sympathetic.

"I know," Devon relented. "I just have to pay you rent soon, and I don't have the money." She sheepishly looked down.

"Hey," he said, his hand landing on her knee, "don't worry about that. I'm sure we can arrange something."

Devon didn't know if she should hear the hidden meaning in that or not, but she chose not to. This was Garrett, and he was madly in love with her best friend. There was no way he was insinuating what she thought he was insinuating. To avoid accidentally spilling her thoughts, she didn't dare open her mouth.

"I'm sure you'll find a job soon, and in the meantime, feel free to stay as long as you like. I've made do without the rent this long, so I think I can manage otherwise. I trust you to pay it back when you actually do get a job. Don't stress yourself into the ground over it," he told her, pulling back his hand.

Devon felt like a shitty person. Was she a completely wrong judge of character? Or was she just so used to people being horrible and taking advantage of any situation that she had assumed someone like Garrett could be like that, too?

"Thanks, Garrett," Devon said. "I appreciate it, but I'm still going to look for work as hard as I can."

"I'll see if I know anyone that's hiring."

"That would be really helpful," she told him, breathing a sigh of relief.

They sat back then and enjoyed the next two episodes of Heroes before Garrett had to get ready for work. Devon wanted to be out of the house before Hadley got back anyway. It had been easier like that lately.

***

ALMOST ANOTHER WEEK WITH no luck was sending Devon's already spiraling depression farther down the rabbit hole. Garrett's search had come back with grim results. No one was hiring. She couldn't believe it.

How hard was it to find a job in this town? Seriously, it shouldn't be this difficult, she thought, crossing the street.

May had disappeared so quickly. How had she already been here a month without finding a job? It felt like it was just yesterday when she had pulled up to Union Station with Dustin's music blasting in her ears. She was amazed she had made it this long. She had never thought she would be strong enough, but here she was. She was still searching for a job, so she could find a way to stay two more months.

The route Devon normally had taken walked past Jenn's Restaurant, but kept her out of sight. She had been in the city long enough that it would be really strange if she just suddenly showed up there. She and Hadley weren't all buddy-buddy anymore, so they hadn't spent their afternoons together in Jenn's, but Devon knew Hadley still frequented the locale. Devon wasn't about to force an encounter with Hadley. Devon's anger hadn't fizzled, and she didn't know if she was just that irritated with Hadley's presence or if it was because of her drug use. She wanted to help, but Hadley wasn't going to allow her in anytime soon. How could she help if Hadley was avoiding her at every turn?

Devon crossed to the other side of the street, and as she did, she glanced into the windows as she passed Jenn's. She tried to tell herself she did it to see if Hadley was inside. Devon was pretty good at fooling herself. Sometimes, she had even searched out for the familiar blonde hair, but Hadley had never been there when Devon walked by.

In truth, Devon was generally hoping to see someone else. It was silly. Brennan didn't know she was in the city. She had turned him down. She had a boyfriend. But she still walked this stretch to see if he was working the bar, so she could catch a glimpse of him.

No Hadley. No Brennan. Devon kept walking. Reminiscing about her first week in Chicago wouldn't help her find a job.

Turning the corner, Devon immediately jumped out of the way as someone came barreling directly toward her. She got off a few choice words for the person as he passed her. People in Chicago are so rude! People just didn't act like that in Nashville.

When the person abruptly skidded to a stop, Devon retreated a few steps. She hadn't thought her cussing at the person would cause him to stop. She didn't want to draw attention to herself. She certainly didn't want to set off some street thug, or worse, tilt the emotional imbalance of some crazed serial killer.

When the person turned around, Devon's fear dried up. It was immediately replaced with what she could only describe as an oh-fuck face.

"Devon?" Brennan said tentatively, facing her.

Breathing heavily from his run with a sheen of sweat on his forehead, he looked astonished by her presence. She couldn't blame him.

"Uh…hey, Brennan," she whispered. She was ashamed that they had to meet like this after what had happened between them. "You looked like you were in a hurry—"

"What are you doing here?" he asked, ignoring her statement.

"I, uh…didn't leave," she murmured softly.

"What?" he asked, looking confused. "You were supposed to be gone like three weeks ago. Why would you stay?"

She had clearly shocked him enough for him to speak plainly. Normally, she thought he was so reserved, but his face was giving him away as clear as day. He hadn't wanted her to leave, and now, he was glad to see her. Could she possibly be reading him correctly?

"I decided to stay and…help Hadley," she told him. It was the truth…mostly.

Brennan's eyes narrowed in response. "I've seen Hadley almost every day for the past three weeks, and she never mentioned that you're still in the city."

Devon shrugged. Well, that looked seriously implicating. It wasn't that she had told Hadley not to tell Brennan. It was just that Hadley wasn't talking about Devon at all. Now, it looked like she had been avoiding him. Well, she had.

"I haven't been succeeding…" she said. That much was also true.

"So, she's avoiding you like the plague because she wants to keep using," he said intuitively. "I've seen that before. You're going to have to try harder." He paused, glancing down and then up, like he wasn't sure what to say. "Maybe you should swing by Jenn's. It might help."

"Oh," she whispered, looking away from him. Why did he insist on complicating things?

"To see Hadley," he added.

"Maybe," she said. "I'm kind of busy looking for a job, so I don't know when I'll have a lot of time."

"You're looking for a job? You're staying?" he asked.

She clearly continued to shock him every time she opened her mouth.

"Oh, yeah, I'm staying through the summer."

She could see the question on his face. He wasn't on guard like he normally was. He seemed to want to know why she hadn't come to see him since their last encounter. Still, he should know why. She had given him reason enough when she had broken the kiss in his apartment.

Instead, he said, "Come with me." Then, he turned on his heel and walked away from her.

Devon stared after his retreating back. What the fuck is he thinking? But he wasn't waiting for her, and she had to jog to keep up with him. She didn't even know why she was following him. She knew it wasn't a good idea to be around him. That had become blatantly obvious after he had kissed her.

She was too messed up. She had too many of her own issues to deal with, and she couldn't drag anyone else into it.

Brennan walked right into Jenn's, the place she hadn't walked into for three weeks straight. She followed on his heels to the back of the mostly deserted restaurant. Some regular customer called out a snide remark to him as he passed, and Brennan flipped the guy off. The guy laughed through his smoker's cough.

When they reached the door to the kitchen, Brennan said, "Wait here."

Devon stood around, twiddling her thumbs. She wished she knew why he had brought her here. She didn't know what had compelled her to follow him, except that it had all been so sudden. She hadn't expected to see him any more than he was expecting to see her.

Loud strong language from the back broke her out of her thoughts. All she could really grasp from the conversation was that he was late for work. That must have been why he had been running. She didn't suspect he was the kind of person who was usually late, but she didn't really know him all that well. Maybe it was a regular thing for him to show up late. Maybe that was why his hair had always been rumpled.

A couple minutes later, Brennan walked back out of the kitchen with a woman in tow. Devon had never seen her before when she had spent time in Jenn's, but that didn't surprise her. The woman wasn't wearing the typical uniform. Instead, she was clad in a form-fitting dress. She looked well-kept, and Devon wondered what she was doing back in the kitchen.

"Devon," Brennan said, facing her, "this is Jenn Yarrow."

"Pleasure to meet you," Devon said, sticking out her hand.

"Brennan said you are looking for a job," she said with a thick Northern accent. "You have any waitressing experience?"

"Yes, ma'am. I worked as a waitress in Nashville for a few summers," Devon said, her hopes flaring.

"First off, don't call me ma'am. That's my mom or my mother-in-law, God strike her down," Jenn said, tilting her head to the sky. "Second, we work with test-runs only. You make it through today, and I'll hire you. Otherwise, you can keep your tips and have a nice day."

Jenn threw a towel at her, and Devon caught it, feeling shocked.

"So…is this like an interview?"

"What does it look like?" Jenn rolled her eyes and looked at Brennan as if she were asking what kind of person he had brought into the place. "There's a change of clothes in the back. I'll check on you at closing time." With that, she turned and walked away.

"What just happened?" Devon stood completely still, holding a hand towel.

"The owner just gave you a job as long as you make it through today," Brennan told her. "So, make it through today."

D EVON PEELED OFF her uniform in the women's restroom at the back of Jenn's Restaurant. As she changed back into her street clothes, her arms and feet ached, her mind was whirring, and she felt an overwhelming sense of exhaustion coursing throughout her entire body. The whole thing made her wonder why she hadn't gotten a job earlier. She was so busy that she had forgotten everything else, like her reason for being in Chicago, her best friend on drugs, and Brennan's eyes always finding her in the room.

Okay, she wasn't busy enough not to notice Brennan, but it

felt different now. She couldn't react or respond like she normally would have because there were simply too many customers who had kept her occupied.

Jenn had met her at the door when the bar closed. Apparently, she wasn't one for long-winded conversations. She told Devon to keep the towel and the extra uniform if she didn't have any other clothing that would work. That was lucky because Devon hadn't brought anything like it with her. She would have to use some of her tips to buy new clothes and more comfortable shoes. Jenn had told her to come in every night for the rest of the week. She hadn't bothered to ask if the closing shift was okay for Devon. Jenn had mentioned that she would give Devon an official schedule the following week, and Devon suspected she would remain on the night shift.

She rolled her shoulders backward and forward a few times, trying to work the kinks out of them, but it was no good. At the very least, she would be sore for the next week. The roll of bills in her pocket made up for the stiffness she would surely face in the morning.

Jenn's was in a nice area, and customers were always floating in and out. The tourists that managed to find the place tipped like crap, but the regulars tipped bucketloads. They had tipped way more than the people at the small pasta place she had worked in Nashville.

She stuffed her work clothes in a to-go bag and walked through the kitchen door into the main dining area. The other waitress had already disappeared, grumbling the whole time about how she didn't need any help. Devon suspected it had something to do with sharing tips. Though, Devon wasn't sure how the woman had managed working the busy restaurant with just Brennan's help in the first place.

"You ready to get out of here?" Brennan asked, sliding his hands into the front pockets of his jeans.

Devon hadn't realized that he was waiting on her. She owed him big time. She wished she didn't feel the wave of awkwardness that ran through her at his nearness. Then, she might be able to show her gratitude more.

"Uh…yeah," she said, glancing away from those eyes.

"I'll just lock up." He ducked into the kitchen and then returned a minute later. "Let's go."

Brennan flipped off the bright red open sign in the window, and then they exited through the front doors. He took the time to lock those doors as well, and then they walked to the L station together.

Devon took in the surprising silence of the city. As they passed through streets lined with tall skyscrapers, fear seemed to seep into her conscience. She wasn't afraid to be alone with Brennan. In fact, it wasn't Brennan at all. It was just that no one else was on the streets. She knew it was late. It was well past the hour most people would be awake and walking around the city, but she had thought that the city would still be bustling, like New York. Apparently, that wasn't the case in the area where Jenn's was located.

She swallowed back her fear and tried to remind herself of the good job that she had done today. She had a new job, a way to stay in Chicago, and a way to escape. But in this moment, she felt the loss of her escape. She felt it all closing in on her. Why were the streets so empty? Why was it just her and Brennan?

Her breathing hitched, and then she realized that she had suddenly stopped breathing altogether. Fear poisoned her blood system, starting in her chest and crawling through her veins like a disease. She felt her chest rising and falling rapidly, and her teeth were chattering as if she were freezing, but she knew these were the sure signs of hyperventilation.

But she couldn't hyperventilate. She had to run. She had to get away. That was the answer. Run.

Brennan touched her arm, rocketing her back to the ground, to the city, to his hand resting lightly on her, to the pads of his fingers grazing her soft skin.

"Hey, are you okay?" he asked.

When she could finally see him through her blurred vision, she saw concern etched into every line of his face.

Devon held up her hand as if to silence him, and that only seemed to make him more concerned. She took a deep breath and bent her knees, crouching there in the middle of the sidewalk. She held her knees to her chest and tried to let the déjà vu of her dreams sluice off of her. She knew where she had come from, where she was, and where she was going. That was all that mattered. This wasn't like her nightmares. No one was chasing her. No one was grabbing her. No one was throwing her down. She took another breath and reminded herself of these things again and again.

When she finally stood, Brennan seemed to have a million

questions on his tongue. Devon didn't want to answer any of them, so she immediately started walking. Brennan strode to her side and walked next to her, allowing her the silence she desired. She should thank him for that as well.

A job and silence. What more could I ask for? she wondered.

The ride on the L was short. Her stop came before Brennan's, but he didn't seem ready to let her go. He hopped off the train with her, and they walked in together to Marina City. At least this area was well-lit, and people were still milling around outside of the House of Blues.

"Thanks for walking me back," Devon said, finally breaking the silence.

"Are you going to tell me what happened back there?" he asked.

Devon looked away from him, not wanting to answer. "I think it was just exhaustion," she murmured.

It was a lie, and he knew it. She was exhausted, but exhausted people didn't hyperventilate in the middle of the street.

"Exhaustion…right," he said in disbelief.

"Thanks for your help today. I really needed the job," Devon said, changing the subject.

"If I'd known you were looking for one, I could have helped sooner," he said pointedly.

The question about why she had avoided him for three weeks was written all over his face. If he didn't matter and she had a boyfriend, then why did she skip past Jenn's every day? She refused to let her mind think about it.

"Well, glad I ran into you when I did then," she said with the only smile she could muster.

"Devon, about that night—" Brennan began.

She held up her hand again, not wanting to talk to him about that. He had been drunk, and she had been an easy target in his apartment. She couldn't blame him for trying or for walking out without waking her up the next morning. He didn't know about her nightmares or that she might scream herself awake the next morning. After what had just happened and the amount of time she was likely to spend with him at work over the next two months, it was probably better that he didn't know.

"I'll see you at work tomorrow," she whispered, desperate to get away.

He sighed and nodded. "Good night."

Devon rushed to the elevator as quickly as she could. She couldn't be under his scrutiny any longer. His intense gaze seemed to weigh and measure her, and she felt her insides squirm under it all. And when she was trying to avoid it all, how did she seem to notice more and more how attractive he was?

She shook her head, trying to dispel her thoughts. The image of him stretching his hands over his head, showing off the muscles in his arms and the tightness of his stomach, rushed back to her then. When she tried not to think of something, why did it always flash back to her at that exact moment?

Her cheeks were still hot when she exited the elevator. She scolded herself for thinking of a boy at a time like this. Another guy in her life right now was the last thing she needed. Period.

Devon flung open the apartment door, forgetting that it was four in the morning. As the door knocked into the wall, she cursed and lunged for it to keep it from banging a second time. Hadley and Garrett were asleep, and she had no desire to awake them at this hour. Slowly closing the door behind her, Devon crept to her bedroom and changed into a loose-fit tank top and her silk sleep shorts. After everything that had happened tonight, the last thing she wanted to do was crawl into bed and have another nightmare to match her freak-out on the street.

She padded out into the living room and turned on the TV. She didn't care what she watched as long as it was something that would captivate her thoughts and pull her out of her funk. When nothing caught her attention, she flipped to old Bugs Bunny cartoons and tuned in as he eluded capture over and over again.

A few minutes later, the front door creaked open, and Devon straightened in her seat. Who was coming home at this hour? It was well past the time Garrett typically got off work, and Hadley had to go to work in just a few hours.

"Hello?" Devon called softly.

"Hey," Garrett said, materializing into the living room.

Devon's body relaxed at the sight of him. It was just Garrett. No need to be alarmed. Why he was out this late was his own business. She was just glad to see him, especially since she could finally pay him some rent for the apartment. It wasn't much, but it would do until she got her first actual paycheck.

"You're in late," she said with a smile and a yawn.

"I'm surprised to find you up." Garrett kicked off his shoes and took a seat next to her on the couch.

"I got a job today," she told him brightly, facing him and crossing her legs pretzel-style.

She was happier about telling him than she had thought she would be. He believed in her. He had given her a chance. He was the one who hadn't kicked her out when she couldn't pay up right away.

"Congrats!" he said with a warm smile.

She liked his smile. It was so genuine.

"Hold on one second." Devon jumped up and rushed into the bedroom. She pulled out the wad of cash, kept a twenty for herself, and then crept back to the living room. "Here you go."

Garrett's eyes widened as Devon handed him the roll of bills and sat back down next to him. He pulled it out of her hand and judged the sum.

"Where did you get all this?" His eyes moved from the money to her face and back.

"They're my tips from work," she told him.

Garrett flipped through the cash with trepidation. Devon couldn't figure out why he was acting so strangely.

"Devon," he said softly, "when I said not to worry about getting a job and that we could arrange something if need be…I really meant it."

Devon looked up at him in confusion. What was he insinuating?

"You didn't have to…do this," he said, pointing to the money, "just because you were worried about rent."

"It's not a big deal. I like the work. It clears my mind." She wasn't even sure why she said it. She hadn't talked much to anyone about what was going on with her. She wasn't about to start now.

Garrett's eyes traveled the length of her body, and Devon grew conscious of the little clothing she was wearing. She hadn't been expecting him, or else she would have put on sweats.

"I'm sure you're...good at the work," he said, treading cautiously. "I just don't think stripping is the answer."

Devon sputtered loudly, her mouth gaping open. "What?" she gasped. "I'm not stripping!"

The breath seemed to explode out of his mouth all at once. He looked very relieved. She couldn't believe he had thought she had reduced to stripping to get money to pay for rent. That would look great on her resume!

"You're not?" he gasped out.

"No!"

"What do you expect when you hand me what looks like a hundred single dollar bills?" He shook his head in disbelief.

"You have to give me more credit than that. I'm sure everyone wants to see me with my clothes off, but it's not like I'd actually do it. I'm a bit more behind-closed-doors than that." She rolled her eyes skyward.

They looked at each other then, and suddenly, they were both laughing. Devon was doubled over, clutching at her sides. Garrett had his hand on her back as he tried to hold in his laughter. He wasn't very successful. Both shot furtive glances at Hadley's closed bedroom door. The last thing they wanted was to explain why they were laughing so hard so early in the morning. Hadley would surely take well to Garrett thinking Devon was a stripper…or not.

Devon leaned back on the couch. Garrett's hand slid across her back and into his lap. She could feel every inch he had touched, and when she checked his gaze, it registered that he had noticed as well. Turning away, embarrassed, Devon tucked her legs back up and scooted over. A conversation about stripping sure shifted the mood.

"So," Devon said, clearing her throat, "why were you in so late from work?"

"I'm working on some foreign investments. They like to have someone there to work the markets when they're open. We alternate who gets the worst hours," he said with a shrug as if this all made sense to her.

She knew nothing about stocks, except that her parents had invested well and that had paid for her college education.

"Sounds boring," she told him honestly.

"Definitely not as interesting as stripping," he said with mischief in his eyes.

Devon laughed and swatted at him. It felt nice to laugh and feel this carefree. "Oh, stop it!"

"Tell me, do the men cry in your corner? When they say, 'no touch,' do they mean no touch?" he asked with humor in his voice.

"Crying is a definite," Devon said, playing his game. "And the no-touch rule only applies to those I don't want to touch me."

She couldn't figure out why her voice changed or when the carefree had shifted away from carefree. Somehow, her teasing had strayed without her permission, and her body was now responding to his assessment of her. She didn't know why, but it was like, all of a sudden, she realized she was attracted to him. He was her best friend's boyfriend and pretty much the nicest guy she had ever met. Why was she allowing herself to be attracted to him?

Garrett laughed at her playfulness, and she tried not to read into the edge in his voice. He certainly wasn't attracted to her. She was reading into it. It wasn't there. She had just had a rough night and was exhausted. That was all.

"I, uh…think I should go to bed," Devon said with a smile. Even if she was reading into it, she needed to be far away from this moment.

"Are you sleeping any better?" he asked, keeping her from her departure.

She nodded her head even though it wasn't the truth. "Much."

"I'm glad to hear that."

His gaze never left her, and she tried not to squirm.

"Night," Devon whispered, easing out of the room as fast as she could.

As soon as she closed her bedroom door behind her, she rushed to her bed and threw herself against it. What the fuck was she thinking? First Brennan, and now Garrett? Was she out of her fucking mind?

She couldn't get a grasp on it. Why was she acting like this?

She had gone a month without sex…only a month. It hadn't been that long of a period of time without Reid.

Her body was betraying her mind. She wanted to scold herself for acting like a hormone-crazed teenager. Was she such a carnal animal that she couldn't go a month without wanting to fuck everyone who got close enough to her? It didn't make sense. She refused for it to make sense.

Devon stuffed her earbuds into her ears and blasted Dustin's music as loud as she could manage. It had always had a calming effect. She let the angsty music rush over her body with its anger and rebellion seeping deep into her pores. She had initiated her own rebellion and needed to see it through. She couldn't be distracted by anything. There was no way she could risk bringing anyone down with her.

She'd had the strength to propel herself into action—to finally leave. She now needed the strength to stay away. Devon couldn't help but remember how it felt to be back in St. Louis, helpless to her own desire for acceptance. As much as she had tried to escape everything that had happened, her life pinwheeled her through time and space. She felt upside-down and right-side-up. She felt lost and so alone yet completely surrounded.

All she wanted to do was to give her body a release and free herself from her own trap. But she wouldn't let herself. She wouldn't orient herself in that way. If she did, then she would only be accepting her attraction. It would be better for her body to ache and her mind to remember that she would have to go without... she could go without. She wasn't beholden to her body's demands.

She could initiate her own rebellion.

CHAPTER 11
Getting Through to You

THOSE NEXT TWO weeks were the best Devon had experienced since coming to Chicago. Working at Jenn's was so taxing that when she came back to the apartment, all she could do was fall into bed, exhausted. And she hadn't had one nightmare during that whole time.

She worried that once the routine started kicking in—when she didn't feel the constant pain in her feet, or the rush to always be moving, or the ring of orders in her brain—the dreams would return. She didn't want to think about it. She preferred to believe that she had made the right choice, that the depression was sliding off her, and that she was improving. Devon didn't want to face the alternative.

Either way, her attitude was much improving with her mind occupied.

The main thing holding her back was that Hadley still hadn't gotten over what had happened. Not that Devon could blame her. She had basically blackmailed Hadley into allowing her to stay. But Hadley didn't know why Devon needed to stay. If Hadley knew, then she likely wouldn't have been as pissed. Devon just couldn't tell her. Even before Hadley had avoided speaking with her for nearly a month, Devon hadn't felt comfortable telling Hadley about what had happened in St. Louis. Now with the strain in their relationship, it seemed even less likely.

When Hadley had found out she was working at Jenn's, it had been a disaster. Hadley had walked into the restaurant with her normal bounce in her step, slapped her ass right down on a seat at the bar, and ordered the chicken from Brennan. Devon had walked out of the kitchen, balancing a tray of drinks on her shoulder. As she had walked to the booth to deliver the drinks, she caught Hadley's eye. All of her bounce had disappeared. She had muttered something to Brennan that Devon couldn't hear before she had stood and strode right out of the place.

Brennan had glanced between Hadley's retreating form and Devon. "You guys in a fight?"

Devon had shrugged and averted her gaze. She had walked back into the kitchen, but Brennan followed her.

"You going to tell me what that was all about?" he had asked.

"No." She had placed the tray down and loaded it back up with food for another table.

"Aren't you guys best friends?" Brennan had prodded.

"Yes," she had answered simply.

"Devon," he had said, reaching out and grabbing her arm, "is everything all right?"

That had become his mantra. She didn't know how many times he had asked her that or how many times she had lied. She was fine. Fine.

Hadley hadn't shown up in Jenn's since that day, or at least, she hadn't shown up anytime Devon was working. In fact, Devon had only seen her in passing at the apartment, too. It was like Hadley was avoiding the apartment as much as Devon had before she had gotten a job. Devon had tried stopping Hadley to talk, but she always pretended to be busy before she immediately left. Devon worried that she would go the rest of the summer without seeing her friend. What she had done was wrong, but she wanted to help Hadley if only Hadley would let her.

***

THE DAY THAT Hadley walked back into Jenn's Restaurant, Devon was so surprised that she nearly dropped her tray. She had been lugging that thing around for how long, and she almost lost control of it? When Amy, the other waitress on duty, glared at her, Devon quickly recovered.

Devon slowly tried to go about her business and not pay any extra attention to her friend. She wasn't a particularly perceptive person to begin with, but Devon noticed everything about Hadley that day. Her business suit was as pristine as ever. Her blonde hair had been tied up into a French twist at the back of her scalp. Her makeup had been carefully applied. She looked perfect.

Except where she didn't.

Living with Hadley for two-and-a-half years had given Devon a certain insight into her behavior that most people wouldn't normally pick up on. Her eyes seemed a bit more hollow than normal. Her suit was too loose, like she had lost weight. The bounce in her step was missing entirely. Hadley was in a low place even if she appeared perfect on the outside.

Hadley sat down in her normal seat. She lifted her head, looked directly at Devon, and then snapped back to face the front.

Devon sighed. So, that was how it was going to be. This was some kind of turf battle. Devon certainly didn't have a problem with her being there. She just wished it were under different circumstances.

Brennan approached Hadley and took her order. Instead of her typical drink, he passed a glass of water across the bar. Hadley looked up at him, and Devon could only guess the seething look she was giving him. Brennan knew as well as Devon did that Hadley was in over her head. Devon was lucky to have him on her side…or at least, she thought he was on her side. He hadn't seemed particularly perturbed the night he had told Devon that Hadley was using, but he had been extra cautious about the subject ever since Hadley had stormed out of the restaurant.

When Hadley's order was ready, Brennan motioned Devon over.

"What's up?" she asked innocently, like she didn't know that this was Hadley's food.

"Will you take this out to Hadley?" he asked just as innocently, like he didn't know anything about Hadley and Devon's relationship.

Devon bit her lip. "Are you sure she won't throw it at me?"

"You're the one not answering questions," he said.

Devon didn't even have a retort for that. She couldn't answer questions—plain and simple. She wasn't confident enough to tell anyone what had happened. Maybe when she went back to St. Louis in the fall, she would find that it was all in her head.

Instead of responding, she took the tray from Brennan and walked through the swinging door. Brennan followed hot on her heels, stopping within a safe distance in case he had to intervene. Devon took a deep breath and walked right up to Hadley. She placed Hadley's food down in front of her, and Hadley didn't look up once. Devon tucked her tray under her arm and waited.

"You can go," Hadley said coldly.

"Hadley, I'm sorry," Devon whispered.

"No," she said, shaking her head. "I just want to eat lunch."

"Can't we talk?" Devon asked.

Hadley stood fiercely and glared at Devon. She turned on her heel and walked toward the door, and Devon just stood there, dumbfounded. Devon had never known Hadley to hold a grudge, especially not one this ferocious. Were the drugs addling her brain this much? How much more was she using since she and Devon had last spoken?

Devon rushed around the bar, but Brennan was already there, striding toward Hadley. He reached her right before she got to the door and pulled her aside. Devon was close behind, but Brennan shot her a warning look, so she retreated a few paces. She was just close enough to make out some of what they were saying.

"Come on, Hadley," Brennan said, dropping his arm.

"Why are you sticking your nose in this?" Hadley asked.

"Why aren't you giving her a chance? Didn't you say she was your best friend? Haven't you known each other for years? What could possibly be keeping you from making up with her?" he asked pointedly.

"Oh god, not you, too," she said. "Don't become a hypocrite. I don't need to hear it from you as well."

"Hadley, I don't give two shits about what you're doing in your free time. I only care about who you're hurting—yourself and Devon. This goes beyond you. Just give her a chance."

Devon could see the hard look in his eyes even from where she stood. She marveled at his smooth words. He wasn't one for conversation when they worked together.

"I can't deal with this right now," Hadley said, pushing him away.

He reached out and took her arm again. "It doesn't all have to be better today. But don't you think she's hurting, too?"

When he lowered his voice, Devon strained to hear.

"Don't you see that she's here for a reason?" he whispered.

Devon lost the rest as her stomach dropped. How could Brennan know that? Was she that obvious? Or was he a good guesser? Either way, it terrified her that he was that perceptive when they didn't even talk all that often. She had let her guard down without even knowing it.

Retreating a couple more feet until she was entirely out of earshot, she contemplated how she had let this happen. When had she allowed herself to be this secure? When had she forgotten how tenuous the thread was, and how easily it could snap, bringing down all her nightmares around her?

This wasn't just about Brennan because she hadn't even known she was weakening around him. This was about Garrett, too. He was just so incredibly nice, and she hadn't met anyone quite like him. They had spent more and more time together, staying up to watch Netflix late at night after they had gotten off work, laughing about the absurd hours of their jobs, and marveling in their shared love of dessert. How many times in the past week had she wanted to tell Garrett? She had held her tongue, but the more comfortable she got, the more she wanted someone to know.

Devon bit her lip and tried to hold in all her emotions. She had to deal with Hadley first.

After her conversation with Brennan, who had immediately made himself scarce, Hadley approached her.

"Can we talk...in private?" Hadley asked, obviously still unsure about it all.

"Yeah," Devon said. "Let me just tell Amy that I'm taking a break."

***

HADLEY AND DEVON sat in the break room in the back of Jenn's. Devon missed her friend, and it was in that moment that she fully realized it. She wished she could unload all her problems on Hadley and have her put them all together in the right order, but Hadley already had too much to deal with. She couldn't also suffer from Devon's issues.

"So…" Hadley said.

Devon nodded. "So…"

"I see you have a job at Jenn's."

"Yep," Devon said. She didn't know what Hadley wanted to say, and she thought it was best to allow her to direct the conversation.

"How did that happen?"

"Brennan helped me out when I couldn't find anything else."

"He's a nice guy, that one," Hadley said absentmindedly.

"So it seems." Devon said.

"I guess I'll just go ahead and say it. I'm pretty pissed at you, and it's not going to get better right away," Hadley said. "You violated my trust, not to mention my hospitality. It's going to take a while before I start to trust you again."

Devon nodded slowly, not sure what to say. That much was true.

"But…I know that I violated your trust, too. I'm not going to talk to you about my problems. They're mine. When I'm ready, we'll figure it out, but until then, I don't want you to interfere."

"Hadley," Devon interrupted. Hadley had to be reasonable.

"No," she said, holding up her hand as she stood. "They're my issues. I'm not begging you to tell me yours, and I know you have some. I've always known, but it's your business."

"I think you need help, Hadley," Devon said softly, feeling like a hypocrite.

"I think you don't know everything about what I'm going through. All I'm saying now," Hadley said, taking a step toward the door, "is that I'm tired of tiptoeing through my life. I'll come and go as I please. I'll be at the apartment and Jenn's. Brennan has a gig coming up soon, and I'll be at that, too. I'm sure you'll be there, and I'm tired of it being awkward. Let's just go from there. We'll let the trust rebuild naturally."

"Hadley, please," Devon said, desperate to reach her friend. "I am sorry about what happened." She choked on her words, wishing that it could all go back to the way it was.

"It's too late," Hadley said, reaching for the door. "The damage is already done," she muttered before exiting.

Devon stared at the closed door. She was beyond frustrated. Was this what it was like for people to deal with her? No. Nobody knew what her problem was. Maybe that made it even more frustrating. She didn't know. She just didn't know.

All she knew was that Hadley was using, and likely, she was using more than she was before. She was irritable and uncompromising. Devon wasn't sure how she could reach her, but she would try however Hadley let her.

CHAPTER 12
The Runaway

IT WAS WELL past closing time. Jenn had been complaining about their work, and Devon was tired of hearing about it. So, she took extra care in cleaning the restaurant. Each table was sprayed down and scrubbed clean. Then, she moved on to the chairs and booths. She mopped the floors and cleared away any excess dust from behind the bar. Brennan had soaked down the bar, so she didn't have to touch his area.

Moving out of the main dining room to the kitchen, she set to work on washing the piles of plates, cups, and silverware in the sink. After putting them back where they belonged, she mopped the floor in the back and then cleaned the countertops of any additional residue. The kitchen staff was pretty good at wiping down the counters, but Devon put extra effort into it anyway. She rearranged the cleaning supplies in the closet, and then she closed the door with a satisfied grunt.

Jenn wouldn't have any complaints in the morning, at least not about the cleanliness of the restaurant. Devon had made sure of that.

Locking up, Devon turned around and began walking toward the nearby L station. Even late at night, she was getting accustomed to the walk. Brennan typically waited and walked with her. He had some intuitive knowledge that she didn't like to walk in the streets at night by herself, but then again, he didn't think it was safe for her to be here by herself. He was probably right. She wasn't sure what he was doing tonight. She wished he had stayed.

Taking the first right, she headed down the dark street, holding her purse close to her side. It would be just her luck if someone mugged her on her way home. She should have asked Brennan to stay. That would have been smart.

She walked for a while, her paranoia getting the better of her. She knew that Chicago wasn't all that safe, but the area near Jenn's was pretty nice. Plus, it was less than a ten-minute walk to the L station. She knew cleaning had taken her longer than normal, but she hadn't realized how much more deserted that would make the streets.

She didn't like it. The feeling was unnerving. She increased her pace in an effort to reach the train quickly, so she could get back to the apartment. There was no reason to be out on the streets longer than necessary.

The faster she walked, the slower it seemed like she was moving. The buildings seemed to stretch farther and farther down the street until she wasn't making any progress at all. She checked over her shoulder to see if she was just imagining things, but the buildings in front and behind her were unbelievably long… impossibly long.

Her stomach twisted, and goose bumps broke out on her skin as fear prickled her body. She could feel it then. Eyes were watching her, following her every movement. She didn't see anyone, but she knew they were there.

Taking a deep breath, Devon tried to rationalize what was happening. She had hyperventilated before over something like this. Perhaps she was just imagining what was ahead and behind her. Her mind was playing tricks on her. But she had been walking an interminable amount of time, and it didn't look like she was any closer to the L. Wasn't she supposed to take a left up ahead? She definitely hadn't come upon a cross street yet.

Devon broke into a jog, hoping to put as much distance between her and the strange city buildings as possible. The faster she went, the farther the buildings stretched. Her mind couldn't process it. How was it possible that she wasn't even moving when her breathing was ragged from running?

Finally, she saw her turn up ahead. She took off toward it,

ignoring the nagging feeling that someone was following her. Devon cut the sharp corner and saw the L station up ahead in the distance. A stitch was forming in her side under her ribs, and she pushed her fingers up into it to try to dull the pain. She wasn't a runner and never had been. Devon wondered why her pursuer didn't just run her down. She wasn't very fast, her speed was already slowing considerably, and soon, she would have to stop. Adrenaline was the only thing fueling her on.

But the person stayed a distance away, her pursuer's eyes locked on Devon.

She reached the stairs in a hurry and scrambled up them, wanting to put as much distance between her and the person after her as possible. She swiped her card, pushed through the metal turnstile, and stepped out onto the platform. She flew up the second set of stairs and prayed that a train was waiting for her.

The footsteps on the stairs below her told Devon that the person was fast approaching. She knew the train schedule, and it would likely be another couple minutes before it arrived this late at night. She paced back and forth in front of the railway, debating her options.

If someone was coming after her, she didn't have the luxury of time to wait out a train. She needed to act now. Biting down on her lip, she decided to make a move. She sprinted down the platform to the opposite end where the elevator stood. Her finger repeatedly mashed the down button. She could hear the rhythmic rise of the machine as it took its time approaching the top floor.

Devon cursed its slowness. Even if she made it inside before the person reached her, her pursuer might be able to get to the bottom floor before the elevator.

Her head whipped around and saw that the person had made it up the flight of stairs. Devon didn't have another choice. She bolted into the elevator as soon as it opened and slammed her hand down on the button to close the door.

Bouncing up and down on the balls of her feet, she watched the doors slide shut just as her tracker realized where she had gone. She didn't get to see what his move was. Was he rushing down the stairs now? Would he beat her there? She didn't know. She just didn't know.

As the elevator slid down the shoot, Devon jumped up and down, wanting it to move faster, but of course, it took its sweet time. It was old equipment, and it wasn't likely to listen to her pleas for help. Finally, it reached the bottom floor, and the doors dinged open. Devon didn't think twice. Vaulting through the doors, she hoped that if the person had already made it to the bottom floor, he wouldn't be expecting her to run straight at him.

Her burst of speed was unwarranted because her body collided with a soft white bed that came out of nowhere. She face-planted into the mattress, sending her legs flying behind her. Devon shouted out in surprise, trying to right herself.

As she did, she felt a hand grasp her arm and hold her in place. She kicked out and smashed into something solid. She heard the person grunt, but he never loosened his grip on her arm. Her face was shoved into the mattress, muffling her cries and tears. She wasn't sure if she could breathe properly, but the person didn't seem to care as he held her in place. Her heart hammered in her chest as she tried to judge what the person would do to her.

"You thought you were safe," the voice said, "but you'll never be safe."

***

TEARS WERE STREAMING down Devon's face even before she woke up. She heard the television, and the bright light from the screen hit against her closed eyelids. She had the good sense to know that she wasn't alone. Someone else was in the living room where she had fallen asleep after she had returned from work earlier that night. It was most likely Garrett since he was always up this late with her. She couldn't face him like this.

A shuddering sob raked through her body. She wished that she had been able to hold it in, but it burst out of her unbidden.

She felt his eyes on her like she was back in her dream. While watching her, he was likely worried as he wondered why she was weeping in the middle of the living room when she had been fast asleep only a few minutes earlier.

Devon had thought the nightmares were gone. She had thought the dreams were in the past and that she had moved on. It had been weeks since she'd had one, and then this…

It was so close to reality. It was like her nightmares were getting closer and closer to the truth. The dream had felt so real.

She remembered the feeling of exhaustion, the pride in a job well done, and wondering where Brennan was. But Brennan had walked her home earlier tonight, just like he had every night since she had started working there, since her mental breakdown on the street.

The words rang in her ears over and over again. "You thought you were safe, but you'll never be safe."

They were painful words that breached her subconscious on a regular basis. Who was she to think that she was safe? How could she believe that everything she had run from would just be back to normal when she returned?

Sitting up, Devon bent her legs up to her chest and rested her forehead on her knees. She couldn't open her eyes and face Garrett. She didn't know what he was thinking. He probably just thought she was a nutcase. She had told him that she was sleeping better, and now, here was proof that she wasn't.

She heard the chair creak, and then footsteps crossed the carpet. The weight behind her shifted as Garrett sat down on the couch. He softly stroked her back a few times, and she cried harder at the comforting touch. He didn't say anything. He didn't need to. Nothing he could say would help. Nothing he could say would be better than the soft embrace as he pulled her into his arms. Devon leaned into his chest and let her tears stain the neck of his polo shirt. He rested one hand on the back of her head as he held her in place, letting the pain rush through her. At times, he would rock her back and forth while stroking her hair. Other times, he would place his chin on the top of her head and just hold her.

When it felt like all her tears were gone, Devon pulled back, and Garrett released her. Finally opening her eyes, she looked up at him and saw the worry on his face. It was far deeper than she had even anticipated. How could he even look at her? She was an ugly crier and probably looked red and splotchy with a swollen face and tear-battered cheeks.

"Are you all out of tears now?" he said, his thumbs wiping the streaks of tears from under her eyes.

As he asked the question, more tears welled in her eyes as she blinked up at him through her blurred vision.

"Hey now, it's going to be all right."

Devon shook her head and looked away from him. She couldn't face him. She couldn't bear for him to look at her like this. He was the only piece of sanity that she had been able to grasp on to recently. Hadley was so distant. Devon hadn't been able to reach out to her at all. Even though she had still been physically present, she was no longer mentally there. Brennan was a dangerous circumstance to consider. He watched her too intensely, and she was sure that he hadn't forgotten their kiss. He kept his distance because he knew about Reid. But for how long? Garrett had been her rock, her only sense of normalcy.

"I thought you said you were sleeping better," he said accusingly.

Devon swallowed hard, trying to find her voice. After that terrible nightmare, she wasn't sure she could even think straight. "I thought I was, too," she said, her voice hoarse.

"You're back to crying when you wake up. Next, you'll be

screaming again. What changed?" he asked.

"I don't know." Staring down at the white carpet, she tried not to think about it.

"Do you remember the dream? Can you tell me about it?" he asked cautiously.

She wanted to shut down. She didn't want to discuss her dreams with anyone. She didn't even want to think about them. But here Garrett was, comforting her and helping her. It felt like no one else even cared. Even though she hadn't told other people, he was here, and he was so damn nice. Maybe she could trust him. Maybe...

Devon slowly nodded her head. "I…I remember," she said softly.

"Will you tell me about it?" he repeated.

The silence that lingered between them was thick with tension. He was waiting for her to answer, and she was determined not to. What could she say to make him understand? She couldn't tell him everything. She couldn't tell him what had really happened. How would he react? What would he do?

"You don't have to tell me," Garrett said finally, staring down at the same space of carpet. "I understand if it's personal. I just want to help you. Maybe talking about it will make the dreams stop."

Devon hadn't thought of that. She didn't think the dreams would ever stop. They had stopped for the longest stretch of time recently, and still, they had returned with a vengeance.

Garrett sighed softly as if he thought he had lost. "If you don't want to talk, that's fine," he said, beginning to rise.

Devon reached out and touched his arm. "Don't go," she whispered.

His eyes met hers then, and she was sure that all he saw was a hollow shell looking back at him. She felt pitiful and worthless. She just needed someone to believe in her.

He nodded and sat back down. "Are you going to tell me about the dream?"

"I've never talked about it before," she answered finally. "Not really."

"Well, I'm all ears. You don't have to be afraid to talk to me."

Taking a deep breath, Devon began. She told him what she had been experiencing in her dreams—how the person would always chase her and how the landscape would alter but it would always be the same person. She didn't know how she knew that it had been the same person each time, but she just did. She told him about the fear that had gripped her, the inevitable end when she had been caught, and more recently, the times she had been thrown down on the snowy white bed in the matching white room. But she didn't tell him the words the person had spoken. She wasn't prepared to release that much of herself.

Garrett listened intently the whole time as if he was trying to really soak up what she had experienced. The longer she talked, the more invested he seemed to become in her story. He never laughed or made light of her dream even though at times when she was telling the story, it didn't actually seem as scary as it had been in her sleep.

As the story came to a close, she ended in a huff and just sat there in front of him with her fears laid out in his lap. She didn't know how he would respond or what he would say. She felt exposed and more than a little bit silly.

"That sounds scary, Dev," he finally said. "No wonder you wake up in tears."

His eyes were filled with sympathy, and she suddenly didn't feel as silly. His acceptance was invigorating. She felt justified in her fear rather than feeling childish.

"Why do you think you keep having these dreams? Do you have any idea?" he asked, taking her very seriously.

Another crossroad. How much could she tell him? Not the truth, not all of it. Maybe just a piece. Definitely not the root cause. She wasn't ready for that. She didn't know if she would ever be ready for that. She had to tell him something though.

"I have my suspicions," she said softly.

"Any you would like to share with me?"

Devon sighed heavily. Here goes nothing, she thought.

"I, um…can only guess. They're not reality. I mean, I've never had anyone chase me," she told him.

"Right."

"Well…I didn't come to Chicago for a vacation," she said as fast as she possibly could.

He nodded. "When you decided to stay, I figured that, but I didn't want to pry."

Devon hadn't told anyone this even though she knew Hadley

and Brennan had speculated about the circumstances of her staying. And she couldn't tell Garrett why either. She just wasn't ready.

"I kind of ran away from my life," she whispered softly. She was ashamed to even say it out loud. It sounded just as foolish as when she had recounted her dreams.

"What could be so bad that you would want to run away?" he asked curiously.

He didn't sound like he was judging her, like she had expected. He just sounded interested in her problems. She could trust him. She could begin to trust him.

"Well…I was kind of tired of my life," she said, tiptoeing around the real problem. "I told my boyfriend that I was in Paris with my family for the summer, and I told my family that I was staying in St. Louis with my boyfriend. Then, I called Hadley and hopped on the first train here. I needed to get away. There were too many things I couldn't take anymore. Sometimes, I feel like I was just being melodramatic about the whole thing, like maybe it wasn't as bad as it seemed."

Before speaking, Garrett seemed to consider what she had said. "So, you think you're having these dreams because you ran away?"

"Maybe. I don't know," she said, not wanting to be any less vague.

"It must not have been easy to get on a train like that. I don't know if I could do it," he said, looking at her admirably. "Sometimes, I wish I could."

"You?" she asked, not hiding her shock. "Why would you want to leave this?"

He laughed bitterly. "For someone so smart, you aren't terribly perceptive, are you?"

She shook her head. "Never have been."

"I have my own demons that I'd be happy to run from. My father, for one," Garrett said, resting back heavily into the sofa.

Devon wondered then what she hadn't wondered before. Perhaps his life and the perfect relationship she had thought he had with Hadley…wasn't as perfect as she had suspected. He didn't know about Hadley's drug use—that much she was sure of. But how much of that put a rift in their relationship?

"He's controlling and demanding. He doesn't see me for who I am. He doesn't care about anything that I care about. He doesn't even like Hadley," he said heavily.

"How could anyone not like Hadley?" she asked.

He shrugged. "I'm not sure. He just doesn't think she's good enough for me," he said. "What he means is that she doesn't have enough money."

"But she has a wonderful job," Devon broke in, feeling like she needed to defend her friend.

Garrett shook his head. "Old money. Status. Prestige. She's from small town Missouri," he said as if this was sufficient explanation.

Devon understood then. She had dealt with prejudices her entire life. She could see the weight on Garrett's shoulders as he fought for the girlfriend he wanted, and the strain it had put on Hadley because she felt she would never be able to live up to it. As Devon recalled the first time she had stepped foot into the apartment, she understood the statement Hadley had made about Garrett going to his dad's. Devon hadn't realized how anxious Hadley had looked until now.

Devon's parents sometimes acted like that, and she thought it was ridiculous. Her family had lived in Nashville for as long as Devon could even remember. Old Southern money was a privilege that afforded a person more luxuries than just status. Devon had taken it for granted a lot in her life. She knew the pros and cons of that lifestyle. She could empathize with what Garrett was going through.

"I've been there," she said, reaching out to him and resting her hand on his. "My parents are like that sometimes."

"Thanks," he said, shrugging like he didn't want to talk about it any longer.

It was sure easier to talk about him than her. This conversation did seem to strike a bond that Devon couldn't shake.

"Sorry for changing the topic. I was trying to help you out with your dreams," Garrett said.

Devon smiled. "I think you helped."

"Yeah?" he asked, raising his eyebrows.

"Yeah, I think so. It was...nice to talk about it and get it off my chest," she said.

"I hope you sleep better now. I think you have too many good things going for you to keep you from waking up in tears from your dreams. Maybe getting away from everything is exactly what you needed." He turned his hand over and squeezed hers gently.

"Maybe it is," Devon said.

She wished she could believe it as easily as he had said it.

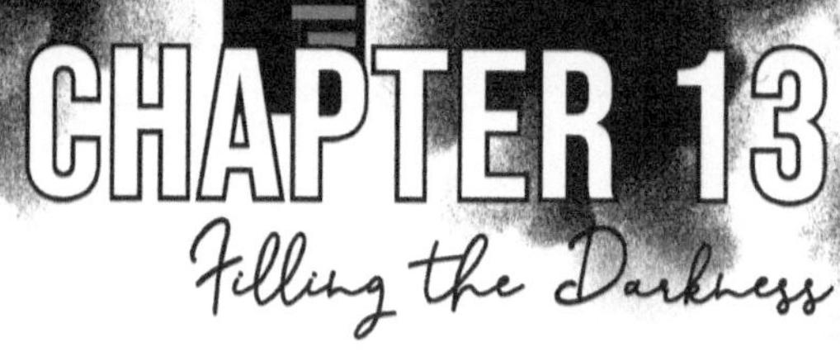

CHAPTER 13
Filling the Darkness

ARKNESS HADN'T YET fallen on the Chicago summer evening. The weather was muggy after the series of storms that had dotted the horizon the past week. When Devon had visited the Navy Pier earlier in the week, waves had been crashing so hard that she had been forced to leave. Thankfully, the rain was holding off for now as she teetered down the street in her impractical high heels and form-fitting dress.

The club was supposedly just around the block, but Devon wasn't familiar with this neighborhood. She wished she had taken

Garrett's offer and went with him and Hadley when they left a little later, but things were at a standstill with Hadley. She wasn't giving any ground, and anytime Devon had tried to push, Hadley would close off completely. Devon was hoping that tonight would be a good starting point to rebuild their relationship.

She double-checked the GPS on her phone to make sure she was going in the right direction. She took the next right and then found what she was looking for about halfway down the street. It was kind of a small, seedy-looking place. The only indication that it was a club was the unlit sign that read Open Mic Tonight.

As she walked into the place, she immediately felt overdressed. No one had told her what to wear for this, and she was too used to the music clubs back home. She always used to dress up to watch performances. Sometimes, even big names would show up out of nowhere to drink and play their favorite tunes. Devon didn't think this was that kind of place.

Devon paid the cover charge and walked into the main seating area. When she entered, eyes followed her around the bar, and she immediately became self-conscious. She didn't think she looked that great tonight, but the men here appeared ready to eat her alive. It was a discomforting sort of feeling, especially since Garrett and Hadley wouldn't be here for a little while. She scanned the crowd, hoping to see someone she knew.

The room was set up in a flat-tiered fashion with four to eight tables on each tier that formed a semi-circle around a small stage. A single microphone and a beat-up wooden chair were the focal point. A black curtain hung against the back wall as the only decoration. The room was dimly lit and clouded with smoke.

Devon craned her neck, looking around. She knew other people from work were supposed to be here. Most of them didn't like her because she was the new girl, but it would be better to sit with them than to sit alone. She was pretty sure she recognized someone when she felt a hand grab her ass. She squeaked in surprise and whipped around faster than she probably should have in her heels.

"Whoa there, honey," the man said, eyeing her like he wanted to find out how many licks it took to get to the center of a Tootsie Pop.

Devon glared at the man, and he smirked.

"You lookin' for a place to sit? I've got a place right here," he said, patting his lap. His friends roared with laughter while the guy just continued to look her up and down.

"No, thanks," she said and turned.

The man reached out and grabbed her arm, and Devon froze.

"Where you think you're goin', baby?"

This wasn't good. Devon could tell what would happen next. This guy was already belligerently drunk even if it was early in the evening. The room was dark, and no one was going to interfere. It felt just like one of her dreams.

Wake up! Wake up! Wake up! she yelled in her head.

But she wasn't waking up, and usually by this point, she was in that stupid bedroom with that stupid white bed, face-planting into the stupid soft comforter.

The guy was just holding her arm. However sinister he appeared, this was not like her dream. This was reality, and she had to face it.

Devon tried breathing in and out to keep from hyperventilating as she turned back toward the guy. "Let me go," she said softer than she would have liked.

"Oh, come on," he said, tugging her closer to him.

"Is there a problem?" Brennan asked, materializing out of thin air.

Devon released her breath as the guy loosened his grip on her arm.

"No concern of yours," the guy said.

"Mind letting my friend go, so we can get to our seats?" Brennan asked, raising his eyebrows.

The guy carelessly flung her arm back at her, and Devon immediately took a step away from him. She massaged her arm where he had gripped her. Her mind was racing.

That terrible voice from her dream spoke into her mind then. "You thought you were safe, but you'll never be safe."

"Come on, Devon." Brennan ushered her in front of him without pulling his gaze away from the guy.

She could tell Brennan didn't trust the guy not to swing on him or worse.

Devon had been approached by these kinds of guys before, and they were all the same. She tried to push the incident aside, but it kept creeping up on her. Was she a walking target for these idiots? Did people just find it funny to mess with her? She must have looked as bad as she felt because Brennan pulled her up short.

"Hey, are you all right?" he asked.

She wondered how many times he had asked her that question and how many times she had denied anything was wrong. It had been at least a dozen times a week since they had started working together.

This time, she didn't have to pretend. She wasn't okay. The guy who had grabbed her was two or three times her size. He could have easily overpowered her, and he knew it. She had seen the flash in eyes that said he had all the power. He was reveling in her helplessness, and that was scariest of all.

"No," she finally said, shaking her head. "I don't particularly like being manhandled."

"I don't think many people do," he said.

When a group walked past them, Brennan placed his hand on the small of her back, moving her to the side. Her body warmed at his touch, and she tried to push aside her growing attraction to him. She had spent too much time with him at work, and she didn't need this right now.

"Thanks for getting me out of there," she said softly.

"Thanks for answering my question," he replied with a smile unlike any she had ever seen from him.

Her cheeks heated, and she looked away.

"And for coming to my gig."

She cleared her throat. "You've been telling me about it for weeks. How could I miss it?"

"You're sneaky. I thought you would find a way."

"I'm not sneaky," she said defensively.

"You're proving me wrong," he said, nudging her forward. "Amy and Hannah are over here. We couldn't get anyone else out of work."

"Sounds good."

"Do you know if Hadley and Garrett are going to show?" he asked, glancing at her apprehensively.

"I think so. Garrett told me they planned to," she told him, wondering if she had said too much.

"Still not really talking to Hadley?" he asked intuitively.

Yep, she had said too much.

"Oh look, I see Amy," Devon said, ducking out from under his arm.

"About you answering questions," Brennan muttered as he followed her.

Amy and Hannah seemed to be deep in discussion about something when Brennan and Devon walked up, but the women welcomed them to the table. Devon took a seat next to Amy, and Brennan sat next to Devon. She didn't know when Hadley and Garrett would show up, so she was left with just Brennan's company.

When she realized Amy and Hannah were going to continue ignoring her, Devon turned to Brennan. "So, what are you singing tonight?"

"I've opted for originals."

"You write your own lyrics?" she asked, surprised.

He hadn't mentioned that part. It made her want to pull out her notebook. With how busy she had been, she hadn't had a chance to open it recently. It made her heart hurt to think about the last time she had written anything. Lyrics had always come so naturally to her. It was likely due to her parents' profession even if she didn't like to admit it. She still carried the notebook everywhere with her, but writing had fallen to the wayside since she had taken the job at Jenn's.

Brennan shrugged, like it wasn't a big deal. "Some. They're not great, but I've been particularly inspired recently."

"That's good," she said, finding she actually wanted to contribute to this conversation. "I like when I feel like that…most of the time."

"Me, too," he said, looking her straight in the eyes.

"Sometimes, it's like ripping my heart out and writing with the blood." She clutched her chest.

"Sometimes, it's like that," he agreed. "And other times, it's like the sun only shines for you, every breath of oxygen was designed for you to breathe, and life has a new purpose."

Devon swallowed and nodded. "Yeah," she whispered. "Sometimes, it's like that, too."

"But I like either as long as someone feels the music."

A pause followed in the conversation. Devon didn't know exactly what to say. When her phone vibrated in her purse, it kept her from saying anything. She pulled it out and stared down at the message. Reid. He had only sent a message to her once since she had supposedly left for Paris. Her heart sped up. What if she got caught? How would she respond?

Taking a deep breath, she pulled up the text.

I know you won't get this message for another month, but I've been missing you here. I wish I could get in contact with you because I have free time. Paris for a week sounds like a dream. Paris with you sounds even better. Call me as soon as you land, so I know you're safe.

As Devon finished reading the message, her hands continued to shake even though she knew she hadn't been caught. She closed her eyes and then opened them slowly. In a split-second decision, she deleted the text from her phone. She didn't know what had come over her, but she couldn't have his words staring at her, making her feel guilty, for another second.

Since she had left, she had received three or four emails a week from him. She hadn't answered any of them. He was probably starting to wonder why she wouldn't even answer emails, but she didn't care. What could she say anyway?

"Anything interesting?" Brennan asked, leaning over to her side.

She closed her phone quickly and looked up at him. She hadn't realized how close he was until that moment. Devon wet her lips as she gazed into the depths of his eyes. His pupils were especially dilated tonight. She didn't know if it was from the lack of light in the room or if he had smoked pot before arriving. He didn't smell like it. Actually, he smelled great. How had she never noticed that?

He cocked a lazy smile at her, like he could read her thoughts. Maybe he could. He just stared right back at her, exploring her face in ways that made her feel even guiltier for deleting Reid's text message.

The more she was around Brennan, the more she noticed him, and that was a slippery slope. Had he always been this good-looking? Had she just not noticed before because she had been blinded by Reid and all the problems she was working through? Or was it more than just his appearance? After all, he hadn't changed his looks. It was just him. It was something about him that she just got. It was something a person could only experience. Now that she was staring at him, she couldn't fathom not noticing.

If she had thought coming to this show would at all dampen her rising desire for the man sitting in front of her, she was wrong. Dead wrong.

"No, nothing interesting," she said, finally pulling her eyes away from him.

Devon was saved from further conversation when the lights began flickering to draw attention. A woman in a black dress walked onto the stage with more confidence than Devon could muster and took the microphone in her hand with a smile. She announced the start of the club's open mic night, resulting in a boisterous round of applause. While she talked, she strutted back and forth across the small stage like she owned it. A few men let out catcalls. Devon hoped that didn't continue and that it was only because the woman was clearly an MC of sorts.

Suddenly, the lights shut off, casting the entire bar into darkness. Devon looked around in confusion even though she couldn't make out anything at all. She didn't particularly like the dark, not after all her nightmares. She hesitantly began to rise, but then Brennan's hand found hers in the dark, stilling her. Devon could feel Brennan staring at her even though she couldn't see him, but this seemed to settle her rather than unnerve her.

Leaning into her, he whispered, "Just wait."

A spotlight hit center stage a minute later, and the opening chords of a song strummed through the speakers. Then, the woman launched into her song, and the cheers followed. Brennan released her hand, and Devon tried not to fidget.

As the woman held the last high note, ending beautifully, the crowd grew even louder. Then, another person took her place on stage and began singing. Devon wondered how many acts were performing tonight and where Brennan was in the lineup. If this was going on indefinitely, she would need a drink.

"When did you say Hadley and Garrett are getting here?" he asked, checking his watch after the last singer.

"They didn't say."

It was getting late. They should have been here already.

"I have to go backstage soon. I hoped to catch them before I left, but I guess I can't help it. Tell them I said hey, and I'll see them after the show," Brennan said, rising from his seat.

Devon fiddled with her phone and contemplated texting them to find out where they were. Hadley was a compulsively late person, but Garrett wasn't, so they usually balanced each other out. A new person anxiously walked up onto the stage and began awkwardly strumming a guitar. Devon knew this one was going to be a nightmare.

She leaned over to Amy and Hannah. "How many of these people are generally terrible?"

They both looked at her like she was being rude.

"They all have the guts to go up there at least," Amy said with a shrug, not meeting her eye.

"Yeah, it's not easy to get up on stage like that," Hannah agreed, crossing her arms.

Remind me to never try to make conversation with you again, Devon thought.

"I'm going to get a drink," Devon said to no one in particular.

They weren't listening anyway.

Careful to avoid the table that had harassed her earlier, she ambled over to the bar and saw there was a long line. Devon sighed, debating whether it was worth it. She decided to wait anyway since she didn't have anything better to do.

She spent the time scanning the room more closely. Earlier, she had only been looking for her friends, but now, she could simply people watch. A group of girls in the corner were dressed in nothing short of hooker attire. She wondered if they were actual prostitutes or if they just dressed that way for attention. If it was the latter, it was working. A couple was pressed up against the wall in the corner. The woman's leg was hitched around the guy's waist, and that was pretty much all Devon could see of her. The couple would be leaving soon if they didn't prefer the convenience of the restroom stalls. More than a few groups of guys had similar appearances to the meathead who had come on to her earlier. This place seemed to be a breeding ground for them. She would have to tread more carefully to evade their wandering hands on her return to the table.

She looked away from a large group of guys making less than playful banter with one of the hooker types. The girl must have been pretty headstrong because she looked like she was ready to take them on…or maybe she was taking them on in other ways. Devon didn't want to think about it.

Just as she was finishing her assessment, her eyes landed on a couple near the entrance to the restroom. They appeared to be in the midst of a heated conversation. Devon took a step forward in line and narrowed her eyes. It was dark, but she could just make out the shape of those shoulders, the style of the guy's hair, the thinness of the girl's waist, and the flash of blonde hair in the light. It was Hadley and Garrett.

How long have they been here? Devon wondered.

Devon observed their body language because she was too far away to hear anything they were saying. Hadley looked out of sorts. Her hands were flying, and her mouth was moving nonstop. From the looks of it, she appeared to actually be yelling at Garrett, but that didn't make any sense. Garrett was standing far enough away from Hadley to not look domineering. He seemed to be listening intently, but his posture showed that he was uncomfortable. It was a weird look on him. Devon had spent hours and hours with him, acting completely silly and also completely serious, and she had never seen him look uncomfortable.

She watched as Hadley pushed Garrett away before she turned her back to him. Garrett reached out and grabbed her wrist. He yanked her back toward him, crushing her against his chest, and then slammed his lips down on her mouth. Hadley struggled against him, beating at his arms and shoulders, before she caved and sank into his embrace. When Garrett finally released her, Hadley slapped him across the face and stormed into the restroom.

The girl behind Devon nudged her forward in line. It was her turn to order, but Devon just stood there and stared on in shock.

WHAT THE FUCK had just happened?

Seriously. What the hell had just happened?

Devon ordered her drink, so the woman behind her would stop bothering her. Finally, with her drink in hand, Devon turned back to the place where Hadley and Garrett had just been. Neither of them was standing there, and she searched the area to see if she could spot them. They weren't in plain sight. They must have moved on.

She couldn't understand what had happened. Hadley and

Garrett were in a realm of perfection that didn't exist in other relationships. Devon was surprised Hadley didn't have a ring on her finger already.

Devon knew it was ridiculous to think that. It was easy to see the perfection on the outside, but she lived with them. She knew what their schedules were like and how little time they actually spent together. She knew that Garrett's dad didn't like Hadley, and she knew that Garrett didn't know about Hadley's little coke problem.

Devon stopped in her tracks. Had Garrett found out about Hadley's drug problem? She ran back through the scenario in her mind, recalling what she had seen. No. No, it didn't make sense. He wouldn't have kissed her like that. Would he? Maybe he had asked her to choose him over the drugs. Maybe the kiss had been an act of desperation on his part to convince her, to try to keep her. Gah! She didn't know, and she really, really wanted to know.

She returned to her seat to wait for Brennan's performance and stress about Hadley and Garrett. Amy and Hannah continued to act as if her appearance at their table was of little importance, and right now, Devon was happy for the reprieve. She had too many other things on her mind.

Coming to Chicago to escape her life in St. Louis wasn't working out exactly as she had planned. Not that anything ever did. Not that she had really planned it out to begin with.

Hadley was supposed to help ground her. Garrett wasn't supposed to take her place. Devon didn't want to be more comfortable with him than Hadley. Brennan wasn't supposed to be so appealing. She had too much to work out in her life without dealing with the intruding thought of Brennan's lips against hers again. She couldn't do that…not with everything else.

"I think he's next," Amy squealed.

Devon glanced over at them and noticed what she hadn't seen before. They liked Brennan. She hadn't paid any attention at work, but it was pretty obvious now that she was looking for it. Maybe they had heard about how she had gotten the job at Jenn's and that was why they didn't like her. They must think she was competition. It would explain a lot.

Well, if that was what they thought, they were wrong. After Devon had turned down Brennan, she couldn't fathom him trying again. She had made it clear that she was off-limits. Even if he wanted to cross those lines, she wasn't sure he would act on it again.

Ugh! She couldn't even think about it all. It just made her head hurt.

Devon placed her palm on her forehead and tried to massage out the growing ache in her head.

"You feeling all right, Dev?"

As Devon's head flew up in surprise, she found Garrett standing over her. "Garrett! You're here!"

"Yeah, sorry about being so late," he said.

She looked around, wondering where Hadley was. Was she still in the restroom? Was Devon a bad friend for not following after her? Devon hadn't felt like it was her place to step in. Garrett and Hadley didn't know that she had seen their argument, and they probably didn't want her to know about it. Still, maybe she could go check on Hadley.

"Where's Hadley?" Devon asked, knowing the answer.

If she wasn't with him, then he had left her in the restroom.

I guess it is just going to be a guilt-ridden night, Devon thought.

Garrett took the seat Brennan had left unoccupied. "Oh, she really, really wanted to come, but she's sick tonight. I couldn't even drag her out of the house. Are you okay? I hope you don't have the same thing that she has."

Devon stared at him blankly. He was lying. He was looking her in the face, straight in the face, and lying. And he was damn good at it. She couldn't even tell. She knew he was lying, and she couldn't even tell that he was. He actually made her doubt what she had seen with her own two eyes earlier.

"Wha…what's wrong with her?" Devon asked in disbelief.

"Headaches, body aches, exhaustion. She has been really moody all week, so it could just be PMS," he said with a shrug.

PMS? He was really going to use that. Hadley had just slapped him across the face, and he was going to blame her behavior on PMS. Yeah right!

It's more likely the amount of cocaine she is using, Devon thought.

"That sucks," Devon said finally.

"Yeah, she really wanted to come," he repeated.

"I'm surprised you came out at all if she wasn't feeling well," Devon said accusingly. Why wasn't he chasing after her? Why was he letting her go? Wasn't that what was supposed to happen? She felt deluded about Garrett and Hadley's relationship. She had wanted so badly for it to be as perfect as it looked from the outside.

"She told me to go. After all, I couldn't do anything for her," Garrett said. He leaned back into the chair, his ankle crossing over his knee.

"Of course," Devon said, trying to hold back the sarcasm from her voice. "I sure hope she gets better soon."

"Comes once a month. I'm sure she'll be fine," Garrett said over the applause from the last performer.

Devon rolled her eyes and looked toward the stage. Garrett wasn't going to give any clues as to what had happened between them. She would have to ask him later, or maybe she would have to ask Hadley. Hadley had been the one who was pissed off, so she might be more likely to spill. For all the confidence that Devon and Garrett had been entrusting each other with, she wasn't so sure he would tell her, but maybe she would ask him about it again later anyway.

Her eyes focused in on Brennan as he walked onto the stage, carrying an acoustic guitar. Her body tensed as she stared down at him. She could hear murmurs coming from the women in the audience as he plugged in his guitar, adjusted the microphone, and sat down on the chair. Everyone was noticing what Devon had just realized moments ago. He looked great up there. He had taken off the blue button-up that he had arrived in, and now, he was just wearing a fitted green T-shirt with his dark jeans.

If she didn't know him better, she would have thought he was completely comfortable up there. But his hands twitched as he plucked at a chord, and she watched his lips move as he muttered to himself. He had an easy, lazy look to him that helped him appear more relaxed than he was. She wished she could do something to calm his nerves.

After Brennan finished his adjustments, he leaned forward toward the microphone. "Good evening. I'm Brennan Walker. A couple of you out there might have seen me up here before. I'm sure a few of you booed me off stage the first time I tried this. Thanks for coming back and giving me another shot."

The crowd chuckled. That was a good sign. Devon found herself rooting for him.

"For those of you who are new to the open mic routine, you picked a damn good night to be in the house. I'm playing a selection of original tunes, and I hope you like them. This first one is titled 'Headstrong.'"

Devon wasn't sure what she had been expecting, but whatever it was could never compare to this. She knew music. She had grown up around music, dated musicians, and listened to every genre imaginable. Her heart craved music. And that was exactly what she was getting tonight.

Brennan's voice wasn't the best out there. He wasn't a master on the guitar. He didn't have the stage presence of the artists she had encountered at home. But he had a certain quality about him that seemed superior to all of that. It was like when she had tried to tease apart her feelings toward him, and all she had discovered was that she couldn't. That was what his music was like. It was more an emotion than anything, like the way she felt when she got butterflies in her stomach, or when she rode a roller coaster, or when she caught the first glimpse of the horizon across the ocean. It was all and none of those things.

And maybe she was the only one in the room feeling that. But wasn't that what made art so beautiful in the first place? She could stand in one place and experience the same thing as a hundred other people, and everyone would come out of it with something different. She felt like she was soaring, and the world was flying beneath her feet. Brennan's smooth voice was music to her ears, and music brought her home.

When the song ended, Devon realized her eyes were closed, and she slowly opened them. As her vision adjusted to the dim lighting, she focused down on Brennan.

What are you doing to me? she wondered.

The crowd cheered, and Devon followed, clapping her hands hard.

"He's good, right?" Garrett leaned over, so Devon could hear him.

"Yeah! Wow!" she said, wearing the biggest smile on her face since she had been in Chicago.

"You should have come to his last performance. The audience gave him a standing ovation at the end. I don't know what it is about the guy, but everyone goes nuts for his music. Hadley even cried at the end of his last show, and he only played for like fifteen minutes," Garrett told her.

"He's good. I should know," she said with a laugh. "I know music."

"You should pitch him to the people you know," Garrett suggested.

Devon wrinkled her nose. "I don't know people, except for my parents."

"I'm sure you can think of someone," Garrett prodded. "His music made you smile brighter than you have since you got here. Anything that can put that pretty smile on your face should be playing on the radio."

Devon blushed at his words. "Thanks," she said, staring back down at Brennan.

She probably did know someone. Most of her contacts were with country music, and he clearly didn't sing country. In any case, she could likely get him an in…if that was what he wanted. It would be something worth thinking about…maybe.

Before she could think about it any further, he started the next song. The next two were ones that Garrett knew from previous shows. He told her that Brennan normally added a couple originals in here and there among the covers he did. Garrett had never been to a gig where Brennan did all originals. Devon couldn't imagine the show any other way. No one else's music would have felt right.

As Brennan's short set drew to a close, Devon found she didn't want it to end. How could it be so close to being over already? It felt like he had just started.

"I want to thank you all again for coming out. This is my last song for the night, and it's kind of personal to me. It's about loss, pain, and silence…about how hope blossoms in the smallest of packages and in the least likely of circumstances. This one is titled 'Moving Forward'," he said into the microphone, his eyes seemingly finding her in the crowd.

As he played the first few chords, his eyes never strayed from her. She wasn't even close to the stage, but he seemed to know right where she was. Amy and Hannah sighed heavily next to her.

As soon as the lyrics started flowing from his mouth, Devon could tell the song was different from the others…more personal. She hadn't thought it possible, but this song was better suited to him than the others. He couldn't have described the lyrics any better than in his introduction.

She felt like her heart was breaking as he sang about a loss she could understand. She felt a stabbing sensation in her body as she experienced his pain. The words made her feel like she wasn't alone with the dreaded silence from which she suffered. And finally, she could feel her heart being stitched together. The needle wasn't gentle, and the thread would heal the wounds in time, but there was hope that the scars would heal.

When the song came to a close, Devon felt tears welling in her eyes. The song was painful. It actually caused her physical discomfort to even hear it, but that made it even better. People who had ever willed themselves to silence needed the hope from Brennan's song. Maybe it would help mend their hearts, too.

Brennan stood as the house came down with applause. People were on their feet. Some people were swiping at their eyes from the emotional song. But Brennan never broke eye contact with Devon, and her eyes never left his gaze until he was ushered offstage for the next performer. That poor soul.

"I don't know how he does it," Garrett said, nudging Devon lightly. "Look, you're even crying. I thought we talked about this. No more crying from you."

Devon laughed through her tears and sniffled. "Right. Right. No more crying," she said, wiping under her eyes.

"If I had a voice like that and could play guitar, I could bag so many girls," Garrett said with a fake dumb expression on his face, making fun of all the guys who actually talked like that.

"I'm sure he does," Devon said, laughing softly at his joke.

If Brennan's advances toward Devon were any indication, he was surely getting exactly who and what he wanted.

"Who? Brennan?" Garrett asked incredulously. "No way. That guy is a saint. Girls are magnets for musicians, and he manages to fend them off like a lion tamer."

"No way is he a saint," Devon said, rolling her eyes. "I don't believe it. Half the girls at work like him."

"Well, you ask him then," Garrett said with a shrug. "I've known a lot of guys with musician complexes. He doesn't have one."

"Oh, you've known guys with musician complexes?" Devon asked, again rolling her eyes to the ceiling. They could never compare to what she had seen.

"All I'm saying is that Brennan could sleep with any girl here tonight, and he won't bring any one of them home. At least, I've never seen him do it."

But he brought me home, she thought. She wasn't going to

stick around to find out if it would happen with someone else.

She could see Brennan backstage now, sliding his button-up back on. Soon, he would be back at their table. She couldn't face him. That song had struck home. The lyrics were so personal and so touching that she felt like he had spoken directly to her. It was as if she had opened up her notebook filled with lyrics and let him read the pages with her heart laid bare in the words. She was the one moving forward, pushing through the pain to find herself once more. And it was then that she felt like the final song had been about her, like it had been written for her. She couldn't prove it, and she didn't want to. She couldn't get more entangled in him than she already was even if Garrett said he wouldn't make a move…another move.

She would be interested in pursuing her little sliver of hope but not under these circumstances. It wouldn't be fair to him, or her, or Reid.

She needed to leave before she did something stupid.

"I'm actually not feeling all that well, Garrett." Devon put her hand on her forehead again. "I wanted to see Brennan's show, but I think we should probably go. I'll see him at work this week, and I'll talk to him there."

"You sure?" Garrett asked, clearly confused.

"Yeah, I'm ready to go home," Devon said, feeling like that wasn't an appropriate name for the apartment she was living in.

She had found her home in Brennan's music.

CHAPTER 15
It's Going Around

"Fuck," Devon cried, impatiently tapping her pen back and forth on her leg on the train.

An old lady sitting down near Devon glared at her. Devon didn't have the patience for it right now. She was late for work. It was the first time she had ever been late. What made it worse was she knew that Jenn was going to be in today.

She hadn't meant to be late. No one ever intended to be late. But she had managed to sleep right through her alarm.

Last night had been the worst dreams she'd ever had. She had woken up twice in the middle of the night with the exact same dream that she'd had a dozen times already, the one where she was being chased through campus. She shuddered even thinking about it. Then, this morning, it had raided her sleep once more and held her hostage through her alarm. Each time she had awoken drenched in sweat or crying her eyes out, remembering the feel of the man's hands on her as she lay sprawled face-first on the bed. Her hands were shaking now at the thought.

She hadn't had time to shower or cover up the dark circles under her eyes, and she was pretty sure she looked like shit. It would be just another thing Jenn would love about her showing up late. Jenn didn't necessarily have a code for appearances at her restaurant, but her idea of looking nice certainly involved a shower and makeup. Devon had done what she could with her mess of hair tangled from her trio of nightmares. Although she would have normally preferred to tame her waves with her straightener, she had only had enough time to run her fingers under the faucet and comb them through her hair.

It wasn't like Devon had anyone to impress anyway. Jenn could get over it, and Brennan wouldn't be in anyway. He had called in sick every day since his gig. Jenn hadn't said what was wrong, but it must have been serious. He never missed work as far as Devon could tell.

She cursed a second time and openly glared back at the old woman until she broke eye contact. Devon was not a woman to be messed with right now. Since Brennan had not come into work, she hadn't talked to him in four, going on five, days. He probably thought she was a super shitty person for walking out on his show without a word. When she had found out he was sick, she had sent him a text, but she hadn't received a response. She could only assume he was pissed or deathly ill. Neither were preferable options.

As the train came to a halt, Devon pushed her way through the doors before they opened all the way. She brushed her hair off her face as the heat of the city hit her full-on. She wanted to run straight to Jenn's, but she knew if she ran, she would be sweating by the time she got there. That wouldn't help her case any.

Not able to help herself, she rushed down the flight of stairs to the street level. When her phone started ringing loudly in her purse, she cursed again. Now was not the time.

She grabbed the phone out of her purse, stared down at the screen, and sighed. Not the best time, but she had been avoiding her mother for too long.

"Hey, Mama," Devon said, leaning the phone against her ear as she pushed through the turnstile.

"Hey, honey! How are you? I've missed you so much this summer," she said, gushing like always.

"I've been fine. How are you and Dad? How is Dani?" Devon said, asking the requisite questions.

"We're all great, Dixie."

Devon rolled her eyes. She would never live down that nickname.

"Your father started a new song that would bring tears to your beautiful blue eyes."

Devon's thoughts drifted to another song that had brought tears to her eyes last week. She swallowed down that thought. This would be a good time to ask her parents about helping out Brennan. She opened her mouth to say something, but then she closed it again. How would she explain Brennan when her mom didn't even know she was in Chicago? Devon cringed.

"I really think this one is going to be a hit. Dani was almost emotional," her mother said.

"Another sad one?" Devon trotted down the stairs, barely listening to her mom. She didn't want to think about how she would explain Brennan to her parents, but now, all she was thinking about was how to do it.

"No! It's so happy that you would just cry with happiness," her mother said, giddy. "It's really, truly beautiful."

"That's good, Mom," Devon said dryly.

"We can't wait to see who the record label chooses for it."

"Mama, I'm kind of busy. Can we talk later?" Devon said, treading the familiar track to Jenn's.

"Oh, I'll just be quick and tell you why I called! So, I bought our plane tickets to New York. I bought one for you—" she began.

"Mom!" Devon whined, drawing the word out as long as she could. "I'm not going."

"Now, Dixie, be reasonable. It's refundable just in case you can't make it, but really, you should be able to make it. It's a nonstop flight from St. Louis to LaGuardia. I even got first class," her mother cooed as if that would make up for it.

"Mom!"

"It's going to be really fun! Your father and I have been nominated for an award, honey!"

"Mom!" Devon tried again.

"It's going to be so nice to have the whole family back together," her mom said.

"I'm not going, Mama. I'm too busy."

"I'll send you the flight information in an email. Dustin thinks that he and Kelly aren't going either, but I've already sent their itinerary along. I'm sure they'll come around," she said, oblivious to Devon's frustration. "Did you need me to get Reid a ticket as well?"

"No," Devon said flatly.

"Are you sure? I'd be happy to get one for him, too," she said in a singsong tone.

"I'm not going, so if you got Reid a ticket, he would be going without me," Devon said.

"Dixie, please," her mother said, turning on the waterworks like a light switch.

Devon sighed, hating when her mother did this. She couldn't deal with this right now.

"I've got to go to work. I'll talk to you some other time," Devon said hastily.

"Work?" her mom asked.

Devon stopped in the middle of the street. Shit!

She hadn't meant to say that. She was slipping. Her mother wasn't even supposed to know that she was working. She needed to come up with something quickly. No one was supposed to know what she was doing. If one person found out, the whole thing would come tumbling down.

"Yeah, I'm just filling in for a friend at a restaurant. They were shorthanded, and I offered to help," Devon lied, trying to cover up her mistake.

"Do you need extra money, Dixie? I'd be happy to put some into your account," her mother offered.

"No, I'm fine," she said quickly.

"I don't like the thought of you working when you're already so busy."

"I just…have to go," Devon said, cursing herself for fucking up. "Bye, Mom."

Devon threw her phone back into her purse in frustration. She was already at the back door to Jenn's, and she needed to get her shit together.

She headed inside and waited for the shitstorm that was likely to surface. Quickly stashing her bag in the break room, she surfaced just in time to see Brennan walk into the kitchen. She stopped in her tracks, surprised to see him. Jenn had said he wouldn't be in all week, and he still looked pretty sick. What was he doing here?

"Hey," Devon said, wanting to say something before he did. "Sorry about running out of the show last week. I wasn't feeling well."

Brennan shrugged, not looking directly at her. "I guess it's going around."

"Yeah, but I feel bad. I should have waited," she said. "You put on a great show."

"Thanks," he said. "I thought it went well."

He still hadn't met her gaze. What was up with him?

"I really liked the last song." She bit her lip, hoping he would look at her.

"I think it still needs some work."

Devon tried to figure out a different angle. He seemed even more off and withdrawn than normal. "Are you feeling any better? Jenn said you were sick."

He shrugged again. "I guess. Some. I just came in for my check." He waved it dismissively in the air.

"Oh. So, you're not staying?" Her stomach sank.

"Jenn won't clear me even though I told her it wasn't that bad. She said I handle food, and she doesn't want me to contaminate her customers."

A faint smile touched his face when he finally looked up at her. He really didn't look good. No wonder Jenn was sending him home.

"That sucks," she said, not sure what else to say.

He felt so far away. Through his music, she felt like they had connected on a different level, one that even she couldn't figure out. Yet, she had left, and now, it was like he was an empty vessel.

"Hey, how did your medical exams go?" She hoped changing the subject would bring him out of his funk. She had forgotten to ask him about it at his show.

He visibly flinched at the words. "Fine."

She wasn't sure how she had managed to make him even less

comfortable. "Do you think you'll get into the schools you want?"

"We'll just wait and see," he responded dryly.

It was the same tone she had used with her mother. That wasn't good.

"Well…good luck," she muttered.

"I've got to get out of here. Not feeling as well as I thought, I guess. I'll see you around, Devon," he said with a half-smile before he walked out the back door.

She watched him leave with a heavy weight on her chest. Hadn't she left St. Louis to escape her problems? Why did it feel like the farther she ran, the more problems kept piling up? Nothing was working, and she couldn't hide out in Chicago forever. She would have to face what had happened to her before school started or else it would only get worse.

Somehow, she would have to factor Brennan into all of that because whatever she was feeling wasn't going away. Her stomach twisted at that thought. Brennan didn't need to be anywhere near her problems…they could get him killed.

***

JENN WAS BEYOND bitchy when she finally found Devon. Devon couldn't really blame her; it was a holiday. Who was late on the Fourth of July? She was missing all the fun with parades, barbeques, and American flags everywhere outside. She wished that she could have had the day off, but Jenn's was slammed.

Hannah had called in sick, and there was no way that Jenn was going to let Devon leave early, especially after she had shown up twenty minutes late.

The only good part about being this busy was that Devon didn't have any time to think. She was on her feet all morning, literally running at some points to get through orders faster. Her head was pounding by noon, and her feet hurt like the first day she had started working there.

Just as she was taking her first break of the day, Devon saw Hadley walk into the restaurant. Hadley had been as scarce in the apartment as when Devon had first confronted her about the drugs. This time, Devon was pretty sure that it wasn't her fault though. She had never found out what had caused Hadley's argument with Garrett. Hadley hadn't been around all week, so Devon hadn't gotten the chance to ask her.

Garrett hadn't been acting any differently toward her. He clearly didn't know that Devon knew about the argument. The more time she spent with him, the more she thought it must be Hadley's fault. He wouldn't be that carefree about the situation if it had been his fault. She knew because she felt terribly guilty for leaving St. Louis, like it was her fault for not facing her problems, for not somehow being better.

Garrett didn't show any signs of feeling bad about the argument, whereas Devon knew Hadley was using.

Hadley's eyes roamed the restaurant, and when she found Devon, she bit her lip and nodded her head to the side.

Hmm…

Devon was on her break, so she did have some time to talk to Hadley, but all things considered, it was weird that Hadley wanted to talk to her. It was also strange that Hadley was alone. It was a holiday. She should have been with her family, or with Garrett, or with Garrett's family.

What the hell? Devon thought, deciding to go find out.

"Hey, do you have a minute?" Hadley asked when Devon reached her. "I know it's packed in here."

"I'm on break actually," Devon said.

Hadley looked relieved and motioned for her to follow her outside. Devon's curiosity was getting the better of her. She wasn't going to miss a chance to talk to Hadley even if Devon wasn't sure of the circumstances.

They walked around the side of the building and stood in the alleyway facing the street. It wasn't exactly private, but it was more privacy than they would get inside. Plus, if Jenn saw Devon in the break room, she would likely flip, and Devon's fifteen minutes would be up. Devon leaned back against the brick building and waited for Hadley to say something.

"Hey," Hadley said awkwardly as if she wasn't talking to her best friend.

"What's up, Hadley?" Devon asked, knowing there was something to this.

What was she going to ask for—money for her drugs? Devon couldn't help thinking the worst of Hadley, and it made her feel bad. Hadley was her best friend, and Devon needed to act like it. Just because she was going through her own issues didn't mean she couldn't keep trying to help Hadley. It was something Devon could work toward, but it was another thing she had just as little control over.

Hadley sighed and looked down at the ground. "I didn't know who else to talk to," she whispered.

She sounded more like the Hadley that Devon knew before she had found out Hadley was on drugs.

"About what?" Devon asked carefully. She didn't want to scare Hadley off.

Hadley swallowed and fidgeted. "I've…I've been trying to quit."

"That's great, Hadley!" Devon cheered.

"I'm still working on it," she said, fidgeting some more. "I didn't really come to talk about that though. I just…just thought you should know."

Damn! That was the best news she'd had all day. Devon didn't know exactly what it meant, but at least it showed that Hadley knew she had a problem. Progress was progress.

"I'm really glad you told me," Devon said honestly.

"There's, um…more." Hadley bit her lip and moved from the ball of her foot to the other. "Garrett and I got into this huge fight the other night."

"You did?" Devon asked, feigning surprise. Now wasn't the time to reveal that she already knew this much.

"Yeah. You might have noticed I haven't been at the

apartment much."

"I did."

"Well, I just got so angry at him. I…I slapped him, Dev," Hadley said, her hands shaking. "Gah, I mean…what happens if we break up, and he kicks me out of the apartment? It's his place. He could do it if he wanted."

Hadley was blabbering on, and Devon was just staring at her, surprised that Hadley had told her.

"Wait…wait…back it up," Devon said. "What were you even fighting about?"

"That's the thing. I don't even know. It all just escalated and got way out of hand," Hadley said, glancing off into the distance.

Devon knew that look anywhere. She was lying. Everyone was lying to her. It was only fitting, considering she was lying to everyone else, too.

"Hadley, come on. I know you too well. What happened?" Devon prodded. She took a chance and reached out to touch Hadley's hand.

Hadley flinched but let her take it.

"You can tell me what happened."

"I wasn't in a good place the night it happened. I was trying to stay off of it for the show. It was…bad. Then, he kept acting so funny, and he made some fucking cocky remark. I freaked out and started yelling at him. I don't know, Dev." She stared at the ground with an expression on her face like she did know. "I think he might be cheating on me."

Devon stared at her with her mouth hanging open. Garrett? Cheating on her? No. That didn't make any sense. That just didn't add up. When would he have time to do that? He worked all day when he didn't live in the gym. His body was a testament to his dedication in that area. The only other time he was awake and not with Hadley was when he was goofing off with Devon late at night.

Also, how could Hadley even freak about him doing something like that when she was doing drugs and hiding it from him? Okay. Devon would give Hadley some credit. Devon would freak about that too, but it was kind of hypocritical, not that she would ever say as much to Hadley, who looked devastated.

"Oh, Hadley, no way. How could you think that? He's so into you," Devon said.

Hadley shrugged. "I told you. He's been acting so weird. I thought he was just as into me as you said, but lately, he hasn't wanted to come to bed with me. I mean…fuck, we haven't had sex in two weeks. Two weeks! We used to not be able to go two days!"

Devon didn't want to think about Hadley's sex life right now. Hers was nonexistent at the moment.

"You guys have both been under a lot of stress. I'm sure it's all just a misunderstanding," Devon said, trying to reassure her friend.

"If you knew anything, Dev, you would tell me, right?" Hadley asked, staring at her straight in the eye.

"Of course!" Devon said automatically.

Hadley looked at her for a second before nodding and looking away.

"Maybe you're right," Hadley said finally with a heavy sigh. "I have this Fourth of July dinner with Garrett and his family tonight. I was freaking out about it. I even considered canceling. I don't know. His family is even weirder around me. I wish you could come with," she said impulsively.

"I have to work," Devon said, wanting to be as far away from that get-together as possible. After a day like today, she would prefer to be in bed before the fireworks.

"You think it'll all be fine?" Hadley asked.

"Just be yourself. How could they not love you?"

"You're right," she said, regaining the strength that Devon had always loved about her.

"But I wouldn't…use anything before you go," Devon cautioned.

Hadley shook her head. "I wouldn't."

Devon really wanted to believe her.

SWEAT BEADED ON Devon's temple, and she wiped it off her forehead and out of her eyes. The party had been going on all night, and it was nice to loosen up and get lost in the music and dancing. She hadn't partied in so long, and she couldn't resist when Amy had actually invited her out. Either Amy was getting over her hatred for the new girl, or Devon had just been there long enough that she wasn't considered the new girl any longer.

People were packed into the club, shoulder-to-shoulder, many even closer than that. The music was earsplitting while the crazy lights traversed the warehouse-sized room before they alternated to strobe lights. Everything began moving in slow motion. She hadn't had much to drink, but she was dizzy from dehydration and the energy in the room. Her tank top was sticking to her back, and she had long since pulled her hair up off of her neck into a ponytail.

God, I need another drink, she thought.

Her eyes moving around the room, she took in as much as she could from her vantage point, but it only ended up being the two feet circling her. Amy had to be somewhere inside the building. How had she lost track of her?

Well, she knew how. There were too many damn people in the place. It was easy to lose one person, especially when that person was as short as Amy. Still, Devon should have been better at keeping track of Amy. Devon didn't like being alone in dark places. Whether she was surrounded by people or in a back alleyway at night, she was still alone.

She craned her head to look for Amy, but she was having no luck. It felt like more and more people were being crushed into the space. How was this in line with the fire code? Surely, the place would be shutdown soon.

Walking in the direction of the bar, Devon tried to find Amy in the crowd. Seriously, it was getting harder and harder to maneuver through the room, and she had to elbow people out of the way. This wasn't okay, and it wasn't fun. They shouldn't let any more people in. Things could get out of control.

Devon looked up over the heads of people in front of her and sighed. It felt like she was never going to reach the bar. There was a huge line anyway. She thought maybe the restroom would be a better alternative. At least there, she would have some privacy.

She turned to walk the other direction and slammed right into a meaty guy who glared at her as she lost her balance and tumbled to the floor. Someone stepped on her hand as she tried to get up. Devon swore and hissed, pulling her hand away from the ground so no one else could do the same thing. She stood as best as she could, cradling her aching hand. Pushing through people with one hand pressed between her breasts to keep someone else from smashing into it wasn't easy. All it did was cause people to unknowingly smash into other parts of her. She hadn't made it more than a few feet toward the restroom, and she had already been elbowed in the arm, gotten her foot stepped on, and been drunkenly body slammed, knocking the breath out of her. The club was getting dangerous.

As a space opened in the crowd, she took advantage, rushing forward through the throng of people. It got her closer to the restroom but not close enough.

Then, she felt it—eyes on the back of her head. She didn't even know how it was possible. Hundreds of people were in the place. No one could be focusing that intently on her, but she could swear that someone was watching her. The feeling crept up her spine, forcing her to move faster. She didn't know where Amy was, but getting away from this place felt like it made more sense than looking around for her.

Finally bursting off the dance floor, she rushed past the huge line of people waiting for the restroom. They all cussed at her as she passed them by and walked to the front.

"Just checking my hair." Devon looked over her shoulder and rushed into the restroom before someone could say anything further.

As soon as she walked through the doors, she felt water underneath her heels. As she slid across the floor, she tried to right her balance, but instead, she crashed down on her hands and knees. Devon cried out as pain shot up her arms and legs. Shock hit her like a tidal wave. Her right knee had taken most of the impact, and it was on fire. She was sure that she had broken the skin. Tears rushed to her eyes as the pain hit her full-on.

How can I be so clumsy? she wondered.

Devon wondered if anyone would help her. She wasn't sure if she could stand by herself. When she dragged her eyes up from the floor, she noticed that she wasn't in the restroom of the club. She was in a beautiful all white bathroom with a Jacuzzi tub and a walk-in shower. Her heart raced as she took in her surroundings.

"Aww, what did you do to yourself?" the all-too-familiar voice asked.

Her body rattled, Devon slowly stood, using the bathtub as leverage to hoist her up. She felt the blood from her knee trickle down her leg, but she wasn't going to let that stop her. Without another thought, she sprinted as fast as she could toward her pursuer.

He chuckled and moved out of the way. Then, he approached her and pushed her back with just enough force to send her stumbling toward the snowy white bed. She could have avoided the bed if he hadn't been at her side. He grasped her wrist, swung her arm behind her back, and pushed her into the bedspread.

She tried to scream through her tears as he all but pulled her arm out of its socket. The pain in her shoulder was so blinding that she bent easily at the waist, forgetting about her hurt knees.

"Let go. Let go. Let go," she muttered, trying to ease the pain off her shoulder. "Please. Let go."

"Isn't this what you want?" the voice asked.

With a chill running through her, she softly said, "Please let go." She didn't even know if he could hear her.

A hand came up and fisted in her ponytail, yanking her head back roughly. As he pulled her off the bed by her hair, she squeaked as he tugged some of the strands out. He released some of the tension on her shoulder, but he tightened his grip on her wrist. She was already starting to lose blood circulation in her fingers.

He brought her head back toward him but kept her facing the wall. He whispered in her ear, "You don't really want me to let go. Do you?" His voice was gruff but seductive.

She felt some her shoulders loosen, but her heart was still racing.

"I don't want to let go, so I don't see how you would want me to."

Devon trembled in his twisted embrace. She tried to clear her mind. She needed to go blank. She needed to forget since she couldn't stop it or fix it.

This is my fault. Why did I think I could run away? I brought this on myself, she thought.

He lifted her skirt and pushed her back over the bed.

***

Devon awoke with a start as someone shook her shoulder.

"Dev, wake up," Garrett said, shaking her again.

"I'm awake," she said hoarsely.

She was having a hard time thinking or even breathing right now. Garrett was hovering over her bed, and he reeked of alcohol. She was glad he had awoken her, but after that dream, the smell of alcohol was the last thing she wanted to wake up to. The nightmares had never gotten that far before. As the reality of what had happened sank into her, she realized she had always woken up terrified before, but now, she wasn't sweaty or crying or shaky. She felt numb. This whole time, she had been letting her walls crumble all around her, but with the memories of that dream, she had tightly locked it all up again.

"Have you been drinking?" she asked just so he would stop staring at her in the darkness. She needed to compose herself.

"Yeah. It's the Fourth of July…well, it's the fifth now," he said, sitting heavily on the bed.

The covers fell down past her breasts, which were only covered by her thin nightshirt. His eyes followed the movement, and for once, Devon was glad for the cover of darkness.

She pulled up the sheet. "Why are you back already?" She yawned as she read the clock. Midnight. "Aren't you supposed to be out with your parents or something?"

"Change of plans."

She could tell something was wrong by the set of his shoulders. Her brain hadn't caught up with her body. She had crashed as soon as she had gotten home. Waking up in the middle of the night made her groggy. She couldn't figure out why he would be home or what could be wrong.

"And you woke me—"

"Come drink with me." He grabbed her hand and tugged lightly, prodding her out of bed.

Devon yawned. "I'm really not up for a drink."

"You're never tired this early."

"I worked my ass off all day."

"You can sleep in tomorrow. Come have a drink with me. I brought a bottle back," he said with a boyish grin, his hand running back through his hair.

Devon sighed and nodded. He wouldn't be asking if something wasn't wrong. "All right. It better not be tequila."

"Would I do that to you?" He chuckled.

"Only if you hated me."

"Which I don't. So, let's go." He stood and padded out of the room.

When he left, Devon kicked out her feet from the bed and stood shakily. She couldn't believe that she was actually going to get out of bed to have a drink right now, and she didn't want to face why she was doing it. All of it hurt too much.

How long could a person go without sleeping? She would do

that if she never had to dream again. Alcohol sounded like a better option than closing her eyes and living that dream all over again.

Still in her nightshirt and sleeping shorts, she slung a cardigan on and walked out into the living room. Crashing down on the couch, she cuddled up with the throw pillow and tried to hold back her yawn.

Garrett walked out of the kitchen with two full shot glasses. He set them on the table next to Devon. She stared at them warily as he walked back into the kitchen. He returned a second time with two whiskey glasses full of a dark brown liquid.

"You weren't joking," Devon said.

"Did I sound like I was?" he asked, staring at her.

"Guess not. I'm going to get fucked up."

"That's the point." He handed her a shot of bourbon.

Garrett held out his glass, and Devon raised hers to meet his.

"To living the life," he said.

Devon cracked up, thinking how far from that she felt, but when she looked up to his face, she could see the feeling was mutual.

"To living the life," she repeated, taking the shot back. It burned like a bitch, but she was from Tennessee. She would have gotten nowhere if she didn't know how to take down a good shot of bourbon.

Garrett slammed the shot glass down on the table. "Fuck that." He returned to the kitchen and reappeared a second later with an expensive-looking bottle of liquor.

Devon's eyes widened when she saw the label. She had seen

people drink it, but it was usually served neat out of a fancy crystal decanter.

Who did shots off of a two-thousand dollar bottle of scotch? Apparently, they did.

Not being able to help herself, she asked, "Where the fuck did you get that?"

"I told you. I got a bottle."

"From who?"

"My parents," he said with a shrug.

"Should we be drinking this?"

"That's what it's meant for." He poured another shot and handed it to her.

She stared at the liquid with a newfound sense of appreciation. Her shot alone was probably worth a couple hundred bucks. As the liquid slid down her throat again, she was glad that she hadn't choked on it the first time. Were people allowed to choke on really expensive scotch?

When Garrett started pouring another, Devon shook her head.

"No more for me unless you want me throwing up. I need to stagger." Her head already felt heavy.

He shrugged and took the shot without her.

"So, why are you home?" she asked.

"Got into a fight with my dad," he admitted. The alcohol was clearly loosening him up some more.

Devon sat up as his head lolled backward.

"Tell me about it."

"He hates Hadley. He thinks she's a waste of time and a waste of space. He thinks I can do better. He thinks I stay in the job that he helped me get with no ambition and no motivation to move up in the company. He refuses to see that I hate the job and would do anything to get out of it. But the thought of disappointing him any further kills me," he said in a rush. "He's just a selfish bastard who hates his only son."

Devon didn't know what to say to that last part. Her parents had expectations for her life. How could they not? But everything they did was out of love. They would never push her so hard that they pushed her away. Even now, when she was lying to them on a daily basis, she never thought that they would try to force her into anything.

"I'm sure he doesn't hate you," she said softly, touching his hand.

Garrett scoffed. "You don't know the man."

"But I know you. I don't know how anyone could hate you."

"Well, I think you're the only one left who doesn't."

"Garrett, what happened?" she asked. "It can't be as bad as you say."

He offered her another shot, and she took it from him only because he seemed so desperate.

"Hadley and I show up at my parents' house in the suburbs for the holiday. Everything is going fine. We barbeque, play football in the yard, and the girls are laying out by the lake. Right before the fireworks, it all goes to shit. My dad asks me about my job, and I say one thing that he doesn't like. One thing! He flips out and starts lecturing me. We start yelling back and forth loud enough for all of the guests to hear. I wouldn't back down. I was tired of him always trying to assert his dominance over me. I'm a grown man! I told him I was going to quit."

Devon gasped. "Quit?"

"I'm really thinking about it. I hate the work. But it gets worse," he said miserably.

How could it get much worse?

"When I refused to take his shit, he brought Hadley into it."

"Oh no," Devon whispered, imagining Hadley hearing all the things that Garrett's dad thought of her. She knew her friend too well to assume she would sit out of the conversation.

"Yeah. You can imagine the things he said about her. I'm ashamed to even repeat it. Small town, white trash, gold digger." Garrett shook his head. "He even called her a fucking drug addict right to my face. I don't know where he gets the nerve."

Devon froze. So, Garrett still didn't know. She wanted to tell him. She really wanted to, but he was already so down right now. She couldn't be the one to break it to him.

"Hadley flipped out at all of his accusations. Her screams only fueled my father, not that she didn't have every right to yell back, but I think it proved to him what he thought of her all along. And then she thought that I was somehow in on it."

"What?"

"Her anger went from my dad to me, and then she just left. I was seeing red after that, and I ended up punching through a wall in my parents' house. Hadley left upset and took my car. I took this bottle of scotch and my dad's Mercedes and got out of there, too. Hadley won't answer her cell. I think we're done," he said, ending his story.

CHAPTER 17

Obsession

After his declaration, Devon and Garrett sat there in silence for a while. Hadley and Garrett were done. It couldn't be true. Hadley was head over heels for Garrett. She had come to Devon just that afternoon, worried that he was cheating on her. Hadley wouldn't have left him for good. She had probably just overreacted.

And that wasn't a pleasant thought either. Hadley's overreaction in her state of mind was a recipe for disaster. She had been trying to quit, but stress made people do stupid things. Who knew where she was right now? She could be out there somewhere overdosing on drugs.

Devon shuddered and pushed that thought out of her mind. No way would Hadley be that stupid.

Garrett poured them both another shot, and Devon gladly took it this time. She wanted to get that image of Hadley out of her head. Devon was all sorts of dizzy, and she dreaded the thought of standing. The scotch sure was potent. She hadn't allowed herself to drink much ever since her last vomiting experience after she had first arrived in Chicago.

"Hadley will come around," Devon said softly. She wasn't sure who she was convincing.

He nodded. "Can we just...talk about something else?" He leaned his head back on the couch.

"Sure." But she didn't have anything else she would like to talk about. "What do you want to talk about?"

He was silent, considering an answer. "Why did you leave St. Louis?"

"Uh..." she muttered.

"You said you ran away from your life. What were you running from?" he asked, suddenly staring at her intently.

Devon glanced down at her feet. "I think I'm going to need another shot for that."

Garrett complied, and the fourth shot of scotch gave her courage.

He slid his hand on her shoulder and squeezed. "It'll be okay."

She hadn't realized that she had started shaking.

Devon moistened her lips and then turned to look at him. This was just Garrett. It wasn't some stranger. He had poured his heart out to her, so she could trust him with her secret. Couldn't she?

"Well, since you told me a story, I'll, uh…I'll tell you one of my own."

"All right." As he straightened some in his seat, he stared at her.

She swallowed and tried to meet his gaze. How drunk was she? Could she do this?

Taking a deep breath, she began. "My mama always told me that once in a lifetime, you are given a chance at true greatness. That you would know it when it happened, and it would be true love at its finest. I believed her." Tears were already hitting her eyes.

"I wanted greatness, just like my mom. Her greatness is my dad, and they found each other in their music," she told him. "When it hit me, I didn't know how I could have ever lived another day without it. I don't know how to explain it, except to say it was like the universe was suddenly in alignment."

"So…you fell in love?" he asked, scrunching his eyebrows together.

She could see he was wondering where this was going. She didn't blame him for his confusion.

"It's…more than that," she said, fumbling for the words. "It's not like fate or soul mates because that makes it sound silly, but it's a sense of rightness of the way things are meant to be."

"All right. I'll buy that," Garrett said.

He has no idea, Devon thought.

"Having that with someone opens everything up. Everything is on the table. Trust isn't even a consideration because there could never be anything or anyone else."

Garrett shifted uncomfortably.

"I know what you're thinking," Devon said.

"I doubt it."

"Well, tell me," she insisted. This was hard enough without trying to read him, too.

"Sounds a bit like…obsession to me."

Devon sighed. "That's what I thought you'd say. I can't explain it any other way, so try to be open-minded," she said. He would need to be open-minded. "I'm not sure when it started exactly, but the sex changed."

Garrett's ears perked up at that. "Changed…for the worse?"

She shook her head. "For the better." Devon bit her lip. When she saw that he was watching, she stopped. She couldn't believe she was telling this story.

"Not to say the sex was bad before because it wasn't. It was amazing. In fact, I didn't believe it could get better. But one day, it was one way, and the next day, I was being held to the bed, forced to comply."

"What?" Garrett snapped. "Forced?"

Devon nodded. "I didn't think I would like it. I mean, it sounds really bad. It's probably why I never talk about it."

"Isn't that…rape?" he whispered.

"Don't use that word," she said immediately, drawing her

knees to her chest. Not that word. Anything but that word. "It wasn't like that."

"Okay, sorry. I didn't mean to say…I don't know what. Just keep going," he urged, brushing her blonde hair away from her face.

She looked back up at him, and he smiled. Her mind blurred from the alcohol, and she scooted closer to him. It was better to feel him comforting her through this. "So, after that started, it never stopped. It only escalated. I don't know if you want details—"

"If it helps you," he said, allowing her to continue.

She took a deep breath. Here goes nothing. "He started getting creative—demanding me to do things at any time or any place, holding me down, sometimes choking me. He would come home to find me in the shower and turn the water to the hottest temperature it would go. He would bend me over into the scalding spray, and we would have sex like that. I remember him waiting for me when I got home from school late one night. He threw me over the hood of his car and told me to be a good girl. We had sex at the end of the driveway under a streetlight. Anyone could have seen us. And I let him."

Garrett was staring at her with a mixed expression. She wasn't sure how much she should read into it. He looked really interested in what she was saying. How could she blame him? She was talking to a guy about sex, about a particular form of rough sex that he had likely never experienced. The interest was mingled in there with something resembling disbelief. She didn't know if that meant he didn't believe that she would put up with it or he didn't believe someone would actually do this. All she really knew was that he had adjusted his pants, and Hadley had been right about the size of the contents that lay within.

"I didn't think I would like it at first, but as you can imagine… maybe…" She shifted her eyes away from him. "Well, it kept things interesting. I never knew what he was going to do. That came with a price at times, but the more it happened, the higher the price I was willing to pay. I trusted him completely…until something tipped the balance further."

"Tipped the balance…how?" Garrett asked curiously.

"It stopped being about sex. I have zero complaints about the sex. When it stopped being about us, it got out of control," she said, trying to explain. "If I told people about this, I would tell anyone I know to try that kind of relationship. I have never felt more safe and sexy and wanted. You're looking at me like you don't believe me, but try it out first, and you'll come around."

She crossed her arms against his disbelief. She would never be able to explain this to someone who had never experienced it, and she would never want to change how it had happened. She would never take it back.

"It was more about him being in control that changed everything."

"Wasn't he in control during sex?" Garrett asked, looking more curious than judgmental.

"No, not exactly. It was mutual. He might have looked like he was in control, but it was consensual. He would only give me as much as I could handle, and I wanted him to push those limits. It's a hard thing to grasp…" She trailed off.

How could she explain the next part? How could she make Garrett see the difference? Sex was not the problem. He was the problem.

"He changed, and it had nothing to do with the sex. He needed to control me. He had always been one of those people who asked where I was going and when I would be back. He always had to know. But then, he started asking why was I going there, and he started telling me when I had to be back. Then, I wasn't allowed to go at all. I just wanted to make him happy because I love him so damn much, but he wanted all the control in my life, which left me with none. That's when I realized I was no longer a person anymore. I was his object."

Devon stopped trying to explain and went back into her story. "I was home early from school one day. I wasn't expecting him, but I could tell something was wrong. And it might sound strange, but I never thought he did any of these things out of anger. He did them out of love."

"You think he held you under boiling water out of love?" Garrett asked incredulously.

Devon glared at him. "I didn't say you would understand. The sex was not a threat. It had nothing to do with him being angry with me."

"Sorry," he said sheepishly. "Keep going. It was my question. I want to hear the answer."

Devon didn't want to continue. She didn't want to tell him the extent of her story. How could he ever understand what she had gone through and why she had allowed it? "I don't know. Maybe it's not the night for this," she said, standing on wobbly legs.

Holy shit, how much did I drink? she wondered.

"Whoa," he said, jumping to his feet to steady her.

She didn't know how he was more stable than her. He had shown up drunk, and then he had proceeded to drink twice as much as her. His hands were on her hips, holding her up, as her head spun so fast that she had to close her eyes. She gripped the collar of his shirt to keep herself standing, and she felt more than heard his intake of breath.

Whoops!

"You should sit back down," he said, guiding her back to the couch. "I'll get you some water."

When he returned with a glass of water, Devon took a few sips of it, thankful for the distraction. The more she talked about this story, the more she missed St. Louis, and the more she wanted to go home. Her heart ached to feel that all over again, for it to be as it once was. Maybe it could be like that again.

"Dev," Garrett whispered, taking the drink out of her hand and placing it on the table, "what happened that day when you came home early?"

She didn't want to recall the memories. Suppressing them was easier than reliving them. She tipped her head to the side and settled it against his shoulder. That was easier than facing him.

"That day, he came home and hit me until I was knocked unconscious."

She definitely heard Garrett's intake of breath that time.

"I remember waking up, lying on the floor of my bathroom. It was really cold, and I found I had been stripped naked. I couldn't stop shivering, but I was careful not to move too quickly. My head was throbbing, and my body was splattered in bruises. At first, I couldn't remember what happened, but when he walked into the bathroom, it all came back to me. I started crying from the pain and the disbelief that he would do this to me. I remember his words. 'How could you make me do this to you?' It was my fault. It was all my fault that it had happened."

Garrett squeezed her knee softly. "Devon, it wasn't your fault."

A tear fell from her eye, and she let it roll down her cheek. "It was my fault. If only I had been better to him or if I had done more, he wouldn't have gotten so upset." She took a shuddering breath. "I never wanted to make him that unhappy ever again. We had greatness, you know?"

"Dev—"

"I swore I would do better and try harder. I wanted us to work. We had to work. I asked him to promise he would never do it again," she whispered.

"But he didn't?" Garrett asked.

"No, it happened again," she said. "Not right away, but it did. I just couldn't figure out how I could do any better. I was everything to him. I tried so hard to be what he needed."

"If you think that, then why did you end up coming to Chicago?"

Devon could hear the desperation in his voice. He didn't understand. He didn't get what she had gone through. This was why she had never told anyone. She couldn't break the silence only to suffer through disbelief. She couldn't stand the thought of people judging her, or worse, people pitying her decisions. She had made the right choices for her at the time. Now, what happened if she returned...

Her heart sank at the thought she'd had every day since leaving. Would it all be as it was before? Would he do worse? Or would he realize that she was everything he needed?

"We started in this cycle that I didn't think would ever break. He would get so angry, and I would take the brunt of it. Sometimes, I just cowered and cried until he forgave me. Other times, I would get angry and storm out. But then, I stopped getting angry. Leaving was not an option. It only made things worse. It made his anger more frequent."

"You just kept letting this guy...hit you?" Garrett asked.

"You don't understand," she said, shaking her head. "I love him."

"Dev—"

"It got worse," she whispered. "I had to cancel classes for a week."

"What for?"

"I could normally hide the bruises...that week I couldn't," she whispered, staring down at the carpet. "He never left bruises on my face again. It raised too many red flags."

Garrett hissed through his teeth at the imagery. He didn't say anything. What could he say? She didn't want to look up at him and read what was clearly written on his face, so she pushed through, just wanting to get this story over with.

"But that wasn't what made me leave," she told him. "I had

just finished my last final for the semester. When I finished, I was supposed to meet my favorite professor in his office to discuss my plans for next year. I got a text, telling me to meet him instead. I rescheduled plans with my professor and rushed to see him. I didn't want to be late. When I got back, I should have smelled trouble. Candles were lit everywhere. There was a bottle of champagne and even rose petals."

"That's a sign of trouble?" Garrett asked.

Devon nodded against his shoulder. "It should have been, but I saw it as a romantic gesture. I saw it as a way to get back to the way it had been. He popped open the bottle of champagne while I stripped down for him. I thought it was going to be that kind of night. It felt like we were finally back on the right track.

"But then, he started asking questions about my professor and why I was going to see him. I told him that I had tutoring, of course, and that my professor wanted to congratulate me for a job well done this semester. It was an odd conversation. I mean, he didn't like that I had tutoring, but that week off had put me so far behind that I had to use every opportunity to get caught up. He didn't believe me.

"He grabbed my arm and squeezed as hard as he could, forcing me backward against the bed. He begged me to tell him the truth. I cried and cried and cried, telling him that I had told him the truth. There was nothing more for me to tell." Devon took a deep breath and then continued.

"I felt like the bones in my arm were going to snap, but the pain evaporated when he yanked a candle off the table and held the flame to my skin. I screamed where it touched me. He said he would stop when I told him the truth. I tried to tell him that I was telling the truth, but he slapped me across the face so hard that I saw spots. He told me I was lying. Whenever the flame neared my skin, burning wax was dribbling down my body. He said that if I didn't tell him, then I didn't leave him any choice. I couldn't convince him, and the pain was blinding. He moved the flames to the area, uh…just above my…" Devon pointed down to her nether region. She blushed but continued. "The feel of my flesh burning so near all those nerve endings was the most intensely painful thing I've ever endured, and soon, I blacked out."

Garrett reached forward and threaded his fingers with hers. She didn't know where it came from, but it was a sign of strength. Devon sighed and used her other hand to pull down the front of her tiny sleeping shorts.

"See," she said, pointing at the scar right above her sensitive skin.

"Fuck," Garrett grumbled.

Devon pulled her shorts back up, ashamed by the conversation. She had made him think she was cheating, so she had pushed him over the edge. Still, even she could see that his punishment was excessive, and her realization had spurred her to action.

He had violated her trust, the one thing she had given over to him completely without him ever having to ask. He had taken everything they'd had and torn it down brick-by-brick for his own deluded sense of control. He had beaten the trust out of her. He had ruined their sex life, ruined their relationship, and ruined her.

"When I woke up, he was gone. A couple days later, I was on the first train to Chicago."

CHAPTER 18
The Only Option

GARRETT DIDN'T MOVE for what felt like forever. Devon wanted to see his reaction. She wanted to know that he didn't think any differently of her. She wanted to know a lot of things, but she wasn't brave enough to look up at him.

She felt his heavy sigh and the shift of his body toward her. She breathed him in. Her mind was still wondering too many things. She couldn't believe she had told her story. It had been a secret for so long. She hadn't wanted to risk someone finding out. What would people think of her…of him? What would they do?

Her mind closed off to that thought.

"Devon," he said finally.

He pulled her toward him and circled his big, strong arms around her. She tensed, unsure where this was coming from. Was he pitying her? She didn't need his pity.

"I hope you see your strength the way I do."

Strength? I ran away. I wanted to yell that at him. I'm not strong. I'm weak. I couldn't face my fears, so I ran.

She didn't know what to say, and he didn't let her go, so she relaxed into his embrace, accepting it for what it was. They were both in a rough spot, separated from their lives. Devon had run, and Garrett had faced his problems head-on. Either way, it had ended with them sitting in the same room. So maybe facing her problems head-on would have turned out the same way. Or maybe she wouldn't have ended up unconscious. Instead, she would have ended up dead.

That thought made her break the embrace. She stared forward at Garrett. She felt the tears on her cheeks, hot and uncomfortable. She hated crying, especially in front of people.

Garrett reached up and pushed her hair off her face. She sniffed as the tears fell faster from his affection. She didn't need someone to care for her. She could take care of herself. That thought made her cry harder.

"Don't cry," he whispered.

His thumbs brushed under her eyes like he had done when she had woken up from her nightmare on the couch. She couldn't stop her tears, and his help only made it worse.

She didn't know how she had any tears left. Hadn't she cried enough? Or were these tears of a different nature? Her throat constricted, and she coughed. She had never once thought that running away was the right thing to do. It was impulsive. It was something Hadley would do. Devon was always the rational one who wanted to work things out. She had stayed with him well past the point she should have. And for what? To be frightened and accused of things she hadn't done? To be hit, burned, and left unconscious?

The whole time she had been in Chicago, she had felt like a coward. She felt like running away from her life was the cheap way out, and the only reason she hadn't returned was out of fear. Now looking at it from a flip side, she understood that running wasn't the right option. It was the only option.

"How did you go through all of that alone?"

Devon shook her head. She really didn't know. She never felt all alone until she left. "I don't know." She hiccupped through tears.

"You shouldn't be alone," he said, stroking her hair. "Is this what your dreams were about?"

Devon closed her eyes. She couldn't face those dreams. He had been haunting them for months. She couldn't escape him even when she had run away.

"Devon, you have to face him eventually," he said.

She thought he meant to sound reassuring, but she wasn't reassured.

"Yeah," she said shakily. "I know...eventually."

"You can't hide out in Chicago forever. Doesn't school start again in August?"

"Yeah, it does."

Garrett squeezed her shoulder and pulled her in closer. "Don't you think it would be better to get it over with than to wait another month or two?"

"Did you not hear what happened?" she whispered frantically.

"I heard, Dev. I'm just saying that you are so afraid of this, and sometimes, you need to face your fears."

Devon shook her head. "It's not about facing my fears. Well, it kind of is. Okay, it is, but you don't understand. You don't know what he's like," she said, her hands shaking violently.

Garrett took her hands in his and held them to keep them from trembling.

"If you knew…if you only knew…"

"Then, tell me. Who is this guy? Who can have this much control over you?"

Devon stared down at their hands intertwined in her lap. She had told her story and left out the most important detail. It was the one detail she was sure people would find hard to believe.

Who would really believe that the perfect couple would ever be entirely dysfunctional?

"Hard to believe," she began, preparing for his reaction. "My boyfriend, Reid."

"Wait," he said, confused. "Aren't you guys still dating?"

"Uh…technically," she whispered. "I did just leave."

"No, leaving means that you guys are done."

Huh. She had never thought about it that way. When she had left, she hadn't really thought of anything. But it made sense to her. Leaving him, even if she hadn't told him what was going on, had made her see that it was over. Still, she hadn't told him though.

"I didn't tell him," she finally admitted.

"But isn't he looking for you?"

Devon shook her head, ashamed. "My parents talked about going on this trip to Paris for months. I told him about it, but we never thought it would actually happen. My parents are just spontaneous enough that when I told him they decided to go last minute, he believed me," she said, looking up at Garrett. "Otherwise, he wouldn't have let me leave, or he would've freaked out and tried to find me. I didn't want to be found."

"So, he thinks you're in Paris for the summer?"

Devon nodded.

"And you've gotten away with that for this long?"

"I told my parents I was staying in St. Louis for the summer to be with him. I shut off my Facebook and Twitter accounts. I haven't answered emails—"

"That's why you didn't want your picture to be taken," he said, piecing it together.

"Yeah, I didn't know if they might show up online or something."

"When you go back to St. Louis and he finds out that you weren't in Paris, what do you think he's going to do?" Garrett asked quietly.

They both knew the answer to that question.

Garrett moved away and poured another shot, and Devon tossed it back. As soon as it hit her stomach, she knew it was one too many. Maybe the one before had been too many. She didn't know. Her head was spinning, and she couldn't feel her legs. That made her giggle despite the terrible thought that had just crossed their minds. Her lips felt heavy, her eyes felt heavy, everything felt heavy. She sat back against Garrett. She was glad he was holding her. Otherwise, she thought she might topple over.

Just as suddenly as the giggle left her mouth, she clamped it shut, and tears streamed down her face. She was royally fucked. She pitched forward and threw her arms around Garrett, hugging her body close to his. His arms dropped to her lower back, pulling her flush against him. Her tears were falling on his shoulder, and she felt too weak and vulnerable and drunk to do anything about it.

Garrett ran one hand through her hair while the other rubbed up and down her back slowly. She hiccupped and then sighed into his embrace. She wanted to just wash away all the pain and all her memories of Reid. She wanted to make it so it had never happened.

"Hey." Garrett slid his hand up her side to her cheek and his other hand met the opposite side to cradle her face in his hands.

When she looked up into his eyes as he held her, the tears came streaming down heavier. He tucked a lock of her hair behind her ear and then trailed his fingers along her jawline.

His lips fell lightly on her cheek, gently kissing away the tears. Closing her eyes, she found the more he tried to comfort her, the more tears continued to fall. His mouth moved to her other cheek, and he erased the tears from the path they had formed. He trailed kisses down to her jaw, and then lightly, almost hesitantly, his lips moved to the corner of her mouth. As she sat very still, Devon felt her breathing pick up.

Then, his lips found hers. He tasted like scotch. The kisses started out slow as Garrett willed a response from her. He threaded his fingers back up into her hair, pressing himself against her. He slid his tongue across her lip, and Devon gasped in surprise. He moved his tongue into her mouth, pushing them closer and closer together.

Then, everything seemed to happen at once. Garrett was leaning her back into the couch. His body moved over her, and she could feel his hips press into her. His hand grazed her breast through her nightshirt. His other hand was still tangled into her hair. His kisses turned desperate and demanding. Devon couldn't breathe, couldn't think. He ignored her unresponsive lips and fumbled with her clothing, pushing as much of it out of the way as he could.

She felt her body sink further and further into the couch as if she were disappearing. She was sure that she would surface on the other side and find this all to be another dream.

His lips traveled to her neck and collarbone, reaching as much space as he could. Devon had the terrible sense of enjoying herself. It had been months since anyone had wanted this from her. She was only human, and her body betrayed her by reacting favorably to him.

The alcohol coursed through her veins, telling her to just enjoy it. Her mind didn't have a response. Had she shut herself off this much? It felt so nice to be wanted, to be kissed. She hadn't been kissed in so long.

Then, her mind did respond. Brennan. Brennan had kissed her last, and she had pushed him away because she had a boyfriend. She had thought then that she had a boyfriend, but in reality, she had walked out on Reid. She had pushed Brennan away for nothing, and Brennan was worth more than this.

When she felt Garrett's hand sliding down her shorts, she yelled, "Stop! Stop! I...I can't do this!"

Devon pushed and shoved him away from her. She fell hard on the ground onto her knees, jarring her body and snapping her teeth together painfully. She grunted and crawled away from him. Her balance was wretched, and she fell twice when she had tried to stand up.

Garrett stared at her, but she didn't want to see his face. She didn't want to see whatever he was thinking. She just needed to leave. If running was her strength, then she would exercise her strength a second time. She couldn't stand the thought of staying in the same apartment as Garrett one more night. How could he try and take advantage of her after she had just trusted him with something she had never told anyone before, especially after *what* she had told him?

Devon wasn't going to wait around long enough to find out. She stumbled into her room and threw on a pair of jeans and her sneakers. Garrett tried to talk to her, but she pretended not to hear him. She couldn't deal with this on top of everything else. She couldn't even deal with her own problems.

***

DEVON WALKED BLINDLY down the streets. She didn't know where she was going or what direction she was even walking in. It was dangerous to walk alone at night through Chicago. It was a really bad idea. Then again, so was dating her boyfriend for three years, lying to her parents, pushing Brennan away, and getting close to Garrett. She would just add those to the list.

Devon walked until the alcohol felt less potent. Why had she drunk so much? Who thought that was a good idea for a depressive? She would have giggled at her own self-realization, but it wasn't funny.

When her feet started hurting, she stopped and looked around. She didn't recognize anything, and that made her even more anxious. Where had her feet taken her? Her eyes traveled the buildings around the area as she tried to place her location.

She had been here before. Realizing where she was, she smiled and walked inside a building.

Standing in front of the door, she made the decision that her feet had already chosen for her. She knocked and waited. When nothing happened, she knocked again louder until she heard someone moving around inside. Her head was spinning, and she didn't know if it was because she was still drunk or if she was nervous. It was fair to say it was likely both.

"Who is it?" a voice called.

She didn't answer.

The door opened, and Brennan's face peered out at her. He left the door ajar, still latched to the wall by a chain. "Devon?" Brennan asked, yawning.

"Hey," she whispered. She suddenly felt self-conscious, like she shouldn't have shown up.

"What are you doing here? It's four in the morning."

"Can I come in?" she asked, surprised by the time.

"It's late, and I was sleeping. It's been a long night. I really don't have time to deal..." He trailed off when he finally looked at her.

"Please?" She tried to hold the tears in, but she didn't succeed.

"Devon, can't this wait until the morning?" he asked, doing a poor job of hiding his sympathies.

"It is the morning," she muttered.

"A normal hour then?" he persisted.

Devon dropped her head and then looked up into his big eyes. They weren't rimmed with red like they had been this afternoon. They weren't dazed like they frequently were when he came into work high. They were just normal Brennan eyes, and she liked them the best.

"I don't have anywhere else to go," she said, feeling defeated.

Brennan sighed. He tipped his head side to side as if debating, and then he closed the door, pulled back the chain, and opened it for her. "Come on in," he said. "I'll make up the couch again."

"Thanks," she muttered, relieved.

Devon took a seat on the couch and remembered the last time she had been here. Her head pounded, and she tried not to think about it. This was Brennan. She could figure things out.

He returned with a pile of pillows and blankets, just like last time. But this time, she could tell that he was still pretty upset. She wasn't sure if it was from earlier or what, but his body was rigid.

"Well, good night." He turned and walked toward the bedroom.

At least, he wasn't one to pry.

"What's wrong with you?" she asked. Unlike him, she was one to pry.

Brennan stopped walking and sighed. He turned around to face her. "How much have you had to drink?"

"Too much," she offered easily.

"That's what I thought. Why don't you just...sleep it off?" he said softly.

"Brennan," she said when he turned away from her again, "can't you just talk to me?"

She watched him clench and unclench his fists at his side. He turned back around and shook his head.

"What do you want to talk about?"

"Can you sit down?" Devon asked, pulling her feet up on the couch.

"No," he said stiffly.

"God, Brennan, what's wrong?" she asked, the alcohol making

her bolder than she would have normally been.

"You want to know what's wrong?" he asked, crossing the room. He took a moment to try to compose himself, but he failed. "You're what's wrong. Everything about you!"

Devon swallowed, looking up at him in shock. Where was this coming from? "What? Me?" she croaked.

His hands shook. "You walk into my life when I won't let anyone in. You walk right in without asking, without giving me an option. Then, you slam that door shut so hard, it could crack the windowpanes. Just when I think you're gone and I can close up again," he nearly shouted at her, "you crash back in all over again. And it's worse now because I'm around you all the time.

"You have this barrier up, and I have no clue how to get through it. And it's obvious that you don't want to let it down, but I can't help but try. When I think there's no chance, none at all, after you leave my gig…when I wrote that song for you…" He trailed off, looking at her fiercely. "Then, you show up here, saying you have nowhere else to go…when the door is always wide open."

Devon's heart was beating so hard in her chest that she thought she might explode. This was what he had been carrying around all this time? She had suspected that he still liked her, but this…how could she even respond?

"I think I broke up with my boyfriend," she said softly.

It wasn't a lie, not exactly. She had left Reid. It was over in her heart.

"What?" Brennan asked, coming up short.

He hadn't been expecting that.

"We're over."

Brennan sat down then. "I'm so sorry."

She didn't believe him, and it made her smile. "It's, uh…for the better."

"God, I'm a dick," he said, his hand brushing through his hair.

Devon laughed. "Far from it."

"Is that why you came by?" he asked, his eyes narrowing.

"Sort of." Devon scrunched up her nose. "Hadley and Garrett got into a fight, and I didn't want to be around that." Also not a lie.

"Everything is falling apart," he said softly.

Devon shrugged. "I don't know about everything."

She patted the seat next to her on the couch, and he moved over to sit by her.

"How are you feeling, you know…about your boyfriend?" he asked with a sigh.

She couldn't tell if it was a sigh of relief or not.

"I'm not sure if it has all sunk in yet," she admitted, wrapping her arms around her knees. "We dated for almost three years."

"That's a long time."

"Yeah," she said, "it is."

Brennan sighed again. "It'll get easier with time."

Devon nodded. "I think so. Plus, time is all I have now, right?" Was she trying to convince herself or him?

"Sorry about yelling at you," he said sheepishly.

"It's all right. I probably deserved it," she whispered.

"You didn't," he said. "I was…projecting."

"That's one word for it," she said with a laugh.

He stared down at the floor for a few minutes. He really was beautiful. He was even beautiful when he had yelled at her.

"I'm glad you're here," he said finally. "That when you didn't have anywhere else to go, you came and found me, so I can be there for you."

He lifted his eyes to hers, and she felt his words hit her.

"I want to be that for you, Devon."

THE SMELL OF bacon filled the apartment, and Devon awoke with a smile. No nightmares. She hadn't had a single one all night. It was the first time in weeks. She had slept soundly, not even waking up when Brennan got up to cook. She checked her watch and realized it was already noon. She couldn't believe it! She had slept for almost eight hours. She couldn't remember the last time that had happened.

"Morning, sleepyhead," Brennan called from the kitchen door.

She yawned and stretched her arms over her head. She was

clad in one of his T-shirts. It was way too big, but it smelled so good and clean and so much like Brennan that she wanted to wear it all the time. Her eyes traveled over his body, and she tried to keep the appreciation off her face. But it was too early, and it must have showed because he smirked at her. What did he expect her to do when he walked around the apartment shirtless?

Devon pointed out her feet until they touched the other end of the couch. It felt so good to just…be for once. She couldn't believe how well she had slept after last night. But she was thinking that discussing what had happened to her, even if everything had gone awry, had helped her…or maybe it was Brennan. She couldn't choose.

"Good morning," she said through another yawn.

"How do you sleep so much?" he asked, leaning against the doorframe.

"I haven't slept this much in months. I feel like a new person."

Brennan laughed, and Devon sighed back into the couch at the sound. She wasn't sure she had ever seen him laugh like that— loose, happy, and free.

"Well, I hope this new person likes bacon."

"She does," Devon said, nodding. She flipped the covers off her body. When she stood, the shirt fell nearly to her knees, and she blushed, remembering that she had taken off her jeans before she fell asleep. She snatched them off the ground and darted into the bathroom. After tugging the jeans back on to cover her exposed legs, she quickly tied her hair in a knot and then splashed cold water on her face. She needed to wake up and not blush so much.

Brennan had a table big enough for two against the wall in the kitchen, and Devon took an empty seat. He placed a plate with eggs, bacon, and toast in front of her.

"Coffee?" he asked with a smile.

"Sure," she said. "Lots of cream and sugar though."

He laughed again, obliging. After pouring his own coffee, he took the seat across from her, and they ate in comfortable silence. Last night felt like a lifetime ago. But Brennan liked her; he had told her. Well, at least, he had kind of told her. He had told her in a completely Brennan kind of way. It made her sigh happily as she ate.

Despite his protests, Devon helped Brennan clear the table, and then she washed off her plate and placed it in the dishwasher. When he finally pushed her out of the kitchen, she walked over to the couch and sat back down. She flipped on the television to some random channel and waited for Brennan to return. It didn't matter what was on TV because she wasn't really paying attention.

A couple minutes later, Brennan walked into the living room. He slid into the seat next to her and wrapped his arm around her shoulders. She leaned back against him, snuggling into his chest, and he intertwined their hands in her lap. It was comfortable and nice. How long had it been since she had felt like this? It had been at least a year, probably longer, since she had done this with Reid. She couldn't remember that far back, back when it had been different, and she didn't want to think any more about it. She wanted to be content.

They sat like this through the mindless television show. Devon couldn't have told anyone what happened on the show, but she knew the rhythm of Brennan's heart, the small movements he made when he nestled closer to her, and the soft caress of his fingers on her hand.

When the show ended, Devon shifted to reach for the remote, but Brennan moved first. He clicked the power button, and the screen went black. Devon turned her face up to him, her eyebrows scrunching together. When she found him staring down at her in adoration, all the tension eased from her face. His hand moved and tugged lightly on the hair tie, freeing her long locks to fall down around her face.

"I love your hair," he said, running his hand through one side, causing her to shiver. "I love when you wear it down. I love when it irritates you, and you throw it all over one shoulder."

His hand brushed her hair to expose her neck, his fingers trailing lightly across her skin. Her breathing turned shallow, and her eyes darted to his lips and then back to his eyes.

"I love your big blue eyes, and the way they can find me in a crowd even when you don't mean to. I love your lips that you constantly bite out of frustration, that you suck on when you're writing lyrics in your journal, that you pucker when deciding on what to order."

Devon swallowed. She couldn't breathe.

He leaned forward, cupping her chin with his hand. "I really love your lips," he whispered softly before pressing his lips against hers.

This time, Devon sighed into him, not even thinking about pulling away. She was lost—mind, body, and soul—to the man before her. Somehow, along the way, he had captured not just her lips but all of her. How had she evaded him for so long?

His tongue stroked her bottom lip and opened her mouth. She met him tentatively at first, and then she wholly indulged in the feel of him. Her senses intensified all at once, feeling the softness of his lips against hers, the calluses on his hands touching her skin, his taut body pressing into her. His scent clouded her mind, and she forced herself not to move too fast. His fingers moved to knot in her long hair, and she moaned lightly into his mouth.

Being kissed this way was like tasting the first strawberry of the season—so sweet and way better than you ever remember.

They remained kissing leisurely, distractedly, happily until Brennan remembered that he actually had to go into work that day. Devon didn't have many days off, and since she had worked so hard the day before, today just happened to be one of those days.

Brennan left to take a shower, and Devon pulled out her phone, trying not to envision him naked. She wasn't having much luck.

She had turned off her phone last night because she hadn't wanted to be disturbed. Mostly, she hadn't wanted Garrett to call her. When the screen brightened and finally reached a signal, her phone lit up with messages, missed calls, and voice mails.

What the hell? she thought, clicking on the first message.

She had expected Garrett to leave one or two texts and maybe a voice mail, asking her to come back. Maybe he would even apologize for his behavior. But thirty-two messages and five voice mails? That was just absurd. What was his problem?

Devon didn't even want to read the messages. She clicked out of them and turned to the voice mails. These were all from this morning. She shrugged and pressed the phone to her ear.

"Devon, you might hate me, but answer your phone!"

She stopped the message, not willing to hear the rest. The next one started playing right after that.

"It's Hadley. She's in the hospital. She's at Northwestern Memorial. I don't care if you hate me, but think of Hadley."

The voice mail ended, and Devon stared down at her phone in shock. All the softness and ease of being with Brennan this morning drained out of her face…out of her whole body. Hadley was in the hospital. Shit!

Devon jumped off the couch in a rush, throwing her phone into her purse. She slammed her hand down on the bathroom door just as the shower shut off. Brennan cracked the door, holding a towel around his waist. He was still wet, and his hair was hanging low, almost over his eyes. She was momentarily distracted by him.

Then, she shook her head and reminded herself what was really important. "Hadley," she gasped out. "Garrett called, and she's in the hospital."

"What?" he cried, rushing past her. "What hospital?"

"Northwestern Memorial."

"That's not far from here," he told her. "Let me throw on some clothes, and we'll go. I'll call Jenn from the car."

Devon wasn't sure why, but her mind focused on the strangest things under stress. Brennan had a car?

FOLLOWING ME

***

Brennan knew his way around Northwestern Memorial better than Devon thought most people should be able to maneuver a hospital. Devon was anxious and kept bumping into him as they walked through the building. The ride over had been extremely short. She had almost felt bad taking a car, considering the L wouldn't have been much more effort. But she did enjoy watching him, albeit reluctantly under the circumstances, driving his little Jetta Hybrid through the busy streets with his Wayfarers on.

He found what he was looking for and approached a desk with a lanky man standing behind it. "Excuse me, we're here to see Hadley Bishop," Brennan told the man.

The man scanned his computer, running his finger along the screen. "Ah, she's in the ICU. Go straight down this hall, then turn—"

"Thanks, I know the way," Brennan said, cutting him off and loping down the hallway.

Devon followed at his heels, wringing her hands like a maniac. She wished she had a pen to flip, but she had already checked in her bag, and she didn't find one. Brennan walked down a few corridors and then stopped when they reached the waiting room to the ICU.

He steadied her before they walked to the nurses' station. "Do you know what she's here for?" he asked.

"Well, I have a guess."

Brennan nodded. "Your guess is probably right."

"I know," she whispered, staring down.

"Are you ready for this?" He rubbed her arm.

"I don't know."

"I wish you didn't have to see her this way. This isn't like her. She should have never overdosed."

Devon gasped. She didn't know why. She knew that was the reason Hadley was here, but saying it out loud sounded so much worse.

Tears sprang to her eyes, and she was suddenly glad that she was outside the room. All the adrenaline from getting to Hadley was wearing off, and she felt exhausted.

Brennan's arms wrapped around her, and she leaned into him, thankful that he was here, that he hadn't gone into work. He kissed the top of her head, and he held her in his arms as she cried through the pain. She was crying for more than Hadley, but the knowledge of what Hadley had done was the most potent at the moment. Why were things falling apart? She felt so guilty for being happy with Brennan this morning when Hadley was suffering all alone.

"You couldn't have done anything about it," he whispered against her hair.

"I know," she said.

"You don't. But she'll be okay, and she'll realize it was her mistake. You can't blame yourself. It's not your fault." He was rocking her gently.

"I know," she repeated.

"You can't have this on your shoulders, too," he said, pulling back to examine her.

He bent down and firmly pressed his lips to hers. Devon sighed into him, thinking she would never get tired of this.

"Chin up. Let's go see her."

"All right," she said shakily.

They turned the corner and walked up to the nurse.

"We're here to see Hadley Bishop," Brennan said to the nurse.

"One moment please. Let me see if she can have visitors," the nurse said, staring down at her computer. The nurse spoke through an intercom to someone and waited for a response. "All right, you two can go on in. She is in room six. Please be mindful of the nurse working."

"Thank you," Brennan said with an appreciative smile.

They walked through the door into the ICU. It was a large hallway of rooms with all glass doors on each side. Each room was easily accessible from the nurses' station. They walked down the hallway to Hadley's room. Just as they arrived at the glass door, Garrett walked out and slid the door back into place.

Devon's stomach lurched at the memory of his body covering hers. He wouldn't meet her eyes, and she was glad. He should be ashamed. He looked the worse for wear, and Devon wondered how long he had been here with Hadley. The pang of guilt hit her again.

"Glad you made it," Garrett said, finally looking at her.

She glanced away, not having the strength to challenge him.

"We would have come sooner, but Devon's phone was off,"

Brennan said with a shrug.

"You had your phone off at work?" Garrett asked, confused.

"I didn't have to work today," Devon said, not sure why he even cared.

"She was already with me," Brennan explained before Garrett could ask another question.

Garrett's eyebrows scrunched together, and his eyes wavered between them. She didn't want to know what he was thinking.

"Can we see her now?" Brennan asked impatiently.

"Oh, of course," Garrett said as if he hadn't realized his body was blocking the entrance. "She's doing a lot better than when they first brought her in. She's sedated, and they pumped everything they could out of her system."

Devon glanced through the glass at her best friend, and a sob escaped her throat when she saw her. Sure, they had been estranged this summer, but Hadley was still her best friend. They had lived together for almost three years, drank at stupid frat parties together, figured out how to cook together, had girlfriend weekends, and so much more. Nearly all her happy memories from college were with Hadley. The worst part of her relationship with Reid had only happened after Hadley left, and it made her sad that six months could change so much.

Her Hadley was the same person as the one who was now lying in a hospital bed, breathing with the assistance of a ventilator and looking as white as the blank sheet covering her body.

"The doctors said that she was lucky to be with other people last night. Her friends brought her in when she became unresponsive, and then they disappeared as soon as they dumped her at the ER," Garrett said. "The doctors aren't sure what she was on. So far, they've found the primary source to be cocaine."

"Which explains the sedative," Brennan said almost to himself.

"Yeah," Garrett agreed. "But she was clearly drunk and had taken some pain pills as well. From listening to the doctors, I gather they were some pretty strong ones."

"She's so pale," Devon said softly.

"I just…I can't believe she would do this to herself," Garrett said. "We fought, but that shouldn't have been an excuse for…for this." He gestured toward Hadley.

Brennan said something quietly to Garrett, but Garrett just continued to stare at Hadley as Brennan talked.

Devon walked inside the room and over to Hadley's side as the guys talked to each other on the other side. She tuned them out and sat heavily in the chair next to the bed. She took Hadley's hand in her own, surprised to find it was so hot it felt like it was on fire. Devon curled her fingers around Hadley's hand anyway and leaned her forehead against it.

"I'm sorry, Hadley," Devon whispered. "I'm sorry for knowing and not doing enough. I'm sorry for putting you in a rough place. I'm sorry for using your weakness to my advantage. That's a shitty thing for a friend to do. I'm sorry for not being your friend since I got here. I wish I could tell you everything I'm sorry for, but I don't think you would want me to be here all day and night. Mostly, I'm sorry that we're not close like we used to be. I don't know who pushed the wedge in between us, but I don't like it. I kept secrets…you know I did. But you were keeping them, too, and then you pushed me away when I was trying to help you. I don't blame you. How could I ever blame you? I'm just sorry it came to this, and I hope that when you wake up, we can fix this. You're my best friend."

Devon squeezed her hand and stood before she the tears came. She couldn't cry again. She had cried too much.

"Is she going to…be okay?" she managed to get out before covering her mouth at the thought.

"Yeah, the doctors said she would be okay physically," Garrett told her. "Mentally and emotionally though will take time."

Hadley would be okay, alive. She would wake up soon and start to recover. She would learn from her mistakes, and then they could all move on.

But today, she wasn't okay, and today, it wasn't all right. Today, it was painful and terrible and heartbreaking. Today, Devon would let herself feel it because it would make her better tomorrow.

"I'm going to…go get something to eat," Devon said, not meeting the guys' eyes as she walked past them.

"Do you want me to come with?" Brennan asked, brushing her arm with his fingers.

She smiled at him and shook her head. She wanted to be alone.

Devon made it out the door and a few feet down the hallway when she heard footsteps behind her. She turned, her heart rate picking up drastically. After all her nightmares about being followed, she couldn't shake that uncontrollable fear.

"Devon, can we talk for a minute?" Garrett asked, walking toward her.

"I'd rather not," she said. Her chest was aching, and she just wanted to find a place to be alone. Couldn't he see that?

"I just wanted to apologize for last night." He shifted awkwardly from foot to foot.

"I really don't want to deal with this right now, Garrett," she said.

"I know. I was an ass. Devon, please…I don't know what I was thinking. I was really upset about Hadley," he said, stepping in closer and reaching out for her arm.

"Please don't touch me," she said, pulling back quickly.

"Sorry." He dropped his arm.

"Can we just not do this right now? Hadley is in there, unconscious. That is what's important. Let's just…deal with that first. I don't even want to think about last night or what happened."

"Devon—"

She held up her hand. "Please…just…no. I can't talk about it yet. I need some time."

Garrett nodded and took a step back. "All right. I can give you time," he said with a sigh.

Devon turned on her heel and walked away from Garrett, leaving him standing alone in the hallway.

Despite all the terrible things that had happened this week, she felt strong, stronger than she had in a long time.

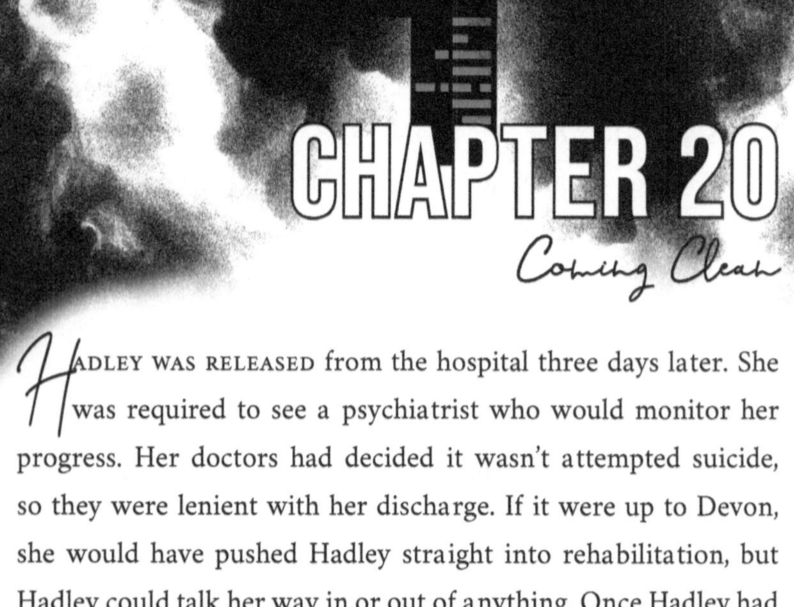

CHAPTER 20

Coming Clean

Hadley was released from the hospital three days later. She was required to see a psychiatrist who would monitor her progress. Her doctors had decided it wasn't attempted suicide, so they were lenient with her discharge. If it were up to Devon, she would have pushed Hadley straight into rehabilitation, but Hadley could talk her way in or out of anything. Once Hadley had regained consciousness, the last thing she wanted was to be in the hospital for any longer than necessary.

Devon had camped out on Brennan's couch until Hadley

returned to Garrett's apartment. She hadn't felt right about going back with just Garrett there. His hospitality had run its course. Still, she couldn't be away from Hadley when she came back, and Devon didn't want her to know what Garrett had done. Hadley had too much stress as it was, and adding Garrett's stupid mistake on top of that would be catastrophic.

Hadley had received a temporary medical leave from work so she could recover. She slept a lot, which Devon thought was good. It was better than feeling the withdrawal pains she was experiencing. Devon didn't even bother to ask how much Hadley had been using because it was pretty obvious that the answer was going to be way too much. Whatever the drug use had started out as, it was far from casual now.

While it was a relief to have Hadley alive and back in the house again, it didn't make the living situation any better. When Devon and Garrett weren't taking care of Hadley, they tiptoed around each other. Devon probably should have been gentler with him at the hospital. They had both been grieving, and she had snapped, but her pride held her tongue. She couldn't admit that to him, but either way, he never should have touched her.

"Hey," Devon said, walking into the living room.

Hadley had taken up residence on the couch ever since she had returned. She was back to watching Millionaire Matchmaker and bad Lifetime movies. At least, some things had remained constant.

"Hey," Hadley said with a smile when Devon walked into the room.

In the few days that Hadley had been home, color had come back to her cheeks. The week off was already doing her some good, but Devon knew the battle was far from over.

"How are you feeling?"

"Not so bad today," Hadley said, staring down at her nail beds. "It's getting easier at least."

"That's really good to hear." Devon leaned against the wall. She was so thankful that Hadley was alive. Not everyone was so fortunate.

"What about you? How are you doing?"

Devon shrugged. "I'm all right. No work today."

"Off on a Saturday? That's a shocker. And here I was under the delusion that Jenn was a slave driver," Hadley said with a laugh.

It was nice to hear her laugh again. Hadley was turning back into her friend.

"Don't let her think otherwise!" Devon said, cracking a smile.

"Hey, Dev. Will you come here for a minute?" Hadley sat up in her seat.

"Sure," Devon said, taking a seat at the end of the couch.

"I kind of wanted to…talk to you."

"What about?" Devon asked, her heart rate picking up before she even knew what Hadley would ask.

"Well, first, I wanted to say thank you," Hadley whispered, staring down at her hands. "You've been really helpful here, taking care of me. Garrett told me that you came to see me in the hospital. I wish I had been awake to see you. But also," she said, looking up at Devon, " thank you for trying to get through to me even when I wasn't listening."

"Hadley," Devon said, waving the thanks away, "you don't have to thank me. I'm your friend."

"I know, I know, but I really wanted to. I want you to know… you're my best friend, and I shouldn't have done what I did," Hadley said.

Devon nodded, reluctantly accepting the thanks. She felt bad taking them, especially after she had taken advantage of their friendship, after Garrett had kissed her, after she had held back all her own secrets. But what else could she do? Hadley wanted her to accept the gratitude, and she couldn't deny Hadley anything.

Hadley cleared her throat. "Well, I'm glad that's out of the way. Now, tell me how things are with you. I feel like I haven't talked to you in forever."

"Oh, things are fine, Hadley," Devon said awkwardly. She didn't want Hadley to know about Garrett or Reid. She wanted anonymity. Most of all, she wanted to move on, and right now, moving on looked like Brennan's handsome face.

"Fine," Hadley said, weighing the word.

"Yeah. Really, I'm fine."

"Look, I don't want this to come off the wrong way because I know I just majorly fucked up. But what's wrong with you? Not knowing makes me feel even worse because you're my friend, and I can tell that you're sad. I just don't know how to help because I don't know what's wrong," Hadley said, staring directly at Devon.

"I just, uh…" Devon began. She didn't know what to say, but

she knew that she had to tell Hadley something. "Reid and I are kind of on rocky footing."

"I knew it!" Hadley shot up, immediately regretted it, and slumped back into the couch.

"I think we broke up," Devon said, finding the reality of that to be truer the more times she said it.

"Holy shit!" Hadley cried. Forgetting how hurt she was, she quickly moved to sit next to Devon. "I can't believe you guys broke up!"

"I know," Devon said truthfully.

"I thought you guys were perfect together. What the hell happened?" Hadley asked in shock.

"I don't know. I came here, I guess."

"Wow. I never thought long distance would be your undoing," Hadley said, shaking her head.

"Well, I didn't exactly tell him where I was going," Devon finally admitted, feeling the weight lift.

"What?" Hadley asked, her eyebrows coming together. "So, he never knew you were here? Did you guys break up before you left?"

"Yeah. Well, sort of. I don't know. Either way, it's over now," Devon said with a note of finality.

"Holy shit! Seriously, holy shit, Dev! You and Reid are no more." Hadley put her hands on her head and shook it back and forth. "I'm totally shocked. Sorry. Give me a minute."

Devon laughed. "Take as long as you like."

"Well, no wonder you've been sad! God, I should have just asked earlier," Hadley said with a giggle.

"To be honest, Hadley, I'm not sure I would have told you. I've been kind of moping around—"

"Ya think?" she asked, nudging Devon's shoulder.

Devon laughed and nudged her back. "But I'm glad you know now."

"Me, too," Hadley said with a smile.

She looked healthier in that moment than Devon had seen since she had arrived. She was happy to have Hadley back to her old self again. Devon just hoped it was sustainable.

"Well, I have to get out of here. Sorry to leave you all alone," Devon said, standing.

"Where are you going? I thought we could have some girl time," Hadley said, sticking out her bottom lip.

"I'd love that, but I'm going somewhere with Brennan," she said, not able to hold back her blush.

Hadley arched an eyebrow. "With Brennan, huh?"

"Yeah."

"Where are you guys going?"

Devon shrugged. "He won't tell me. He said he wanted it to be a surprise."

"A surprise?" Hadley didn't even bother to hold in her smile. "Uh-huh."

"Stop doing that!" Devon said, laughing.

"Doing what?" Hadley asked innocently.

"Oh, you know what!"

"I mean, Brennan's good-looking, Devon. I don't blame you."

"Hadley! Jeez, we're just hanging out," Devon said.

They had been hanging out all week—with their lips locked, playful touches at work, eyes staring across the room, and their hands exploring one another. Devon's cheeks heated as she thought about it.

"Hanging out," Hadley said with air quotes. "I sure hope that involves a bedroom."

"Oh my god, seriously, you are ridiculous," Devon said, shaking her head.

"Just look at you! You're blushing from head to toe. Who knew I was actually the matchmaker?" Hadley said exaggeratedly.

"Go back to watching your silly show! I have to get out of here," Devon said.

"Wait, wait!" Hadley cried as Devon tried to ease out of the living room. "Have you made it to the bedroom?"

"Hadley!"

"All right, all right. Go have fun! I would have already told you though!" she called as Devon rushed out of the apartment.

Devon could hear Hadley's laughter, sweet and melodic, as she pulled the door closed. At least, Hadley was laughing again.

Devon walked down the hallway and took the elevator to the bottom floor. It was early, so Devon started walking toward the L station on her way to Brennan's place. When she pulled out her phone to text Brennan, she found it was already ringing. She hadn't noticed it was set on silent.

"Hey!" Devon said. She was glad to hear from her brother. It had been a while since they had talked.

"Hey, Dev. Can I just tell you how much I hate you right now?"

Devon laughed and shook her head. "Why is that?"

"Because you're in St. Louis, and I'm in New York City with Mom and Dad. How exactly did you get out of this?" he asked.

"I didn't take the bait like you did!"

"This is supposed to be for your birthday!"

"No," Devon said, "we both know it's for Mom."

"Yeah, speaking of, she wanted me to call and guilt-trip you for not being here. I mean, she wanted me to tell you how much she misses you and wished you could be here," Dustin drawled. He had never given up his Southern accent.

"Well, tell her that I'm so sorry even though I'm not, and good luck at the award ceremony, even though she doesn't need it," she said.

"Word for word, Dev. Word for word."

Devon laughed. "Ass."

"That's what I'm here for."

"No, really, tell Mom and Dad good luck and that I miss them. I have to go," she said, wanting to get off the phone before she reached the train station.

Devon couldn't believe that she had actually gotten this far without anyone growing suspicious.

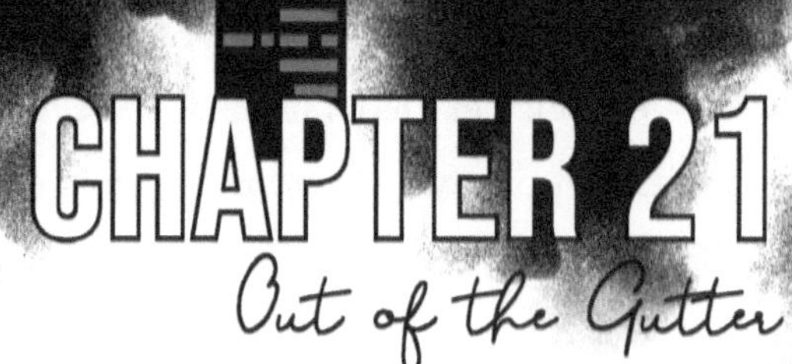

CHAPTER 21
Out of the Gutter

"SO, WHERE ARE we going?" Devon asked, walking up the stairs to the L station.

"You'll see when we get there," Brennan said.

He took her hand and held it in his as they walked. He looked comfortable today, not wearing his work clothes. She liked him like this—in khaki shorts, a blue T-shirt with a lighter button-up over it, and his ever-present Wayfarers.

"Am I going to like it?"

"Would I take you somewhere you wouldn't like?" Brennan asked.

Devon smiled and let him take charge. She wasn't a big fan of surprises, but this one felt different. It was exhilarating. They hopped on the train and sat next to each other. She could get used to this.

"I think Hadley's getting better," she told him.

"That's good to hear."

"I told her I was going out with you, and she turned into a total girl," Devon said, rolling her eyes.

Brennan smirked. "I'm sure I can guess what she's thinking."

Devon looked down at their hands. "Probably. She's entirely predictable."

He leaned forward and kissed her lips. Her eyes fluttered closed as she breathed him in. This had been happening all week, and every time he pulled back, it made her want more. His kisses were intoxicating, leaving a heady haze over her mind when he touched her lips.

She pushed herself toward him, trying to close the distance between their bodies. She snaked her hands up and gripped his collar between her fingers. As their tongues met, Devon groaned softly. Her body was on fire. She couldn't get enough of him.

Brennan's hand trailed along the exposed skin on the small of her back, and she shivered. He chuckled, pulling back to look at her.

"I like when you get all riled up," he said huskily, pressing and lacing their hands together.

"You do it so easily," she said, her voice betraying her desire.

"And in public no less."

Devon flushed all over, glancing around at the people near them. She was sure some of them had noticed, but she hadn't even thought about it. She had never been big on public displays of affection either…but this was Brennan.

"And there's that blush," he said with a laugh. "Damn, do I love that."

She ducked her head and smacked his shoulder playfully. "Shush!"

"This is our stop." He dragged her to her feet and kissed her full on the mouth again.

She wobbled against him, her mind going blank.

When he released her, he chuckled again and pulled her along. "Come on, you."

They walked through the streets until they reached a park in front of the Navy Pier. She had been up here twice before. The first time was with Garrett during her first week in the city. The second time, she had wanted some time to relax. She had brought her journal and sat by the pier, writing lyrics until she thought her brain would explode. Then, big fat water droplets had begun falling all over the pages, and the waves had started crashing higher. She had ducked out of there as soon as she could get away. She hadn't been back since.

"Navy Pier?" She wondered if this was the surprise.

Then, she looked closer. It was packed with people. Children were everywhere, attached to their parents or running around like mad. Boats filled the harbor, stretching out as far as she could see. Big heavy sails held taut on enormous sailboats. The lighthouse stood out in the distance like a beacon against the cloudless horizon.

"Why is it so busy?" she asked.

Brennan's smile was contagious, and she found herself standing on her tiptoes to kiss him again. He laughed and picked her up, swinging her around in a circle. Devon giggled, burying her face into his shoulder.

"I think I'm going to love being with you everywhere I go," he whispered into her hair.

"Me, too," she confirmed.

After setting her gently back on her feet, he kissed her forehead, her nose, both cheeks, her chin, and finally, he planted a firm kiss on her mouth. She tried to keep the kiss going, but he pulled back.

"There are too many people here. We should just go back," Devon said, wrapping her arms around his waist.

"You don't even know what you're in for," he said with a chuckle.

Brennan walked her away from Navy Pier, leading her off to the right toward the park holding her hand once more. His hand was big and warm. She had petite hands, and his dwarfed hers in comparison. She liked it.

She was starting to get really curious about where they were going and what was happening. She was practically bouncing up and down with excitement. Brennan kept looking at her from out of the corner of his eye. His smile grew wider at her enthusiasm.

"So…really, what are we doing?" she asked as they passed through the small park.

"Have you ever heard of the Chicago to Mackinac Race?"

"No." Walking at his side, she stared at all the huge boats docked.

They walked, crossed the end of the park, and stepped out onto a sidewalk leading up to the water. Devon looked up at the building that stood before the docks and read DuSable Harbor on the side.

"Well, it's a huge sailing tournament. Hundreds of sailboats flood the lake to sail from here to the island on the north coast of Lake Michigan. It's over three hundred miles."

Brennan took a right and started walking away from the Pier side of the harbor.

"Wow," she said, surprised she had never heard of this.

"It's hosted by the Chicago Yacht Club, which is that building," he said, pointing it out from their vantage point on the harbor.

"Oh, fancy," she said, wondering if it was anything like the country clubs at home.

Brennan shrugged. "I suppose so. Anyway, I've actually sailed to Mackinac Island a couple times in the competition. Decided to sit it out this year, and I'm glad I did."

"Why?" she asked, trying to keep her mouth from falling open.

Brennan knew how to sail and was good enough to enter competitions? What else didn't she know about him?

"Because now I get to spend today with you." He took a turn, walking down one of the busy wooden docks.

Devon smiled brightly, giddy from his compliments and the impending surprise. They walked down the dock, stopped at the very end, and faced a pretty imposing-looking boat. She didn't know anything about boats. Well, she knew nothing more than the one her parents had at their lake house. Even then, she hadn't been all that interested in much more than tanning, tubing, and drinking.

"This is Alma," Brennan said, gesturing to the boat.

"Alma?" Devon asked with an arched eyebrow.

Brennan shrugged. "She was named after my grandma."

"This is…your boat?" she asked slowly, trying to keep it all together.

"Well, it's my dad's boat, but we're going to use it today." Smiling, he jumped onto the deck like he was more familiar with it than the land.

He extended out his hand to her, and she took it, steadying herself before taking the first step onto the boat. It rocked as her weight shifted it, and she all but fell into his arms. He caught her easily, laughing.

"We'll work on your sea legs," he said, holding her steady.

"I've been on a boat before," she said defensively.

"When was the last time?"

"I don't know." She chewed on her bottom lip. "Like two years ago."

"Way too long. I'm glad I could remedy this," he said. "Come on, let me show you around."

His boat included way more than her parents' lake boat, which was big enough for a couple of people, not much more, to jet around the lake. Brennan had pointed out that this was less of a boat and more of a cabin cruiser. It had plenty of space for hanging out on the deck, and it also had a cabin area with a small kitchen and dining room as well as a door that led to an even smaller bedroom with a double bed taking up the majority of the room. When her eyes landed on the bed, she knew that she should look away, but somehow, she couldn't. Even when she had been staying at Brennan's, she had slept on the couch.

She scooted out of the room and went back onto the deck. It was hard to keep her mind out of the gutter. Her life had been filled with that for a long time. She didn't want to fuck this up. She had so much more to figure out first.

They spent the afternoon enjoying each other's company, leisurely cruising around the harbor and watching the sailboats depart. It was lazy and comfortable and exactly what Devon needed.

Day faded into night, and the soft crash of the waves hitting along the boat lulled them into silence. Lying on a blanket out on the deck, Devon cuddled up into Brennan's arms, leaning her head on his chest. He rubbed his hand back and forth along her arm. As the boat swayed to and fro, she felt herself slipping away toward the sleep that had so often evaded her.

"Hey," he whispered before kissing her forehead.

"Hmm?" she mumbled.

"You can't sleep yet."

"I wasn't sleeping," she said with a big yawn.

"Good." His hand moved from her arm to her waist, pulling her in close.

"Brennan," she whispered, propping herself up on her elbow to look at him.

"Yeah?"

"Thank you for today. You don't know what it means to me." She bit her lip and broke his gaze.

"No, thank you," he whispered, pushing her hair off her face and bringing her back to face him. "I'm not sure I would have gotten through this past week without you."

Devon smiled shyly. "Why is that?"

He sighed softly before bringing her face down to meet his lips. She kissed him until she was breathless. When they broke apart, she melted at the sight of him lying beneath her. How had she gotten so lucky after everything that had happened to her?

"Devon," he whispered. He scooted his body up, so he was facing her, seated on the floor of the boat.

"Yeah?" she asked, mirroring him.

"I don't really open up to many people, so this is kind of big for me," he said, taking her hand in his.

Out of nowhere, Devon's heart rate picked up. She wasn't sure if it was just because she hadn't been completely honest with him or what, but it made her uneasy.

"This, uh…isn't my dad's boat."

"What?" Devon asked, confusion creasing her temple. "Then, whose boat is it?"

"What I mean to say is that it was my dad's boat," he said softly.

Devon stopped fidgeting and stared into his handsome face. Was. That was such a final word. "What happened?"

"Three years ago, he died in a car accident on the Fourth of

July. Sideswiped by a drunk driver," he said, gripping her hands. "They took him in an ambulance to Northwestern Memorial. It was the hospital he had worked in as a doctor for thirty years. He died before I got there."

Devon gasped. "Brennan..." she whispered, clutching his hand more tightly. What could she say? What could she possibly say to heal that wound? No wonder he had been sick and in a terrible mood the week before the Fourth of July. How could she have ever blamed him?

"I don't know why, but when I look at you, I sometimes see myself. I feel like I understand you...like we could understand each other. I don't know if that even makes sense."

"It does," she said quietly, tears welling in her eyes. She leaned her head into the crook of his neck and wrapped her arms around him. She didn't even want to ask, but she had to. "What happened to your mom?"

"They were divorced. I was an only child. She lives in California with her new husband and brood of children," he said, distaste seeping into his voice. "She was only really interested in me after he died. At least, she was until she found out he left me everything, and I wasn't going to give her a dime. Now, she doesn't even send birthday cards."

At the thought of having a parent that cruel, Devon felt a lump form in her throat. And she couldn't even imagine the loss of her own parents. Her problems felt so small next to his.

"Everything just feels better with you in it," he told her.

"It feels better with you in my lifeit, too."

Before she could say more, fireworks exploded overhead, filling the night sky with color. Devon jumped in surprise, and Brennan pulled her in closer, laughing in her ear. They watched the sky light up over and over again, content in each other's arms. It was a beautiful spectacle, announcing the end of the festivities for the day. Devon didn't want the day to end though. She didn't want to let Brennan suffer another day alone.

She stood, pulling him up with her, and led him to the back of the boat. She opened the door, and he followed without question. Wrapping her arms around his neck, she leaned up on her toes and kissed him. He picked her up mid-kiss and deposited her on the bed. Devon shifted under his intense gaze.

Reaching forward, she worked the buttons loose on his collared shirt and pushed it off his shoulders. He dropped it to the floor and stripped out of his T-shirt. She swallowed hard as she stared at his body. When he lay down on the bed, his hand trailed the curves of her body lightly. He moved to her stomach and pushed away the soft material of her shirt from the warmth of her flat stomach. His lips skimmed across the surface, flicking light kisses across the hem of her shorts before he returned north to recapture her lips.

His touch super heated her skin, and she found that she couldn't get enough of him. She couldn't get close enough to him. She pressed her body hard against his and rocked her hips. He groaned against her collar bone and grabbed her hip roughly in his hand.

"Belle, you're killing me," he said. He nipped lightly at her neck, and she shivered.

"Don't stop," she whispered.

A part of her thought about stopping, thought about everything that she had gone through with Reid. Everything she was running away from. But this was different. She wanted this with Brennan. She refused to let what happen to her define her new relationship. She owned her body and everything she did with it. And tonight, she wanted to give it to Brennan.

The pressure on her hip increased as he started guiding her movements to match his. She was straining not to rip his shorts off as her need heightened. His lips returned to hers with a passion, and she let him push her back into the bed. His hands gripped the end of her shirt, pulled it over her head, and then crawled the length of her body exploring what he hadn't been able to touch with her clothes on. She arched her back, and he lifted her off the bed and into his lap. He unsnapped her bra and tossed it off the bed. She gasped and she pressed her breasts against his bare chest.

Brennan smiled and then pulled back so he could trail his fingers down between her breasts slowly. She squirmed against him, but he took his time, running down her stomach and popping the tiny button on her pants.

He pushed her back onto the bed and slid her shorts off her slender hips. She propped her hips up to ease them off, and watched as he pulled off his own. She swallowed as she stared at his body. God, he was gorgeous. She wanted her turn to run her hands over him.

When he had stripped them both down, he moved back over her and rocked his hips against her. She closed her eyes and bit her lip as he slid against her. She wanted to prolong it and continue with all this seduction and teasing, but she didn't know how much more she could take. Her body was already primed and ready to go.

Brennan brought his lips down to meet her. She raised her hands and fisted it through his thick hair, pulling him harder against her. She kissed him like she had never kissed him before like they had lit a fire under them and this was the only way to extinguish the flames. He groaned into her mouth.

She slid her legs up and wrapped them around him just as he slid into her. Devon clenched and rocked her head back as he filled her completely.

He buried his head into her neck with a sigh.

"Oh my God," she breathed, agreeing with the sentiment.

She gasped as he eased out of her again, taking his time before moving back in. Her nails dug into his back as they started a rhythm. Like everything with Brennan, being with him was so easy. It just felt right...like she was finally complete. In a way, it felt like the whole summer had been building up to this moment. Now that she was here, she realized just how much better it all was...how much better life was with Brennan.

She felt her body pushing over the edge as he sped up their tempo. Her heart pounded in her chest and she moaned into his shoulder. "Brennan, I'm close..."

And then they both hit climax together. She saw stars as waves of pleasure coursed through her. Then lay still.

Her heart was racing and Brennan panted into her shoulder. He kissed her forehead and then rolled to the side, pulling her against him again. He ran his fingers back through her hair. She sighed, completely content with him.

"Can we just stay here forever?" she whispered.

He nuzzled into her neck. "If you think I'm letting you leave, you're very wrong."

CHAPTER 22

Fool

BRENNAN'S ARM WAS locked around Devon's body when she woke up. She yawned and snuggled in closer to him. Her thoughts were hazy as she opened her eyes and realized she was still on the boat with Brennan. The bed was comfortable, but lying with Brennan was even better. She hated that it was morning, that their date was coming to a close, that they had to work today, so they couldn't hang out on the boat all day again.

Rolling over to face him, she began to twirl the hair on the back of his neck again. She really liked the longer strands and the way he looked at her when she played with them. His eyes slowly opened, and he smiled when he saw her.

"Morning, Belle," he said before he kissed her lips.

"Good morning." Her heart fluttered at her nickname. She hadn't realized how much she had missed it until last night when he had finally called her that again.

"Can we skip work today?" he asked, nibbling lightly on her bottom lip.

"Uh-huh," she said. Her body was suddenly wide-awake.

"Okay, good."

As his hand slid up the back of her shirt, she arched in response.

"No one will even notice that we're both playing hooky."

"Definitely not."

She did everything she could to keep her focus, but she wasn't winning. Work didn't sound like that great of an idea anyway. It would be better to just stay here all day on the lake and forget the rest of the world. Brennan tracing her rib cage with his fingertips wasn't helping with her motivation to leave.

"It's not like I need money to pay rent or anything."

Devon inhaled sharply as his hand brushed her breasts unexpectedly.

He stopped moving and pulled away. "Oh, that's right."

"That was a joke, Brennan," she said, pulling him closer.

He kissed her lips again. His body shifted over her, covering her. As his hips began grinding into her, she groaned, and her legs naturally moved to wrap around his waist. Her body was pulsing, and all she could think about was getting him closer and closer. She didn't want this to stop. She didn't want any of it to stop. He tried to break the kiss, but she pushed her hands up into his hair and pulled his mouth back down to hers. He growled deep in the back of his throat and gripped her tightly.

"Dev," he said with a painful edge to his voice, "I don't want to stop you."

"Then, don't," she said, willing him to continue.

She knew they had to go, but she didn't want to think about that. She didn't want to think of anything but Brennan—the feel of his body pressed into hers, his heated touch, his passionate kisses.

Brennan sighed and moved back just far enough, so he could look at her face. "But we have to stop."

Devon stuck out her bottom lip and pouted.

"I don't mean it like that. I want to, Dev. I do." He planted another kiss on her lips and then nibbled on her bottom lip again. He stopped and smirked. "I'm not playing around. I do want you, but we have places to be."

Devon rolled out from under Brennan and stood, so she wouldn't tempt him any further. He reached out and took her hand, placing a kiss on it.

"You look good in my shirt," he said, gently pinching her exposed thigh.

She jumped, surprised by the touch. "Don't pinch me!" Devon cried, reaching forward and pinching his arm.

"Who said you could pinch me?" he asked, crawling across the bed. He wrapped his arms around her middle and yanked her back into bed. "On that note, who said you could get out of bed?"

"I'll do what I want," she said stubbornly.

"Not until I let you," Brennan said, holding her tightly and wrestling her back into the bed.

It didn't take much effort because she wasn't really fighting him. Although if she had put up a fight, she was sure it still wouldn't have taken much effort on his part. He was surprisingly muscular.

So, she stopped resisting entirely and enjoyed the fleeting minutes they had left, locked away on his boat. She wished they didn't have to leave, and when they did leave, she wished that they could come back soon. This felt right for them, and she wanted to remember that and cherish it for what it was.

***

BRENNAN DROPPED HER off back at her apartment and escorted her all the way up to the forty-third floor. He stopped her before she could head inside. He picked her up by her waist, letting her feet dangle above the ground. She giggled and leaned forward against him.

"I'm going to miss you." He let her body slide against his as he released her, placing her gently back on the floor.

"I'll see you soon," Devon said, shaking her head at him. She was dizzy from his touch and his enthusiasm. She couldn't get enough of him.

"Too long," he murmured. He walked her backward into the wall and captured her lips.

"Much too long," she said between breaths. "Maybe you could stay—"

"I'd never make it to work on time."

"Not such a bad thing." She fiddled with the buttons on his shirt.

"That's not helping."

Devon smirked deviously, toying with his shirt more. "Just stay."

Gripping her wrists in his hands, he pulled them away from the buttons and lifted her hands up next to her head. "Maybe tonight. I'll stay here, or you can stay with me. How does that sound?"

"Like forever away." She pouted despite her heart feeling like it was beating out of her chest.

"So, is that a no?"

"That's a yes, of course."

"Good." He released her, kissed her one last time on her lips, and took a step back. "I'll see you at work then, Belle."

Devon watched him walk away. Sighing heavily, she wished that he could have stayed, but she knew it was impractical. They actually did have to work. They had gotten yesterday off, and Brennan had missed too much recently because of his dad. She couldn't let him miss work again because of her.

She pushed open the door to the apartment and was surprised when she noticed that Hadley wasn't camped out on the couch already. "Hadley?" she called, tossing her purse on the floor next to the side table.

"Hey," Garrett said, walking out of the bedroom.

"Oh. Is Hadley here?" she asked. Since the incident, she didn't like being alone with him. It didn't sit well with her.

"No. She went to get lunch with her mother, who is in the city for the afternoon," Garrett told her.

"Her mom is here?" Devon asked.

Hadley's mom was the nicest woman Devon had ever met. She was a mirror image of her daughter—all smart, pretty, and bubbly. But she didn't like big cities; they made her feel claustrophobic. So, there must have been a good reason for her visit.

"Yeah. Drove up this morning."

"Why?" Devon asked, narrowing her eyes.

"Hadley didn't say."

"That's…weird," she said. "Does her mother know about the overdose?"

"I don't know. Only if Hadley told her," Garrett said.

"Okay. Well, I guess I'll see her later then. I have to get ready for work," Devon said, turning toward her bedroom.

She shut the door and pulled out her phone from her back pocket. She glanced down at the screen, and her stomach dropped to the floor. Her phone nearly slipped out of her fingers, but she gripped it tighter even though her hands were shaking. There were five texts and a few missed calls from Reid, all from the last hour.

She swallowed hard, wondering what this could be about. Her brain told her not to read them. What good could come from reading them? But she couldn't stop herself. It couldn't be a coincidence that all the messages were so close together.

I saw your parents on TV this morning for some award ceremony in New York. Are you in the States?

FUCK! She couldn't believe he had seen the ceremony.

Devon? I've missed you since you've been gone. If you are in the States, hurry home. I have a bed waiting for you.

Devon shook her head. This could not be happening.

Why aren't you answering me? Are you avoiding me? Answer your phone. Let me know if you're here. I'll fly out to get you.

To. Get. Her. She knew what that meant.

Answer your goddamn phone. Since when do you not answer my texts right away? Are you in New York with someone else? Is that what this is about? You better text me back right away. Better yet, call me. I need to talk to you.

No. No. No. No. No.

I don't know what the fuck you are doing, but if you don't call me, this isn't going to be good. I'm giving you fair warning. Don't be a bitch. Call. Me. Back.

Devon's palms were sweating by the time she finished reading the last text message. Not good. This was so not good. How the fuck had she not thought of this? Of course, he would happen across her parents' award ceremony, the one she had skipped with good reason.

Her hands were trembling, and she was barely keeping it together. What would he do now that he knew she hadn't been in France? Okay, she was getting ahead of herself. He didn't know that. He just knew that her parents were in New York. They could have come back from Paris for it unexpectedly. She could have stayed in Paris…right?

She shook her head. He was too smart. She couldn't fool him into believing her. Not that she could text him back if he was flipping out anyway, not that she had responded to anything he had sent her in weeks.

How did he do this to her? How did he make her feel so guilty for what she had done when he was the one who had hit her? She needed to keep repeating that to herself or else she would end up texting him back. She already felt bad for lying to him. They had been together for so long. Not letting him know that she was all right felt weird. But if he found out, he would make sure that she wasn't.

A knock at her door pulled her out of her thoughts, and then the phone started ringing again. Reid. Fuck.

"Hey, Devon? Can I come in?"

Devon silenced the phone and tried to stay calm. "What's up?" she called out to Garrett.

All she wanted to do was lie down and pretend she was back on the boat with Brennan.

The door cracked open, and Garrett cautiously walked into the room. "Do you think we could talk?" he asked.

"I'd really rather not," she said, not wanting to deal with this and Reid.

"Don't you think we should discuss what happened?"

"I prefer to just forget about it," she said. She really wanted to forget everything at the moment.

"Right," he said, shaking his head. "You would rather run off with Brennan and avoid everything that's happening in your life. Does he even know about the things that went on with you and your boyfriend?"

Devon glared. "It's none of your business what I'm doing and who I'm with."

"I'm just trying to look out for you," he said, taking a step toward her.

"I really don't want to talk about all of this right now, Garrett," Devon said, crossing her arms.

"I'm trying to apologize," he insisted.

"I know. I get it. I just can't even think about it. Reid has been calling and texting me nonstop all morning. He won't leave me alone. I don't know what he's thinking or what he's doing, but I'm just sick and tired of it. So, please just drop it for now!" She turned away from him.

"He's been contacting you?" Garrett asked.

"Yes! All morning. I have to go to work, and I'm going to be late. So, please just drop it Garrett."

"Dev," he said consolingly.

"Please, Garrett," she pleaded, hoping he would actually listen.

"Fine. I just wanted to tell you that I'm sorry. I made a mistake. I don't want you. I want Hadley. And I should have never let any of this happen." He threw his hands out wide and walked back toward the door.

"No, you probably shouldn't have," she said. Her emotions were too high right now for her to have this conversation. She just wanted him to leave, so she could wallow in peace.

"But it was just a drunken mistake."

"Garrett, please just leave. I can't handle anything more right now," she pleaded.

Garrett shook his head and walked through the doorway. Turning around to face her, he said, "I'm trying to do the right thing here, Devon." Then, he walked out of her bedroom, shutting the door behind him.

Devon gritted her teeth upon his exit. It wasn't that she intentionally wanted to be angry with Garrett, but she was just too mentally exhausted. Between her growing feelings for Brennan, Reid's persistence, and Garrett's continual reminder of that night, she was too drained to deal with anything.

Devon quickly changed into her uniform and pulled out her phone to let Brennan know she would be a few minutes late. She clicked out of the new missed call from Reid and sighed, knowing that he wouldn't likely stop anytime soon.

Another message flashed on the screen as she was deleting Reid's call.

I'm going to be a few minutes late to work. Can't wait to see you.

Brennan. Devon smiled.

She exited the screen and sighed. She missed him.

Staring down at her phone, she was full of frustration, doubt, and regret, and then she remembered that Reid didn't know she was in Chicago. As long as he didn't know, then she was safe from him. And she sure as hell wasn't going to tell him. She would deal with him in August when she was on more solid ground.

277

CHAPTER 23
Natural and Easy

EVON SHUFFLED INTO Jenn's Restaurant a full fifteen minutes late. After her conversation with Garrett and those texts from Reid, she hadn't been able to get herself together. The only way she had guaranteed she wouldn't respond to Reid's messages was to leave her phone at home. She had backtracked her steps and picked up her phone at least three times before tossing it back on her bed and leaving it there. The last thing she wanted to do was thumb through her messages at work while Brennan was around. They had too much to talk about tonight after work, and she didn't want him to find out about Reid early.

She stood there as Jenn laid into her for being late. Devon wasn't sure how many more times she could apologize before Jenn would give up and send her out on the floor.

"All right, I will be more aware of the time from now on," Devon said.

"That's right, you will," Jenn grumbled. "I need a drink."

You're not the only one, Devon thought.

"Brennan," Jenn called, finally turning away from Devon, "I'm heading out and leaving you in charge. The morning rush has died down, so I think it should be smooth sailing for the rest of the day. If you need anything, call me."

"Thanks, Jenn," he said as she stormed out of the restaurant.

Brennan turned to Devon with a serious look on his face. "You were late."

"So were you," she said.

"But I didn't get caught. So, don't get caught next time," he said, reaching out for her hand.

"All right, boss. Is that all?" Her response was cheeky, but she couldn't help it.

"I think Amy has the front covered for a bit." He tilted his head toward the break room.

Devon smiled, feeling the weight of the morning drama lift off her shoulders. "I think she definitely has it taken care of," she said, walking through the door.

Brennan looked around to make sure no one else was inside

the room, not that it was a big restaurant with many employees or anything, and then he closed the door behind her.

His hands pushed up into her hair. Tilting her face up to his, he planted his lips down on hers. She gripped his shirt between her hands and pulled him closer to her. He tasted slightly of alcohol, and she became dizzy with his touch as if she had been the one drinking. He smelled good, fresh from a shower and she was glad that his scent wasn't tainted with the smell of pot. Actually, she couldn't remember the last time that smell had been on him.

Never breaking contact, Brennan walked her backward into one of the lockers, and their bodies melded together. It was all Devon could do to keep her mind focused on what they were doing instead of jumping a million steps ahead of where they were. She wasn't succeeding.

Devon clawed at his shirt, untucking it, as she pressed her hands against his flat, toned stomach. The heat from his skin sent electricity coursing through her body, and the room suddenly felt stifling. Her mind couldn't register a time she had ever wanted something this much. Maybe it was the knowledge that they were in a public place and could easily get caught, but mostly, she thought it was just Brennan.

He located the bottom of her skirt and hiked it up. Grasping her thigh in his hand, he pulled it up to wrap around his hip. Between kisses, her breath came out in short spurts as her hands roamed down to the hem of his jeans. Devon felt so rushed, so clumsy that she snapped the waistline of his boxers. Brennan grunted and pressed more firmly against her, like he had enjoyed it. She continued running her fingers lightly along the inside of his boxers, just enough to tease him.

"Belle," he whispered, not pulling back but not moving forward.

"Yeah," she said, her voice strained.

"We have to work," he said, like it pained him.

"Yeah." She would wait for him to make the first move.

"I can't go out there like this," he said, gesturing down.

Devon took the moment to look down, and when she saw what she did to him, her smile grew. "Maybe...I should go first."

He swallowed. "Probably. I'm going to need time to calm down or else we're going to need to finish."

She preferred the second option, and it must have been clearly written all over her face because he groaned and pressed his forehead against hers.

"Belle, you can't look at me like that."

"I'll, uh...just go," she said, easing away from him.

Brennan grabbed her one last time, pulling her in for a slow kiss before releasing her. "You're still coming to my place tonight, right?"

She smiled brightly. "Yeah, definitely."

"Good."

His eyes roamed her body as she backed away from him.

***

DEVON EXITED THE break room and made sure her clothes

were in good enough condition before she went out onto the floor. Jenn was right; it was a pretty light crowd. Amy was having no trouble with the few people in the restaurant. Devon just figured it was slow because it was the weekend after the Fourth of July. Most people wouldn't be able to travel two weekends in a row. Plus, the traffic from the sailboat race was concentrated in the morning and the evening. She would probably get a rush tonight.

"About fucking time," Amy grumbled when Devon walked up. "Think you could be any later?"

"Probably," Devon said with a shrug.

"I mean, was it not enough that you got yesterday off, too?" Amy snapped.

"Amy, lay off, all right? I already got yelled at by Jenn and Brennan for this."

"From Brennan? Riiight." Amy rolled her eyes.

So, that's what this is about, she thought, realizing it was about Brennan.

"Yeah, they were both pretty pissed," Devon told her.

"Well, maybe they'll fire you."

Devon gripped the menu she was holding as tightly as she could, so she wouldn't snap back at Amy. Could she get much bitchier?

"Thanks for the vote of confidence," Devon said sarcastically.

Amy just rolled her eyes again and walked over to one of her tables. Devon busied herself by rolling silverware, filling salt and pepper shakers, and wiping down the tables. At some point, Brennan returned, and she smiled as she felt his eyes follow her around the room. She wondered if he even knew that he did it so frequently.

The day passed with a steady flow of traffic. It wasn't anything that one person couldn't handle on her own, but it was nice to have both Amy and Devon on the shift. The dinner crowd was more obnoxious than normal, and Devon felt like punching one of the customers. She even heard Amy swear at a guy who grabbed her ass. Jenn's wasn't that kind of place.

Devon was more than irritated when she found the shitty tips from the rambunctious groups after they had exited the restaurant. Amy was fuming across the room, and Devon suspected she had discovered the same problem with her tables. What kind of assholes came in with a huge party, acted like hellions the whole time they were here, and then didn't tip? Who had raised them to do that? Devon wanted to throttle them and explain to the worthless human beings that just because they had never worked a day in their life didn't mean they couldn't appreciate the hard work she had done for them. But, of course, she couldn't do that either.

"You go ahead and take a break. You look like you need it," Devon told Amy.

She didn't want to do Amy any favors, but Amy had been there longer. Plus, it didn't help Devon any to have everyone hate her.

"Thanks. I need a fucking smoke," Amy said, pressing her hand to her forehead. "I'll be back in fifteen."

Devon watched Amy's tables and kept Brennan busy with drink orders. Leaning forward, he kept offering her shots of tequila like the first time they had ever really talked. Devon declined, but he just kept offering.

"Just one shot," he whispered, pushing the drink toward her.

Devon shook her head. "Not on the clock. Give it to Amy. She will flip her shit."

"What do you mean?" he asked.

"Oh, don't play dumb. That girl is obsessed with you."

Devon giggled as Brennan poured the rest of her drink orders.

"What? No, she isn't," he said.

"Brennan, really? You are not oblivious to the world. You have to know that her and Hannah are so into you."

"Huh," he said, his eyes going deep into thought. "That explains a whole hell of a lot."

Devon rolled her eyes. "How did you not see that?"

"Only have eyes for you, Belle." He smirked, placing a drink on her tray.

Her stomach flipped as she picked up the tray. She made a round of her and Amy's tables. Amy returned ten minutes past her allotted fifteen minutes with the smell of smoke announcing her presence. She didn't apologize for her tardiness, and Devon suspected it was because she had been late earlier.

"Your turn," Amy said with a shrug.

"Thanks," Devon said.

Devon walked past Brennan into the back and took a seat on the bench. She sighed and stretched out her aching legs, lying back on the bench. She yawned and let her mind wander back to this morning when she had awoken in just a tangle of limbs. Being with Brennan was the only thing that had allowed her to forget her old life. She had tried to push back the memories, but they haunted her no matter how hard she had tried. When Brennan had walked into her life, all of that changed.

When she heard the door creak open, she shifted up to her elbows to see Brennan walking in.

"Hey," he said with a charming smile.

"Hey."

"Came in here to check on you. It was a bit of a madhouse out there for a while."

He walked over and sat on the end of the bench. She scooted down and rested her head on his thigh.

"It was. I'm ready to go home," she said with a yawn. "Someone kept me up late last night."

"Not late enough," he said, running his hands through her hair.

Devon chuckled and closed her eyes as he worked his magic at untangling the knots. He calmed her down, and she could have lain there all night. Everything was so natural and easy with Brennan.

She exhaled softly. "Can I ask you something?"

"What is it?" His hand pulled back through her loose strands.

"I've been wondering about this since you told me, but I don't want it to sound weird," she said, her hands fiddling with the buttons on her white shirt.

"Nothing is weird between us," he said.

"I just…well…your dad left you with money, right?" She felt weird for asking.

Brennan tensed and stilled his hand. "Uh, yeah."

"Then, um…why do you live in a small one bedroom, take the L, and work as a bartender?" she asked, her words coming out in a rush.

She didn't want to sound snooty because that wasn't her intention. But if his dad had worked at Northwestern Memorial for thirty years as a doctor, then he was likely well-off. Why wouldn't Brennan use any of that money?

"Oh," was all he said.

"I don't mean to sound like I like you any less because of it. I don't! I don't care about those things. I like those things," she added hastily. "I was mostly curious."

"Well, truth is…I don't like money," he said with a stilted laugh.

"You don't like…money," she repeated.

"I don't know. I do. I just…it was his money. Everything I buy with it reminds me that he's gone."

Devon sat up, so she could look at him. The pain was clear on his face, and she was sorry that she had brought it up. She took his hand and held it in her own.

"I don't mind the things he owned, like the boat. Those are happy memories, but the house…" He shuddered. "I couldn't live in that house."

"He left you a house?" She wasn't sure why she even asked, but she didn't know what else to say.

The more he talked, the more she wondered why she had asked at all. He sounded so sad.

"Yeah. I didn't know what to do with it, so I just left it as is. It's probably dusty. Sometimes, I go over there to mow the lawn the way he liked it, but that's as far as I can get," he said. "I bought the apartment after that. I try to keep it all low-key and live the way I used to live before it happened."

"That has to be hard," she said, her thumb drawing circles on his hand.

"I've survived."

"Glad I can be here…so you're not just surviving anymore." She pulled him in for a hug.

"With you, I'm living," he whispered, kissing her head.

She leaned her head back and kissed him on the lips. "Me, too."

"And just so you know, I try so hard on those medical exams," he said with a sigh. "He always wanted me to be a doctor, just like him. Follow in his footsteps."

"But is that what you want?" she asked, knowing that it wasn't.

After listening to his music just one time, she knew that being a doctor wasn't what he wanted. How could it be when art called to his soul?

"I'm perfectly content working as a bartender and playing music for the rest of my life…but you can't retire on that."

"No."

"I just don't have the heart for it. I got my scores back," he said.

"How did you do?" Devon asked, her heart jumping out of her chest. Was it that time already? Were the scores already reported?

He shrugged. "Good enough to go wherever I want."

"Oh wow," she said with a smile. "Where have you applied?"

"That's the problem…nowhere. I haven't applied anywhere. I don't know if I can be him…and I hate that about myself," he told her.

They sat there in silence for a bit. Devon knew something of parental approval. She and her mother had never seen eye to eye on what Devon should do with her life.

Devon reached out and took his hand in her own. "You know, my mama always wanted me to be a country music singer."

"Yeah? Is that because your parents work in the industry?"

She was surprised he remembered that about her.

"Yeah. They're lyricists."

"Like you," he said with a smile.

"Ugh…no way. Not like me. My stuff sucks, and I'm never letting people hear it."

"I doubt that, Dev."

"Anyway," she said, not wanting to touch on that conversation right now, "I never wanted that for myself. I never saw myself as the country music artist my mother wanted me to be, no matter how hard she tried, and she tried hard. But my mother also wants me to be happy, and she only pushed me as far as she could without upsetting me. She wants a country music star, but she's okay with me being the person I am. And…I think your dad would want that, too."

Brennan leaned forward and kissed her. "Thank you."

"You're welcome," she said shyly. She felt weird being the one giving out advice for once.

"Come on. Amy will probably be looking for us any minute,"

Brennan said, standing.

"You're probably right."

They walked out of the break room and into the kitchen just as Amy walked through the swinging door.

"Where have you guys been? I need your help!" She glared at Devon like she might stab her.

Devon wouldn't put it past her.

"Sorry." Brennan swept past Amy and headed to the bar.

Devon sighed heavily. She hated when the moments with Brennan were broken. It was like she was in a dream, but unlike her nightmares, it was the best place she had ever been. It was nothing like her past life.

She walked out onto the floor and took orders at the two tables she had acquired. She rushed them back to the kitchen and refilled drinks for another table. Brennan handed her a full tray, and she quickly deposited the contents around the room.

"Here you go," she said with a big smile, giving out the last drink to her customer.

Devon turned around toward the entrance to greet an incoming customer, and her tray slipped out of her hand, clattering to the ground.

"Reid?"

CHAPTER 24
The Right Option

R EID BENT DOWN and collected the tray from the floor. He looked up, his eyes met Devon's, and he smiled bright and beautiful. He had an award-winning smile. Her hands were shaking as he handed the tray back to her, and she automatically tucked it under her arm.

How had he found her? She had thought that she was safe, that she had time, that she would be able to figure things out. He wasn't supposed to be here. He wasn't supposed to be standing in Jenn's, staring at her expectantly. He had only texted her this morning.

There was no way he could have found her in less than a day, right? That wasn't even supposed to be possible.

And Brennan. Oh fuck—Brennan! She hadn't told him. There hadn't been time. Her mind had been elsewhere, running ahead of her as always to his one-bedroom apartment. She had been planning to tell him night when she was supposed to go to his apartment.

Now, what could she do? Brennan didn't know, and she had told him that she had broken up with her boyfriend. But now, Reid was here, and he was staring at her, making it very obvious that she was his property. He had a way of looking at her that made it very clear they were together. She never got hit on in public, and Hadley had been the one that pointed it out the first time. Devon recognized it now as possessiveness, which was part of his problem.

Would Brennan notice? Fuck! He was the most perceptive person she knew. Of course, he would notice. Plus, with the way they hadn't been able to keep their hands off each other the past couple days, it would be strange for her to act any different now.

But if Reid saw her with Brennan, what would he do? She couldn't think about it. She couldn't imagine her life right now without Brennan. He made her feel human, and she never wanted to feel like she was anything less again.

As she saw it, she had two choices, neither of which she wanted to face. She could confront Reid right here, something she had never prepared for, and watch him go ballistic, potentially hurting her and Brennan. Hadn't she thought that if Brennan ever collided with her problems that he might end up dead? She couldn't let that happen, but she knew what Reid was capable of. The other option was to act like everything was fine—leave with Reid and keep Brennan out of it. Figure out what to do from there. It sounded like a suicide mission to her, but it felt selfish to risk Brennan.

All she had to do was figure out why Reid was here and how he had found her. She couldn't do much else.

Devon's whole body was trembling, and she was sure that Reid saw the shock all over her face. Heat rose to the surface of her skin. Her body flushed all over. And all she could do was stand there and stare at him. It had been two-and-a-half months since she had last seen him. It was the longest amount of time she had been away from him in nearly three years.

Devon could see what she had fallen for all those years ago. He wore the requisite prep look like a second skin. It was a trait he had acquired long ago when he had attended an all-boys private school in the Kansas City suburbs. He had perfected it when he had pledged a fraternity at Wash U. His height had gotten him the quarterback position in high school, but he hadn't been good enough to play Division I in college. Pride had kept him from going to a lower division. He had used the legacy factor from his father as the reason he didn't play in college. Most of all, Reid just seemed like the perfect guy—smart, confident, ambitious.

But then, she also saw what she hadn't seen when they had first started dating. His smile was a promise, telling her she was in a lot of fucking trouble without even saying a word. His eyes were icy, threatening her with just a glance. His height didn't just make him taller than her; it was a power struggle. He had to take up the room and break her down, make her less than nothing. His entire presence was sinister.

And she could do better.

It was a scary thought.

"Hey, Dev," Reid said, still not making a move toward her.

"Hey," she whispered. "Wha…what are you doing here?"

"It's good to see you, too," he said, smiling that terribly beautiful smile in her direction.

Devon deadpanned. She couldn't say it was good to see him. It was shocking to see him. It was fucking scary to see him. It made her want to collapse into a puddle on the floor. Good wasn't even in the first hundred adjectives she would have used.

She didn't miss that he didn't answer her question. She hadn't asked what she wanted to know the most. Not what was he doing here, but how had he found her? She didn't think that one would go over well.

"How have you been?" he asked.

Devon swallowed. This sounded like a trick question. "Fine."

"I've missed you."

Devon couldn't bring herself to smile. Her insides twisted, and she did everything she could not to look away.

"You didn't return my messages," he said, taking a step closer this time.

"I accidentally left my phone at home," she told him.

She wanted to run. She wanted to turn around and run away from him…into Brennan's arms. But that was dangerous…too dangerous.

"Well, I'm glad I found you then. We have a lot to talk about."

She knew what his talking looked like. "I have to work," she said softly.

He smiled like he knew she was trapped. "I'll wait."

What could she say to that? No, get the fuck out! Yeah right! He was coiled up like a viper ready to strike, and she wasn't going to poke him.

"It won't be long. I can meet you somewhere," she offered, wanting nothing more than for him to leave right now.

He chuckled, and even that sounded threatening. Maybe everything about him was a threat to her now because she knew how dangerous he was.

"I think I'd rather stay. I could use a drink."

Fuck! No. No. No. He could not have a drink. Bad idea. Really bad idea. Brennan was over by the drinks.

"Take one of my tables, and I'll go get you one," she said, her voice struggling to remain calm. "Crown, right?"

"Don't worry about it, Dev," he said, walking up to her. "I'll just go to the bar. We can talk after you get off work."

"Okay," she whispered, knowing it was anything but okay.

He reached forward and squeezed her hand. "You look good," he said, raking his eyes over her body. Then, he released her, turned, and walked directly toward the bar, toward Brennan.

Her heart deflated, and air burst out of her mouth in a whoosh. She reached out, grabbed one of the booths, and held on for dear life. She couldn't even turn around to look at Brennan and Reid standing at the bar together while Brennan made Reid a drink, offered up polite conversation, and joked around. She couldn't witness it. She thought she might throw up.

It took everything she had to return to her tables and act like nothing was wrong. She had never worked so hard in her life. She was trying so desperately not to look at Brennan and Reid that she worked twice as hard as normal. She needed to keep her mind busy, and that was the only way she knew how.

Devon didn't know what she was going to do when her shift ended. She had been running for so long that she had completely pushed away thoughts of when she would have to face her life again. Now, it was here, sitting right in front of her.

The after-hours crowd started filling the room, which made the distraction a bit easier. She still had a hard time looking over to see Reid sitting at the bar, but at least, Brennan was busy enough that he didn't have to talk to Reid. She didn't want them to ever have to talk.

When Hannah and another waitress walked in to take over for Amy and her, Devon thought she might break down into tears. She couldn't leave. Jenn's was a sanctuary, and her demons were waiting for her outside the door...or even worse, at the bar, drinking with Brennan. She knew that Reid wouldn't do anything in public. He was too self-controlled for that. It was the only reason he had gotten away with everything for this long. She hadn't ratted him out, and no one would guess that perfect Reid would ever do something like hurt his perfect girlfriend.

She wanted to believe that their time apart had showed him how much he had missed her and how wrong his actions had been. She wanted him to see her for the woman he had fallen in love with. She wanted him to apologize and beg her to come back.

But those were fairy-tale dreams. When he had walked in, the look Reid had given her had been enough to show her that none of those things would be her reality. This was Reid after all. He could never be wrong…ever.

"Hey, Devon," Hannah said, walking up to her.

"Hey, Hannah."

"I wish I had the mid-shift this week," she said with a sigh. "But I'm stuck working late. What are you doing tonight?"

Devon stared at her blankly. Hannah never made polite conversation with her.

"Um…nothing."

"Sounds riveting," Hannah said, straight-faced.

That's more like it, she thought.

"Well, have a good time," Devon said, untying her apron. "I'm out of here."

"Lucky," Hannah said under her breath.

If only she knew…

Devon bit her lip and stole a glance at the bar. Both Reid and Brennan were looking directly at her. She averted her eyes as quickly as she could and hurried through the swinging door into the kitchen. Her heart was pounding as she walked stiffly into the break room.

Only a couple hours ago, she had sat here with Brennan while he played with her hair. Before that, they had been kissing, and he had her backed up against the lockers. Could everything that had happened since then be real?

She grabbed her purse and slung it over her head, letting the strap cross her body. She leaned forward against her locker and tried some breathing exercises to calm her racing heart. Tears sprang to her eyes, and her hands swatted them away. They wouldn't help her now. She just needed to be strong.

The door opened behind her, and she hoped it was Amy.

"Belle, you okay?" Brennan asked.

No luck.

She straightened immediately. "I'm fine," she said, the words sounding hollow. Why did that word sound so horrible when she said it?

"Fine. All right. Are you ready to head out then? Kami just walked in to take my spot," he said, walking across the room.

He knew something was different. She could tell by the set of his shoulders. He was waiting for it. She didn't think he knew what it was, but he knew to get ready. He was preparing himself for whatever was to come.

"Brennan," she said softly. God, she hated herself.

"So…you're not fine."

"I…I don't know," she said with a shrug.

His hand reached out to touch her, but it fell halfway through, like he thought better of it.

"Does this have something to do with that guy out there?"

"What guy?" she said, barely audible.

He looked at her pointedly.

"Yeah, it does."

"I figured as much."

"I wasn't expecting him to show up here," Devon told him. She wondered if he could tell how scared she was or if her fake bravery was enough to sway him away.

"Who is he?" He crossed his arms, already closing himself off.

"That's my boyfriend."

Brennan raised his eyebrows. "Boyfriend?"

Devon closed her eyes and shook her head twice. "Ex-boyfriend. Sorry."

"If he's your ex, what is he doing here?" Brennan asked cautiously.

"I'm not sure exactly. We broke up on rocky terms. I think he wants to talk to me," Devon said, looking away from him. This wasn't going to be easy.

"Sounds like trouble," Brennan said. "Devon, look at me."

She obliged, trying not to see the hurt in his face.

"You don't have to talk to him. I know it might seem like you have to, but you said it was over. And you're over him, right?"

He waited for the answer that should have been immediate on her tongue. It was more complicated than whether or not she was over Reid, but she couldn't tell Brennan that without putting him in danger. She cared about Brennan too much to let that happen.

"We didn't break up face-to-face. I think I should at least talk to him," she said softly.

His eyes shut, and he breathed heavily through his nose, like he was holding himself back. She hated herself. She hated herself so much. She never wanted to cause him any pain. She never wanted to see his beautiful face look at her any other way than as lovingly as he had on the boat yesterday. She would never forgive herself, but at least, he would be safe. She needed to keep reminding herself of that.

Brennan opened his eyes and stared so intensely into her own that she blushed and looked away. He grabbed both of her shoulders and pulled her close to him.

"Devon, please," he said, making her look at him. "I can already see it happening. Don't let the life drain out of you again. I can see you retreating. I need you, and I think you need me, too. Please just stay here, stay in the present, in the future. Stay with me."

"Brennan," she whispered, tears coming to her eyes this time.

"No, Devon, no tears," he said, wiping them away from her eyes. "You're too beautiful for that."

She laughed through her tears and sniffled.

"There's that smile, that beautiful smile. I want to keep making you smile, but I can't if you walk out of this place. We pulled each other out of the water once, Devon. I can't bear to see you sink any deeper. Please, please stay with me. Just stay with me," he pleaded.

Devon closed her eyes and tried to steady her breathing. The tears were coming harder, and they weren't helping anything. She wanted to stay so badly. She wanted to run away with Brennan and continue to forget all her problems. She wanted to be with him, but she couldn't keep running. She needed to do what was right even if it wasn't what she wanted.

"I can't," she said, sinking into herself as she forced out the words. "I have to go."

She pushed the tears out of her eyes and brushed past him toward the exit. She had already been in here too long. Reid would notice, and she didn't want him to associate Brennan with her.

"Devon," he said, grabbing her wrist in his hand before she could go, "you're making a big mistake."

She swallowed back her tears. "I have to go," she repeated, pulling her wrist free.

Before Brennan could say another word, she rushed out of the break room and into the kitchen. Pushing her hands up into her hair, Devon doubled over like she had just been punched in the stomach. No. This was worse.

This felt like her heart was breaking, shattering into a million pieces.

CHAPTER 25
Coiled

When Devon finally composed herself, she walked out of the back to find Reid fiddling with his empty drink while he talked to an enamored Hannah. This was going to go over well for her reputation, not that it even mattered. She didn't know what she would even be doing after today.

"Hey," Reid said. He watched her as she walked toward him, like a predator tracking his prey.

"Hey," Devon responded.

His eyes searched her face. She knew that he could tell she

had been crying. She never hid it well, but there was nothing she could do about it now.

Seemingly without thinking, he reached out and took her hand. "Are you ready to go?"

"Yeah," she murmured.

"It was really nice meeting you, Hannah," Reid said with that same award-winning smile. He placed two twenties on the bar and stood.

"Nice meeting you, too," Hannah said sullenly as she watched Reid with Devon.

Devon didn't even have the strength to say anything else to Hannah. She was ready to leave or else she never would. She had already left Brennan in the break room, and that had been nearly impossible.

***

The silence that permeated the space between Reid and Devon was suffocating. There was so much left unsaid, so much that she was waiting for, but she wasn't going to be the one to break the silence. She didn't even know where Reid was taking her. She knew the area, but she couldn't tell where they were going. She should have cared more or been a little freaked out, but it was Reid. He wouldn't do anything to attract attention to himself in public. But if they were walking somewhere more private…

She swallowed hard; a lump that she couldn't get down lodged in her throat. The fact that they were here together right now was so messed up. She had thought that she had loved this man, that he was her greatness. True love had never felt so cheap than it had in this moment.

She had deluded herself into believing in it, in him. Reid wasn't her greatness. He was just a guy who got off on a little power. She had been so blind to him that even when the worst had come—she had still blamed herself. Why couldn't she be better? How could she get him to see that she was trying harder? She deserved what he was doing to her because she wasn't good enough for him.

The longer she had stayed away, the more these thoughts had faded from her mind. She wasn't a coward. She hadn't run because she thought it was easier than facing him. She was brave, and she had run because facing him wasn't possible.

Two-and-a-half months wasn't long enough for her to forget what had happened. It wasn't long enough for her to forgive if she ever would. It was only long enough for the bruises to heal...but not the emotional ones. Those had scarred, and she didn't know if they would ever fully heal.

As Reid walked into a parking garage, Devon's heart fluttered. Of course, he had driven here. How else would he have gotten here so soon? The thought of getting into a car with him and letting him control her course was terrifying. Where were they going to go? Would he drive them straight back to St. Louis and pick up where they left off?

They found Reid's sporty little black BMW parked all by itself.

He had a habit of parking a floor above all the other cars to avoid anyone messing with his baby. Ironic at best.

Still holding her hand, he guided her to the passenger seat, opened the car door for her, and let her slide onto the black leather seat. As he shut the door tightly behind her, she tried not to hyperventilate.

They were alone. Completely alone. 100 percent alone.

She felt like a caged animal, desperate to be released from captivity. Her hair stood on end, and she tried not to fidget. Without thinking, she reached into her purse and pulled out a pen. She absentmindedly flipped it between her fingers. It didn't calm her down, but it helped. It gave her something else to think about. She wanted to write then, to let out all the emotions coursing through her body. She wanted to write more than she had since the first couple weeks she had been in Chicago. But she didn't dare pull out her notebook. Reid didn't like her lyrics, and he certainly wouldn't like the ones she had written about him.

Reid sat himself comfortably into the driver's seat and locked the doors. Devon watched the lock click into place, and she had the sudden urge to lift it and bolt. How far could she get? She wasn't a runner. Could she make it to the elevator? Would the stairs be a better option? Would he chase her? Were her dreams becoming reality?

He revved the engine to life, and Devon sank back into the seat. She couldn't outrun him. Although he didn't work out like he had used to, he still had more than six inches on her in height. Not to mention, he was a natural athlete. And who was she kidding?

Her dreams were already her reality.

"Where have you been staying?" he asked, reaching for her hand and taking it.

"With Hadley and her boyfriend," she told him with a sigh.

"Ah," he said, putting the car into reverse, "I forgot Hadley was in the city."

Devon nodded, not knowing what else to say. Now, he knew. Great.

"Then, we'll go there."

"What?" she asked. Oh God…Hadley! She had told Hadley that she and Reid had broken up and that she was into Brennan. If she showed up with Reid in tow, it could cause a nuclear meltdown. Garrett knew what had happened between them, and Garrett and Hadley both knew that she had been out all night with Brennan. If they said one word about Brennan, it would set off Reid. Reid could not go back to the apartment.

"That's where your stuff is, right?" he asked, turning to face her.

"Uh, right. But I don't have much," she said. She didn't even know why she said that. It wasn't like she wanted to hurry up and head back to St. Louis. She had no escape there.

He smiled and squeezed her hand. She tried not to cringe.

"Didn't you leave your phone there?"

Her stomach dropped. Fuck! Of all the days…

"Oh yeah," she whispered.

Reid pulled the car out of the garage and exited smoothly into traffic on the one-way street. "Where am I headed?"

She bit her lip and stared out the car window before directing him to their destination. She didn't want to bring him back to the apartment. What choice did she have though? She had taken the only choice she could to protect Brennan. Now, she had to follow through with it. Once he was safe, she would try to work things out with Reid. He just couldn't find out. She wouldn't be able to forgive herself if Reid were to hurt Brennan.

Devon had never driven the streets of Chicago, but she knew the blocks well enough. Jenn's wasn't far from Marina City, but she felt a bit disoriented since she always took the L. He grunted when she made another accidental wrong turn.

"I should have just used my GPS."

"Sorry," she squeaked.

It was the least angry he had gotten with her for bad directions in a long time. He had refused to let her navigate anywhere they went because he hated all her mistakes. This was already starting out so well.

He pulled into the Marina City complex and parked. Devon pushed the door open and stood. From her position, she could see out of the building all the way to Lake Michigan. It made her think of Brennan's boat, the boat his father had left him, sitting in the harbor. She pulled her eyes away from the horizon, not wanting her eyes to show the loss of what could have been. Reid might not be able to decipher what it was immediately, but she didn't want to give him cause to consider it.

They walked to the elevator together, his arm locked around

her shoulder. He was using any excuse to touch her. She wanted to run far, far away. Apparently, she hadn't run far enough to get away from him.

The elevator was as quick as ever and deposited them on the forty-third floor of the building. Devon was dreading this with every ounce of her being. She hated not knowing what would happen when they walked through the door.

Devon slid her key into the hole and turned the handle. She took a deep breath for strength and pushed through the door. Reid walked in behind her. Suddenly, the apartment felt very small, much too small. Two bedrooms, two baths, a kitchen, and a living room—it wasn't enough space. She couldn't get away from Reid in here unless she wanted to jump off the balcony and drop forty-three floors. And that wasn't even an option.

"So, this is the place," she said tentatively.

As they walked into the living room, Reid seemed to be examining the apartment. He was probably judging the place.

She heard a noise behind her, and she turned quickly. Garrett was standing in the hallway. His eyes moved from Devon's face to Reid and back. His eyes grew wide as he seemed to realize what was happening, and then his face turned white as a sheet.

Reid turned around just then and smiled. "Hey, man, I'm Reid." He walked across the room and shook Garrett's hand.

"Garrett."

"So nice to meet you. Devon's been telling me all about you. Really nice of you to let her stay in the city for a couple weeks," Reid said.

"Uh, yeah, no problem. She's welcome here anytime," Garrett said, his eyes shifting to Devon.

Reid smiled bigger and turned to include Devon in the conversation. "That's always good to know. Maybe we'll make another trip up here during the school year."

Devon looked away from them. She just couldn't handle this. The implication in Reid's words sliced open old wounds. They were never going to make a trip to see Hadley and Garrett. Once Reid got her in St. Louis again, she wouldn't go anywhere. He would make sure of that.

"So, how long are you here for?" Garrett asked, running a hand back through his hair.

Devon already knew the answer. They would leave as soon as Reid could get her out of here.

"Well, it's up to Devon, of course," he answered, clearly lying.

Reid smiled at her, and Devon thought she might be sick. Since when had anything been up to her?

"What do you want to do, Dev?"

She shrugged. She wanted to go back to Brennan and apologize. She wanted to explain to him that Reid was dangerous and Brennan couldn't come anywhere near him. She wanted to tell Brennan that she didn't trust Reid not to hurt him, and if he did, it would kill her.

"Well, I got my MCAT scores in the mail this week, and it's Devon's birthday soon. Maybe we could all go out and celebrate?" Reid said.

"How did you do?" Devon asked automatically. Hadn't she just asked Brennan the same question?

A muscle in Reid's neck twitched at the question. If she didn't know him so well, she wouldn't have known what that meant. He hadn't done as well as he had wanted. She wondered if his parents would donate a library or something to get him into Wash U's medical school. She wouldn't put it past them.

"Great. They were great," he said with a sinister smile. "So, you want to go out then?"

"Sure," she said softly. She would rather be out than alone with him, and she might as well put off the inevitable.

"I'll have to see what Hadley's doing. I'm not sure if she's ready to go out again. She should be home soon though," Garrett said.

He sounded uncomfortable and out of place, and Devon didn't blame him. He knew what had happened with her and Reid, and he was probably trying to figure out his role now that Reid was here.

"She's not home yet?" Devon asked just to fill the silence.

"No, she and her mom decided to go out shopping. I don't expect them until after the stores close." He looked down at his watch. "That was thirty minutes ago, so she should be here soon."

As if on cue, Hadley walked through the door, loaded with bags. She kicked the door shut with her foot as she stumbled inside, weighed down by her packages.

Garrett reached out to steady her.

"Hey!" she said, bending into him. "Missed you."

Garrett's smile took over his face. "I missed you, too."

"I got way too much," she said, leaning forward and kissing him.

When she backed up, he said, "I can see that." Garrett turned to gesture toward Reid. "We, uh…have a visitor."

"Reid McAllister!" Hadley cried in shock. "What are you doing here?"

Reid laughed good-naturedly and shook his head. "Nice to see you, too, Hadley."

"Seriously, what are you doing here?" she asked, hoisting her bags over one shoulder to redistribute the weight.

"I'm here to see Devon, of course. What do you think I'm doing here?" he asked, his eyes moving to Devon.

"I really don't know."

"Hadley, what did you get from your shopping trip?" Devon asked quickly, cutting off Hadley's next response.

Hadley narrowed her eyes, but she was too much of a girl to not give in. "Ugh…too much. I'll have to show you. Bedroom?" she asked, nodding toward the room she shared with Garrett.

"Sure. Garrett, maybe you should pour Reid a drink," Devon offered, skirting around him.

Reid reached out and grabbed her wrist. When she winced, he released some of the tension. He pulled her into him, and she did everything she could not to pull away. Her wrist would be the least of her worries then. He pushed back a lock of blonde hair from her face.

"I missed you, and I don't ever want you out of my sight again," he said so softly only she could hear. His lips landed possessively on hers. "Don't be in there long."

Devon bit her lip, wanting nothing more than to wrench herself out of his grasp, but she just nodded.

"Good," he said, releasing her. "I think I would like that drink now, Garrett." He walked into the kitchen with a boisterous laugh.

Devon scurried away from him and into the bedroom. She hoped her shaking wasn't noticeable. She closed the door quickly behind her just as Hadley tossed her bags on the bed with a big huff.

"Okay...what the fuck is he doing here?" Hadley asked.

"Shhh," Devon warned quickly, putting her finger to her mouth. "Keep it down."

"Sorry," Hadley said quietly.

"We didn't really break up," Devon said, biting her lip.

"What are you talking about? You said that you did, and then you were gone all night with Brennan," Hadley said, confused.

Devon fiercely shook her head. "Don't talk about him. Reid can't know about Brennan."

"Devon, what is going on?" Hadley demanded, crossing her arms.

"I left St. Louis without telling Reid. I wanted to break up with him, but I didn't know how. So, for all intents and purposes, we were broken up. He just...didn't know..." Devon trailed off.

"Fuck, Dev. What are you going to do?" Hadley asked, sitting back heavily on the bed.

"Wing it?" Devon said with a shrug.

Hadley looked at her skeptically.

"Okay, I'm going to have to act like everything is normal...as much as I can anyway. You are, too. Then, I'm going to try to talk to him, but please don't bring up Brennan. I don't want him to think that is why we're breaking up."

"Isn't it?" Hadley asked.

"No," Devon said, shaking her head. "I left Reid before I had ever met Brennan."

"Fair point."

"I just…have to do this my way, okay?"

Hadley stood up and placed her hand on Devon's shoulder. "Let him down easy, Dev. He's crazy about you."

He's just crazy, she thought.

***

Devon was close to collapsing by the time they made it out to the bar. She really wanted a drink to calm her nerves, but she wanted to stay in control. The last thing she wanted was to confront Reid with an addled mind or accidentally slip and say something she shouldn't while drunk.

Hadley and Garrett decided on a club not too far from their house. Hadley hadn't been out at night since her overdose. Devon didn't want to worry about that on top of everything else. Garrett would just have to take care of her for once.

When Devon walked into the club, her head was swimming. It felt so much like her dream. It really wasn't anything like it at all, except for the dance floor, heavy music, and crowd. That shouldn't have been enough to trigger her terror, but having Reid holding tightly to her arm didn't help anything. As bile rose, she covered her mouth and tried to swallow away her apprehension.

His hand slid across the small of her back and gripped her waist. He leaned down and spoke directly into her ear. "Drink?"

She shook her head. "I'm okay."

"Come with me anyway," he said, pulling her toward the bar.

"Okay," she said because she really had no other choice.

Reid ordered himself a Crown and Coke and her a Cosmopolitan even though she didn't want it. She didn't like cosmos, and she had told him a hundred times that she didn't, but he kept ordering them for her.

"Reid," she muttered as they waited for their drinks.

"Yeah, Dev?"

He pushed his hand up into her hair and massaged her scalp. She didn't want to enjoy it, but it felt good. She wished he would stop, so she could concentrate.

"I think we need to talk," she said, wondering if he could even hear her over the music.

"Let's talk later, okay? I can't really hear you," he said with a smile.

Devon didn't like the thought of later. "But—"

"No," he said sharply, cutting her off. "Later. Let's enjoy our night together."

With that, his lips covered hers as he held her head in place, so she couldn't move. He forced her mouth open and plunged his tongue inside. She wanted to squirm away, but he had her exactly where he wanted her. Her heart pounded as one of his hands slid down her backside. He grabbed it forcefully enough to make her cry out. Back before he had ever hit her, that would have turned her on. Now, she only felt disgusted.

When the bartender slid the drinks across the bar to him, he released her. Reid handed the guy his credit card and told him to keep the tab open.

His eyes found her again, and he laughed. "You're mine. You know that, right?" He grasped her chin in his hand. "All mine."

She swallowed, trying not to react. He didn't care if she confirmed or denied what he had said. In his head, he believed it to be true.

They spent the rest of the night hanging out with Hadley and Garrett. Devon tried and failed to act like her normal self because normal didn't include Reid anymore. Thankfully, for the sake of the conversation, he took over. He had a big enough personality for the two of them, and he seemed to seamlessly hold up their end of the conversation. She couldn't believe she had ever let him talk for her like this before. It felt unnatural.

She wanted to speak up at times, but then she thought better of it. If she didn't hand him ammunition, he would be less likely to pull the trigger.

Reid yawned big and exaggerated. Devon knew he wasn't tired. He was actually wired. Everything about the situation that put her on edge riled him up.

"I think it's time we got out of here."

"Are you sure? It's still early," Garrett said hastily.

Devon didn't know if Garrett's reaction was out of fear for her safety or because he had gotten along with Reid so well. She wasn't really surprised. Reid got along with everyone, but she thought that Garrett wouldn't play into his hand so easily.

"Yeah, I haven't seen Devon in a while. I think we need some alone time," he said, pulling her up with him.

"Reid," Devon said quickly. She did not want to be alone with him.

"Do you want us to come with you?" Hadley jumped in.

"No. We don't want to interrupt your evening," he said smoothly.

Hadley looked at her pointedly. She thought she was being reassuring as if telling Devon, Here's your chance. Devon regretted not telling Hadley the truth. She couldn't be alone with him! This was absurd.

"It wouldn't interrupt our evening at all," Garrett said, standing as well.

"Really, don't even worry about us," Reid said. "We'll see you in the morning."

"Reid, I think they should come with us," Devon said quickly.

His grip on her arm tightened, and she stopped breathing. It felt too familiar. She just wanted to wake up from her nightmare. Wake up. Please wake up. But she wasn't dreaming, and she couldn't get away from this.

"Don't be silly, Devon. There's no reason for them to come with us." He smiled brightly at them. "Night, guys."

Reid all but pushed Devon out of the club and into the empty street. He didn't let go of her arm until he had secured her into his BMW.

"What were you thinking? You say we need to talk, and then you try to get them to come back with us?" he asked, backing out of his parking space.

Devon didn't bother saying anything. She was trapped, hopelessly trapped, and she had done it to herself. Her meager attempts at getting Hadley or Garrett's attention had only upset him.

She hoped that she could keep Reid's anger at bay. She was starting to doubt her own sanity at ever agreeing to leave Jenn's with him. She turned toward the window and closed her eyes. Her thoughts drifted back to Brennan—heated kisses, soft caresses, trusting conversations, freedom. She was doing this for him. After it was all over, maybe he would forgive her.

"Wait…" Devon said, actually paying attention to her surroundings for once. "This isn't the way to Hadley's."

Reid tightened his grip on their laced fingers. "I thought we could use some privacy."

"I thought we were going back early for privacy," she said, her voice coming out hysterical. This couldn't be good.

"Haven't you exploited their hospitality enough, Devon? I think it's a good idea for them to have the place to themselves tonight. I thought it would be a good surprise," he said, smiling.

He took a turn that led them farther away from the apartment.

She didn't even have a pretense to hide her fear. Her heart was hammering, and her breath was coming out heavy. Where was he taking her? She didn't feel comfortable talking to him in a place she thought of as home, so she certainly wouldn't feel any better somewhere else.

"Where are we going?" she asked in a demanding tone.

"Don't you like surprises, Devon?" he asked as calm as ever.

She knew he could tell she was afraid. She hated that fear was taking her over because she was pretty sure he reveled in it. He liked to see her cower and back away. He liked to have control. She was giving him what he wanted, and she couldn't do anything to keep herself in check.

A few minutes later, Reid pulled up to the valet of a tall skyscraper, and the valet helped her out of the car. She then realized where they were. She hadn't thought that she could feel sicker, but he had proven her wrong.

A hotel. Really? A hotel? She couldn't believe this was where he was taking her. Okay, yes, she could. It made perfect sense. She almost made a smart-aleck comment about whether the place charged by the hour. Luckily, she restrained herself. She didn't even want to think about what happened in hotels by the hour. That might actually break her character.

The valet zoomed off with his car, leaving Reid alone with Devon.

He smiled brightly at her. "Nice surprise, right?" He wrapped his arms around her waist and pulled her in close. "I missed you so much, Dev."

Devon stepped out of his embrace. "I can't go upstairs with you, Reid."

"Why?" he asked, his eyes hardening.

"I don't think it's a good idea," she said, trying to remain strong.

Waiting for Reid's reaction was like turning the handle to a jack-in-the-box, knowing it was going to pop in your face.

"You haven't seen me in two-and-a-half months. I get us a nice hotel room in the city, and I'm excited to see you. And you don't want to go up with me?" he asked. "What's wrong with you, Devon? What's changed since you left?"

Devon sighed and looked down at the ground. What was wrong with her? Maybe it wouldn't be that bad. They had a lot of stuff to talk about, and it's not like they could stand outside the hotel all night.

"Are you seeing someone else? Is that what this is about?" he asked.

She heard the tension in his voice, and she tried to remain perfectly calm. If she reacted at all to her thoughts of Brennan, it would be bad. She couldn't let Reid know. She had to keep that one thing from him. She was safe as long as Brennan's identity was kept safe.

"No, I'm not seeing anyone," she said softly, staying as calm as possible. "I just feel like we're rushing."

"We've been together for three years. How could we possibly rush this?" he asked, reaching out for her.

"You know what I mean," she said with a shrug.

"Just hear me out, Dev," Reid said softly. He cupped her chin and lifted her face to his. "I love you so much. I've missed you something fierce. If you feel like I'm rushing you, then I'm rushing you. I want to talk. I want to spend time with you. It's been too long since I've gotten to be with you. Just come upstairs with me."

Devon bit her lip and stared up into the face of the man that she had thought for years was her greatness, her true love. Something in his pleading seemed to weaken her resolve. Maybe it would be different. If he loved her, maybe it would be different.

"Please come with me, Dev. I've been a mess without you." He planted a tender kiss on her lips.

"All right," she said softly, breaking the kiss. "We'll go upstairs and talk."

He smiled like he had won a prize, and then he took her hand and walked her into the hotel. They took the elevator, and after they reached the floor and found their room, Reid slid the room key into the slot. Devon walked in before him and heard him push the lock over to bar entrance. She swallowed and looked around. It was nice enough with a small living area and a king-size bed. She didn't even bother looking in the bathroom. The last thing she wanted was to see another one of her nightmares.

Devon decided to take a seat on the chair in the living space. It faced the door and away from the bed. She wanted a clear view of the exit, and she wanted to avoid the bed at all costs. That was the way she wanted to handle this, focusing on a clear escape route.

"Okay..." Reid walked up behind her and began to massage her shoulders.

When he touched her, she tensed up, and he just rubbed harder. She was so on edge. She didn't know what was going to happen.

"You said you wanted to talk, so let's talk."

"Um…all right," she began.

"Let's talk about how you lied to me. Or we could talk about how you ran away to Chicago. How about we talk about how you've been acting all night or how scared you looked when I found out that you were lying? Maybe we should just talk about the bartender," he said, his voice thick with venom.

Devon felt like she had stopped breathing. Not Brennan. They couldn't talk about Brennan.

"Ah, so it is the bartender then," he said like he had stumbled upon something.

"Reid," she gasped out, trying to find air.

"You said you wanted to talk. I think we can talk about him first. Did you fuck him?"

He pushed into the muscles of her shoulders so hard that she tried to jump away from him, but he held her tightly in place.

"Reid, that's not why I'm here," she cried. "Stop! You're hurting me!"

He only held her more firmly. "Sometimes, I don't think you listen to me unless I force you, Devon."

"I'm listening!" she spat in frustration, trying to wrench herself away from his grasp.

"I don't think you are because you haven't answered my question yet. Did you fuck him? It's a yes or no question, Devon."

She swallowed. She couldn't talk about Brennan. How did Reid know? She had done everything she could to keep Reid from finding out, yet he had still figured it all out. She wanted to break down and cry, but Reid didn't deserve her tears.

"No answer, Devon? You lost your voice somewhere? I'll just assume that means yes." He let go of her shoulders and walked around to the front of the chair.

She tried to stand, but he pushed her back down to a sitting position.

"You were here acting like a whore while I was in St. Louis missing you. Doesn't really seem fair to me, does it?"

He was acting completely insane. She needed to get out of there. This was going nowhere fast. How had she let him manipulate her so perfectly? He had preyed upon her weakness and her desire to make him happy. Even when she was desperate to get rid of him, it was hard to break old habits. For so long, the thought of being without Reid put her in an agonizing state of self-doubt and fear, but now, she realized she had only projected what it actually was like when she was with Reid on to what she assumed it would be like without him. Living without Reid had led her to Brennan, and when she was with him, she had neither self-doubt nor fear.

"You wanted to talk, but I'm doing all the talking," he said. "Don't you have anything to say for yourself?"

He grabbed her arms and hoisted her out of the chair he had just thrown her into. His hands circled her bicep and squeezed, pulling her face-to-face with him. The pressure on her arms was agonizing.

"You want to know why I left?" she asked. "This is why I left. I was tired of you hurting me."

"If you didn't hurt me so badly, I wouldn't have to do anything. Why do you want to hurt me, Devon?" he asked. He shook her forcefully. "Explain it to me. Why would you leave me, lie to me, cheat on me?" he yelled.

A tear ran down her cheek, and there was nothing she could do about it. "Reid, please," she said, blinking back tears. "Don't hurt me."

"I shouldn't hurt you?" he asked in disbelief. He slammed her back into the wall. "I shouldn't hurt you? After what you did to me, you think I should just let you go? You think I should let someone else get his grubby hands on you? You're mine, Devon!" he yelled into her face. "You're mine!"

Reid threw her on the ground, and her head collided with the corner of the side table. She saw spots through her vision while she heard ringing in her ears. She was sure Reid was saying something, but she wasn't sure what it was. Her breath came out in gasps as tears poured down her face, and then the shock of the fall hit her. She tentatively reached her hand to the back of her head and felt the lump that was already forming. It was too tender to even touch lightly with her fingertips.

"Do you hear me?" Reid cried, bending over and forcing her to look at him.

"What?" Devon whispered, her voice light and wispy. She didn't feel too well.

"You're not even listening to me," he cried, looking maniacal. "You've got to be fucking kidding me. How can I make myself any clearer to you?"

"I don't know," she said, trying unsuccessfully to stand.

She felt silly sitting on the floor with him towering over her, screaming at her, but she needed to let the stars clear first. She had seen stars before. Sometimes, she had blacked out from them. She couldn't black out right now. She needed to keep her mind active. No sleeping.

Think about something else. Think about Brennan. What would he do if he were here? He was a doctor's son. He would take care of her, hold her while she cried, and kiss her wounds. He wouldn't do anything to harm her. He would wipe her tears away and tell her he never wanted to see her cry again. He thought she was beautiful. That made her smile.

"Oh, you have something to smile about?" Reid yelled, breaking through her reverie. "Do share what is so funny."

"Nothing," she said, trying to stand again.

Reid grabbed her wrist and yanked roughly until she was on her feet. Her shoulder wrenched, and she was sure he was going to pull it out of its socket. By the time he had lifted her all the way to her feet, her shoulder was screaming at her. She steadied herself on the wall to keep from falling back over. The stars were clearing a bit, but she still felt slow and hazy all over. Her mind needed to start clearing. Reid was going over the edge, and she couldn't afford to be out of it.

"That's right. You are nothing without me. Just look at you," he said, gesturing to her. "You're a wreck."

"I'm a wreck because of you," Devon mumbled.

Reid laughed at her. "You think I made you a whore? I don't even know why I want to be with you, except that I love you. I will eventually forgive you for the things you have done wrong."

"You'll forgive me?" she asked in disbelief. Really? Was he going to try and blame her for everything?

"That's just the kind of guy I am," he said a bit too calmly.

Devon closed and opened her eyes, feeling the haze slowly lift. It was too slow, much too slow. She hadn't had that much to drink so that she could stay alert, and now, with one tumble, she was losing it. She tried keeping her eyes closed longer to see if that would help, but when she opened them again, Reid was standing right in front of her.

When he pressed her backward, she swallowed, wondering what else he could possibly want from her. She was a fool to believe that he would just be able to talk, that he wouldn't hit her like he had every other time. And she would be a fool now to think he was done with her.

Reid reached out and stroked her hair like she was a pet. He was staring at her possessively, and it was terrifying. His subdued demeanor after an outburst frightened her more than the outburst. At least when he exploded, she knew what to expect. The restraint made it more difficult to judge him.

His hand trailed down her side to her waist. Her head started to clear, and all she could think about was escaping. She wanted to run. She wanted to get away, but she couldn't move. He kissed her cheek, across her jawline, down her neck, across her collarbone… anywhere he could reach. Devon whimpered, trying to shift away from him, but his body held her in place.

"Reid, stop," she pleaded.

He picked her up like a rag doll and carried her across the room to the giant bed. Her panic heightened at the thought of what he might be thinking.

"Reid, please stop. Please. No!"

He tossed her back on the bed, and before she could scramble away, he yanked on her ankle and pulled her flat against the bed.

"If you're going to act like a whore, I'll treat you like one. You're mine." He ran his hand up between her legs and massaged the sensitive skin with his thumb. "I'm going to take what's mine."

Devon gasped in shock at his eager touch. It felt so wrong. He had been forceful before, but that had been when she trusted him. This was different. This was…that word she never thought about. No, she couldn't even think about it now. It was demoralizing.

Without a second thought, Reid grabbed her underwear and yanked them down past her knees. Tears burst from her eyes as he probed her body. It was a violation, and it felt wrong, so wrong. She tried to pull away from the touch, but he held her legs open, so she couldn't move.

"Reid, no. I don't want this! I don't want you to do this!" she yelled, feeling more alert than she had minutes before.

"You'll get what you deserve, and I'll take what I want," he said matter-of-factly.

She closed her eyes and tried to think of what to do. She had to get away. She repeated that to herself a few times. She couldn't let him get away with this.

When she heard a zipper, her eyes flew open. Reid wrenched his pants down and moved to position himself. He was already hard. He must have gotten off on the control, at having her weak, at taking what he wanted. It was sick and twisted.

Before he had the chance to do anything further, Devon screamed at the top of her lungs. She didn't know if anyone was around, but her fight-or-flight instinct was taking over, and she couldn't let this happen. She had endured enough. This was too much.

Reid's hand clamped down on her mouth. When he leaned forward over her, she jabbed her fingers into his eyes. He cried out in pain, pressing one hand over his eyes. He used the other hand to backhand her with enough force to knock her off the bed. Devon screamed again as she tumbled to the floor.

It felt like her eye had exploded as blood rushed from her nose all at once. She pressed her hand to her cheek, and it hurt all over, but she didn't have time to think about it. She stood as quickly as she could and rushed toward the door.

Devon had just yanked it open when Reid was upon her. He reached out for her, and she turned and brought her knee up into his groin. Then, she slammed the door open into his head. He fell backward, but she hadn't knocked him unconscious. It gave her just enough of a head start to make it out of the room and run down the hallway.

She jammed the elevator button as many times as she could. Devon heard him rushing down the hallway, coming after her, just as the elevator door dinged open. Adrenaline threw her into the elevator, and the door closed just before Reid got there. She clicked the button for the lobby and prayed to whatever god would listen that she made it to the bottom floor before he could run down the stairs.

In the mirrors of the elevator, her reflection stared back at her. She could already see her face swelling up like a balloon. She would for sure have a black eye tomorrow. He had only ever given her one of those before. She choked back tears.

The doors opened on the bottom floor, and she ran as fast as she could out of the hotel. People stared at her, but she didn't care. A cab was idling in front of the hotel, and she yanked open the door before the valet could even approach.

"Where to?" the cabbie asked, pulling out of the hotel entrance.

Devon leaned her head back against the seat of the cab and slowly breathed out a sigh of relief. She had made it. She had gotten away.

CHAPTER 27
Finding Your Way

THE CAB MERGED into traffic and began to drive her away from the hotel. Devon pulled out her phone with shaky hands. She needed to get a hold of Hadley. She needed to tell her about Reid. That had to be the first place he would look when he came after her. She wasn't stupid. She knew he wouldn't stop until he got what he wanted. He had been holding back since he had gotten here, and the hotel room had pushed him over the edge. She didn't know what he would do next. All she knew was that she needed to stay away from him…or she would never get away again.

"Come on, Hadley," Devon grumbled into the phone as it rang.

Hadley's voice mail picked up, and Devon hung up and tried again. No luck.

"Fuck."

She needed to keep Hadley and Garrett safe. No one else needed to get hurt tonight. Knowing what she had to do, she dialed Garrett's number. He was normally up this late since he didn't have to work in the mornings. He better answer!

Garrett answered on the second ring. "Devon?"

"Garrett, thank God you answered. I've been trying to reach Hadley," she said desperately.

"Where have you guys been? I thought you were coming back to the apartment. I tried reaching you, but you never answered. I was waiting up for you," he said a hint of panic in his voice.

"Reid took me back to a hotel. He said he wanted privacy," she told him.

"A hotel? Are you okay? What's going on?"

"No. I don't know. Reid got out of control." She didn't want to tell Garrett. She didn't want to confide in him. But what other choice did she have? She needed him right now. "He hit me. I just barely got away."

"Fuck, Dev!"

She could practically see him pacing the apartment while he talked to her. It was a common habit of his.

"Do you need me to come get you? Are you safe?"

"No. No. I'm in a cab. I'm safe for now," she whispered.

"Good. I'm glad you're away from him. Are you on your way here? I can go downstairs and wait for you," he said.

She heard shuffling on the other end, like he was pulling on shoes or something.

"Garrett, no. I'm not coming back there tonight. That's where he expects me to go. I'm not safe there," she told him.

"Devon, you're safe here. Where else are you going to go?" he asked.

The words hung out between them. She didn't want Garrett to know where she was going. She didn't want anyone to know where she was. She couldn't risk Reid finding out.

"It doesn't matter. I don't feel safe. I need to hole up somewhere," she said.

"So…you're going to go see Brennan?" Garrett asked cautiously.

Devon closed her eyes and tilted back her head. Brennan. No, Garrett couldn't know that was where she was going.

"No, I'm not going to see Brennan. He's not happy with me right now. Don't blame him. I'll find somewhere else."

"Devon, I don't like this," Garrett said.

"Well, I don't like the possibility of getting hit again," she said with a finality to the statement.

"I…don't blame you. I'm so sorry, Devon. I didn't know. I would have never let you leave if I knew," he rambled on with his apology.

Devon shook her head, trying to understand his words. The adrenaline from her confrontation with Reid was wearing off, and she felt herself slipping toward unconsciousness. The stars were coming back, and her head was pounding. Her cheek had gone numb, and the blood had stopped, but she didn't think feeling numb was a good thing. Numbness meant severe pain later. Her eye was swelling, and she wondered if it would seal shut.

"What are you talking about, Garrett? I'm not feeling that well," she whispered. Her voice was slipping. This wasn't good.

"Devon, I'm so sorry. I know you have no right to forgive me. I don't expect you to. I wouldn't forgive me," he said.

"Garrett, I'm over the kiss. It doesn't even matter anymore," Devon said softly.

"Not the kiss, Dev," he said. "More than that—"

"Whatever you're talking about, it doesn't matter. I'm alive. That's what matters."

Garrett sighed on the other line. "It's not all that matters. It's the most important thing, but it's my fault that it's even a consideration."

Devon sat up slowly and tried to piece together what he was trying to tell her. Something more than the kiss. Something that mattered besides her being alive. Something that was his fault. Her heart sank.

"What are you trying to say, Garrett?" she asked, the fear of his answer creeping into her voice.

"I'm so sorry, Devon. I was the one who answered your phone when Reid called."

Devon felt all the air whoosh out of her lungs at once. Garrett had been the one who had talked to Reid. That was how Reid had gotten to her so fast. She hadn't gotten a chance to ask him, and likely, he would have lied anyway. It just didn't make sense. Why would Garrett do that?

"I know. I'm sorry, Dev."

He sounded miserable, but he knew nothing of misery compared to her.

"I was trying to protect you. I was trying to get him to leave you alone. I never expected him to show up."

Maybe Garrett had been trying to protect her. Maybe he had answered to tell Reid to fuck off. Maybe he hadn't expected Reid to show up, and if that were the case, he certainly wouldn't have expected Reid to hit her. Maybe those things were true, but it was still inexcusable. Garrett was the only one who had known the whole story. He was the only one who knew what it meant to keep it all a secret.

"Devon? Are you still there?" Garrett asked into the phone.

"Yes. Just keep Hadley safe. Don't let Reid inside. No matter what he says, don't let him in," Devon said, sticking to business. She didn't know what Reid would do, and right now, that was more important than dealing with Garrett.

"Devon—"

"Do you not understand that he's dangerous?" she asked gruffly into the phone. "Stop with the self-pity for one second, and tell me that you will do what I told you. I don't want anyone else to get hurt."

"I understand," he said, her harsh words clearly sobering him up.

Devon hung up. That was all the confirmation she needed. As long as Hadley was all right, then Devon just needed to worry about herself. She couldn't think about Garrett right now. That anger would make her boil over. The only benefit from his words was that it shocked her system, keeping her awake long enough to reach her destination.

***

THE CAB PULLED over, and she paid the bill. She didn't feel too bad as long as she didn't touch her face. She knew this was nothing compared to how she would feel tomorrow. Her head was pounding, and that was the worst part. She just wanted her headache to go away. She hoped it didn't last that long.

Devon stood before the door with a sigh. She reached her hand up to knock, but then she dropped it back down again. There wasn't anywhere else for her to go or anywhere else she wanted to be. Still, she felt terrible. Her injuries went far beyond the physical. She hoped, with time, she could rectify everything in her life. Time was all she had to offer. She didn't know if it would be enough.

Reaching out for the source of courage that had pushed her to this point, Devon knocked on the door. A short while later, the door swung inward, and Brennan stood before her, shirtless. She sucked in a deep breath. He looked gorgeous. He was a bit of a wreck with tangled hair and rumpled shorts, but it worked for him. Everything seemed to work for him.

"Devon," he said softly, his mouth falling open at the sight of her. His eyes grew wider and wider as he took in her swollen eye and the blood that had fallen on her dress. "What happened to you?"

He looked shocked, and she didn't blame him.

"Can I come in?" She looked over her shoulder. She was worried that Reid had somehow been able to find out where she was.

She waited for Brennan to say something, but he didn't. He just stared at her. Then, when she opened her mouth to say something else, he moved forward and pulled her into him. She wrapped her arms around his neck, and his arms encircled her waist, holding her tightly. He breathed her in as she tried to hold back the tears. Just being held had never felt this good.

He pulled back and found her lips. He kissed her with a desperation that bordered on delirium. She returned his eager kisses and backed him into the apartment. She wanted this. She wanted him. He was the only thing that had kept her going through the entire ordeal with Reid. Thinking about Brennan had given her a reason to push forward and get away from Reid. She didn't have to be under Reid's hold any longer. She was better than that, and Brennan had been the one to show her that.

Devon broke away long enough to shut and lock the door. She wasn't going to take any chances.

Brennan had his hands back on her immediately, pulling her in and holding her close. "You came back," he said. "You left, and you came back."

He walked backward with her down the short hallway and turned into his bedroom. The whole place smelled so much like him that it made her dizzy. Or was she already dizzy? She didn't know. All she knew was that Brennan felt right.

"I came back," she repeated.

He bent down and brought their lips together again. She felt like everything that had happened since Reid had returned to her was just a fleeting moment in time. Each kiss from Brennan was healing the wounds, pushing all the hate out of her life. Being there with him was like starting fresh all over again.

"You can't leave again," he said when they finally broke apart.

"I'm not going to," she told him.

"I'm serious, Belle," he said, brushing his lips against hers again. "Watching you walk out the door was like hearing that my dad had died all over again. I don't want to let you go."

"I never wanted to let you go," she said, swallowing back the tears. "But…I had to for your own safety."

The tears flowed freely then, and the pounding in her head intensified.

God, it hurts so bad, she thought.

"Shhh," he said, pulling her into him. "It's okay. You don't have to worry about my safety. I can take care of myself. I only worry about you."

"I didn't want him to hurt you," she blubbered through her tears.

"That guy? Your ex?" He really looked at her and examined her swollen eye. "Did he do this to you?" He sounded equal parts shocked and angry.

Well, maybe he was a bit more pissed.

Devon nodded, but that was a bad idea. "I don't…feel too well," she said, resting her hand on his shoulder.

"Hey, look at me." He softly cradled her head in his hands. "What did he do to you? Do you remember?"

"Yeah," she said, trying to focus on the task at hand.

"Hey, hey, now. Just look at me. Look at me." He stared into her eyes, looking at them under the light. "Just tell me one thing that happened."

"He tried to rape me," she whispered, saying it because it was the one thing that stood out.

Brennan hissed between his teeth as his eyes hardened. He looked murderous. She had never seen him so angry before.

"Anything else?" he said through gritted teeth. "Did he shake you really hard? Or did you hit your head when this happened?" He pointed at her eye.

Did she hit her head? She was having a hard time remembering what happened. She had a foggy thought about a side table. Wait… yes, she had hit a side table. Stars. She had seen a lot of stars.

"I hit the corner of a side table," she said, her voice slurring.

"Okay." He scooped her up in his arms before she could collapse. "I think you have a concussion. We should get you to a hospital."

"I can't go to a hospital!" she cried hysterically. "He'll find me!"

"Devon, please let me take care of you."

"No hospitals!" she repeated.

"You're not exactly in a condition to argue with me."

Carrying her over to his bed, with one hand, he pulled the

comforter back on his bed and gently placed her down. He grabbed an extra pillow and stuffed it behind her head, so she would be more comfortable for the time being.

"Please," she said, drawing her knees up to her chest, "I'll let you take care of me. Just no hospitals."

Brennan sighed in a way that showed he was going to give in. How could he deny her anything when she was in such a state?

"All right. I know a thing or two about concussions, but if it gets worse, I'm taking you to the hospital. You might need an MRI to check for brain damage. I'm not going to fuck around with head injuries just because your ex might find you. Deal?" he asked.

"Deal." She was able to relax now that she knew she wasn't going anywhere.

"I'll be right back. I'm going to get you some ibuprofen and an ice pack."

He returned with the medicine and a large glass of water, which she took without complaint. She placed the glass on the nightstand and then leaned back into the bed. He adjusted the ice pack to the back of her head and Devon winced slightly at the tender spot. She already felt much calmer and so comfortable. She just wanted to sleep. Her eyes fluttered closed. It felt nice.

"Hey," he said, sinking into the bed next to her. "No sleeping just yet. I want to make sure you're all right."

"No sleeping. Got it."

Brennan found her hand and circled his thumb against her palm. "Can you tell me what happened? It might help you stay awake."

She nodded slowly. She had been planning to tell him that night anyway. Now, she was here, like fate had reasoned that this was their night together. Too bad fate had taken a pretty disastrous turn.

"Yeah. Where should I start?"

"The beginning, I suppose. Wherever is good for you." He brought her hand up to his mouth and kissed it. "I'm here for you."

Devon smiled and started from the beginning, the very beginning. "When I was in high school, I was dating this guy, Mason," she began. "I'd known him all of my life. His mom was my mom's best friend. I think they had arranged for us to be married while we were still in the womb. I think it's how I got my nickname, Dixie."

"Dixie?" he asked, unable to hold back his chuckle.

Devon nodded. "Mason and Dixie. Mason Dixon. I'm sure you get it."

"How Southern, Belle," he said, squeezing her hand lightly.

"Exactly. My mom still calls me Dixie even though I've told her a million times that I hate it. Anyway, long story short, Mason and I dated through almost all of high school. I was a cheerleader, and he was the quarterback. I know, big surprise. It's really cheesy and embarrassing."

"That sounds like everything in high school."

Devon smiled faintly. "Yeah. Well, as we grew up, we grew apart. It was only natural. We weren't the same people anymore. I didn't want to be a country music singer or Dixie or anything related to my parents' life, which included him, and he just wasn't okay with that."

"I could see that if you had been together all your life," Brennan said.

"We had this abandoned house that we used to meet up at." Devon's cheeks flushed. "I'm sure you can imagine what for. Anyway, I told him I didn't want to see him anymore. He freaked out and slapped me. I started crying and swore I was going to tell everyone, but he apologized and then freaked out even more. It never happened again, but I think it was part of the reason I chose to go to Wash U," she whispered. "When Reid hit me the first time, I just thought that he was like Mason …that he wouldn't do it again, but he did…"

"You made the right choice by leaving," Brennan said, drawing her closer.

Devon shook her head. "I'm not sure my choices were ever right. If I'd made the right choices, then I would have outted Mason. I would have outted Reid. Then, maybe all of this would have turned out differently."

"And maybe then, I never would have found you," he said, softly kissing her swollen cheek.

"I would have found you," she whispered.

"Good. I wouldn't have wanted another life that didn't include you."

"Me either."

He smiled. "Tell me the rest of the story."

And so she did. She told him everything she had told Garrett that night she had mistakenly decided to trust him with her secret.

It hurt just as bad the second time. She hoped that the pain would dampen over time. She also hoped that she wouldn't have to tell the story that much. She knew at least two other people who needed to know—her mom and Hadley. Maybe if she was completely honest with them, they would be able to forge a better relationship again. She knew it would take time.

When she finished, she found that her tears had dried up, and Brennan had his arm around her shoulders. She didn't feel like he was trying to control her. She only felt that he wanted to comfort her...be there for her in any way that he could. She turned her face up to him, and then she felt his lips land softly on hers.

"Belle," he whispered against her lips.

"Yeah?" she asked.

He said stared down at her intensely, and she found herself gripped in his gaze.

"I think I knew you were running the first time I saw you," he said. "I just didn't know what you were running from, but I think, all along, you were running toward me."

CHAPTER 28
Following Me

Sleeping through the night and much of the next morning had been a surprise to wake up to. More ibuprofen waited for her on the nightstand. She smiled and then immediately winced from the pain in her face.

After taking the medicine, she padded into the bathroom to take a look at her face. One of her eyes was swollen shut, the other eye had a large black circle under it, and her face looked like hell. The spot on the back of her head where she had fallen and hit the side table had a huge knot.

Devon swallowed back tears as she stared at the damage to her face. She felt even more defeated than she looked. How had she let Reid get to her again? She had left St. Louis. She had thought she was safe, and still, he had managed to break her. It was even worse this time because she had finally started feeling like herself again. Running away from him was the best thing she had ever done. It was the only reason she had retained her sanity.

She couldn't let this keep happening. She had to do something. She didn't know what that was, but she had to figure it out to move on with her life.

All she really knew was today was going to be roughhh.

Devon walked out of the bathroom and sat down heavily on the bed. Brennan appeared in the doorway with a smile. His smile faltered when he got a good look at her face.

"Oh, Belle," he said, walking over and taking a seat next to her on the bed. He kissed her temple next to her swollen eye, like he intended to kiss away the pain. "It's good to see you're awake. I've been checking on you off and on to make sure you are doing all right."

"I can't believe I slept for so long," she said, leaning into him for support.

"Injuries like that require a lot of rest. It's good that you slept." He kissed the top of her head. "Do you mind if I take a look at you?"

"Go ahead." She didn't even want to look at herself.

Turning her face toward him, he examined her more closely than he had the night before. "Are you sure we can't take you to a hospital to get this looked at?"

"I never went before, and I recovered just fine," she said, wanting nothing to do with hospitals.

Brennan winced. "I hate that you've ever gone through this before, let alone all by yourself. I'm not a doctor yet. I want to take care of you, but I don't know how serious this all is."

"No hospitals, Dr. Walker," she said, poking him gently.

He laughed at the nickname and nodded. "All right, I got it." Then, he stared down at the bruises on her face, and his smile slipped again.

"Give me your best assessment," she said, straightening.

"I think you'll live," he said with a sigh. "At least, it doesn't seem like the brain damage has affected your sense of humor."

Devon giggled and swatted at him playfully. He grabbed her hands before they even made contact with him and pulled her in for a kiss. She wanted to give him more, but even the kiss was hard to manage with her face so messed up.

"Hey, I wanted to talk to you about something," he said, shifting uncomfortably. He reached out for her hands and laced them with his. "And I'm not sure you're going to like it."

"What is it?" she asked, narrowing her eyes suspiciously. What more could possibly go wrong in her life?

"I think you should file a restraining order against Reid," Brennan said.

"What?" she asked, snatching her hands back. That hadn't been what she had expected. "No. No. No. I can't do that."

"Devon, I said you wouldn't like it, but it's a good idea. Then, if he comes near you again, you can take legal action against him. I think you're within your rights to press charges for assault and battery after what happened last night. The least you can do is stop him from doing it again."

"No," she said, shaking her head and ignoring the pain. "No hospitals, no cops, no court. I should have made myself clearer."

"I already agreed to no hospitals. I can't agree to your other two. You're terrified that this guy is going to come after you for a reason. He's dangerous. He could hurt you. I couldn't live with that, and I can't be with you twenty-four/seven to make sure that it doesn't happen again," he said, scooting closer to her. "If you don't get a restraining order, which I still say is the very least you should do, your distaste for hospitals won't keep you from ending up in one."

Devon looked away from Brennan, tears pooling in her eyes again.

"He's applying to med schools in the fall. A record could keep him from getting accepted," she told him. She didn't know why it mattered so much to her, but Reid had mattered for so long. Old habits die hard.

"You want this guy to become a doctor?" Brennan cried. He was beside himself. "Are you out of your mind? Go look in the mirror, and tell me you want him treating patients!"

"No," she said softly. She didn't, but it felt wrong admitting it. "No, all right, I don't."

"Belle, don't cry." Facing her, he kissed her softly. "I didn't mean to yell. I just don't think someone without a shred of compassion should be working in the most selfless job."

"I know he shouldn't," she said. She had known that for a long time.

"You deserve to be with someone who makes you happy. Someone who won't complicate your life. Somebody who won't hurt you."

"Someone like you," she said.

"Someone like me."

***

Cook County Circuit Court was about a twenty-minute drive outside of the Loop in downtown Chicago. Devon stared up at the imposing building with its all-glass entrance. Her hands were shaking, but when Brennan touched her back, she began to relax. She could do this. She could be strong.

The wait was to be expected, and more than a half-dozen times she had tried to convince Brennan that they should just leave. He had smiled at her for strength before he told her that they had made the drive out for a reason. He was happy to wait it out with her.

He had called in at work again. Devon had heard Jenn bitching at him through the line, but he had carefully explained that Devon had a concussion. Jenn hadn't sounded pleased, but really, Devon needed Brennan around to help take care of her. She was doing a lot better, but she didn't trust herself to be alone.

"Devon Sawyer," a woman in a suit called when it was her turn.

She looked over at Brennan anxiously. "I can't do this. I can't. Brennan, what am I going to tell them?" She was panicking.

"The truth, Belle. Just tell them the truth, just like you told me. I'll be here waiting for you when you get done," he reassured her.

"Promise?"

"Promise," he said with a smile.

Devon stood stiffly and walked across the room with her head hanging down. "I'm Devon," she told the woman.

"Come with me," the woman said. She had a comforting voice, not what Devon had been expecting.

They walked down a hallway, and the woman took a seat behind a desk at a cubicle. Devon sat across from her and folded her hands.

"How can we help you today, Ms. Sawyer?"

"I, uh…want to file a restraining order against my ex-boyfriend," she said, trying to keep her voice from shaking.

"Of course. Let me get you the paperwork." She rifled through a file cabinet against the wall and handed it to Devon. "Just fill this out, and then I'll see when we can get you in to see the judge to plead your case."

"Thank you," Devon said softly, staring down at the paperwork in front of her. There was no turning back now.

***

A few hours after her arrival, Devon exited the Circuit Court office with a temporary restraining order in her shaking hand. The judge had approved her case and scheduled an official hearing in three weeks. She didn't like the thought of what might lead up to that. Reid would get served papers. He would realize what she had done—that she had taken legal action. It was a complicated system, and she would have to face him in court to make it permanent. The thought of seeing him again made her stomach twist.

Brennan seemed pleased that it had worked out in her favor. He had suspected it wouldn't take a lot of effort to get a restraining order. Her face was pretty beat-up, and she hadn't even had makeup at his place to hide any of it. She was a pro at covering bruises with makeup.

The drive back into the city had a calming effect, and Devon found her eyes drooping. It had been a long couple of days, and with her head injury, she was just so tired.

"Hey," Brennan said, shaking her shoulder softly.

She peeled open her eyes and saw that they were parked somewhere. She rubbed her eyes, and immediately, she regretted it as pain shot through one side.

"Where are we?" she asked with a yawn.

"Jenn's. I just wanted to stop by and get my check. Is that all right?" he asked, his face showing concern very clearly.

"Yeah. I'm not going inside though," she said, looking around. She could see they were parked in the alley behind the restaurant.

"I didn't expect you to. Want me to grab yours while I'm in

there?" he asked.

"I got mine last week. I don't know how you could even forget."

"Distracted by a beautiful woman, I guess," he said with a smile. He leaned forward and planted a kiss on her lips. "I'll only be a minute."

"All right. See you soon," she said sleepily.

Devon closed her eyes and leaned her head against the window. She could fall asleep again. When they got back to Brennan's, maybe she could sleep through the afternoon. She hoped he would hold her. Being with him calmed her nerves and allowed her to actually rest.

She felt herself drifting away when the handle of the car door clicked. Her reaction time was off, and when the door swung open, she tumbled sideways out of the car. She landed heavily on her hip as her hand struck the pavement.

"Ugh," she grumbled. She wiped gravel off her clothes and picked it out of her hand. A sharp piece had embedded itself into her palm, and blood pooled at the point of injury. "Great. Add that to the list."

She turned her head to look up at what had been the cause of her fall, and her vision blurred. She scrambled backward, but he was on top of her before she moved two feet.

"Did you think I would just let you leave?" Reid grabbed her arm and hauled her to her feet.

He looked terrible. His clothes were a mess. His usually perfectly manicured hair was tousled. His eyes were bloodshot, like he hadn't slept all night. Still, it was nothing compared to how she looked.

"Reid, stop! Leave me alone," she said, trying to pull away from him.

He ignored her and started dragging her down the alleyway. Her balance was shot, and she kept tripping over her feet and falling.

"Stop! Reid, fucking stop!"

"You're mine, Devon. And I said I would have what is mine," he said. "I always keep my promises."

She knew Brennan would return soon, but clearly, it was not soon enough. She didn't know where Reid was taking her. If he got her somewhere private, she didn't know what would happen. Putting all her energy behind it, Devon screamed at the top of her lungs. Someone had to hear her.

Turning around, Reid covered her mouth with his hand and shoved her back against the wall to hold her in place. "Shut up!" he yelled into her face.

Her eyes went wide at the ferocity in his gaze. He had gone crazy, completely crazy. Whatever shred of humanity he'd had left in him had evaporated.

"If you make another sound, I'll knock you out and carry you back to the car."

Devon didn't put it past him. Her heart was beating so hard that she thought it might jump out of her chest. She couldn't stop staring into his eyes and wondering where the man she had once loved was. Where was her greatness? Had he never actually existed and she had only clung on to hope like a child?

"I'm going to release you, and you're not going to make a sound or try to get away. Right?" he asked threateningly.

Devon nodded slightly. She was lying. She would fight him tooth and nail to get away.

He slowly dropped his hand, and she kept her mouth clamped shut. She wanted to take him by surprise. She heard footsteps crunch on the gravel, and Reid's head whipped to the side. Devon used the distraction to her advantage, and for the second time in two days, she brought her knee up into his groin. She hoped he would never be able to reproduce after this.

Reid dropped over, holding himself. She turned to run, but his other hand shot out, catching her in the chest and slamming her into the wall again. The air quickly left her lungs as he knocked the wind out of her, and she cried out. She heard footsteps running toward them, but she didn't look up to find out who it was. She was concentrating too hard on trying to breathe.

"Hey, get away from her!" Brennan yelled as he approached them.

Reid stood and faced Brennan, planting himself between Brennan and Devon. "Stay out of this. She's none of your concern."

"I beg to differ."

"Just get the fuck out of here!" Reid cried.

"I'm not leaving her," Brennan said determinedly.

"Brennan," Devon gasped out.

"I'm not going anywhere. Don't worry," Brennan said to her.

"Don't you talk to her," Reid growled. "Don't even look at my girl."

Brennan stared Reid down. "I think you should just calm

down and step away from Devon. She's hurt and probably needs medical attention. She suffered a concussion last night. Somehow, her head connected with a table." He waited for Reid to react, but he didn't. "If you care about her," Brennan said skeptically, "then you'll let me take her to a hospital."

"You're fucking stupid if you think I'm ever letting her near you," Reid said. "She's fine. She doesn't need to go to a hospital."

Devon slowly straightened, feeling air fill her lungs again. She closed her eyes and opened them again, adjusting to the light. She leaned back heavily against the wall for balance. "Reid, stop it," she said breathily. "Leave him alone."

"You can stay out of it, too," Reid said, not even looking at her.

Brennan started walking carefully toward Reid, like a circus ringleader holding off a lion with a wooden chair.

"What the fuck do you think you're doing?" Reid asked.

"I'm just going to check on her," Brennan said, inching in closer.

"Don't come any closer!" Reid yelled. "We're getting out of here."

Reid turned as if he was going to walk away from the scene, and then he countered and swung at Brennan. With considerable force, his right fist moved toward Brennan's face, and Devon screamed. Brennan must have been anticipating it because he deftly blocked the punch as if it bothered him no more than a fly. Reid was thrown off balance with the force of his own throw, and Brennan took the opportunity to connect his fist with Reid's jaw.

Reid cried out in shock and rushed Brennan. Brennan sidestepped Reid's advance, and then Brennan jabbed his fist into

Reid's kidney, causing him to double over.

"Not as easy to take on someone your own size, is it?" Brennan taunted Reid. "Don't worry. I won't tell anyone you were beat up by someone smaller than you."

Reid glared at him with murder in his eyes. He was bigger than Brennan, and that reminder made Reid try to counter with his size. Brennan saw it coming and ducked Reid's advance, sending him sprawling to the ground. Brennan rushed forward toward Devon, planting himself between Devon and Reid.

Reid scrambled to his feet and charged Brennan again. Reid threw a wild punch, but Brennan landed a hit first, cracking Reid's nose with a terrible popping sound that rang throughout the alley.

"You broke my fucking nose!" Reid screamed at Brennan.

Devon rushed past Brennan to stand between Reid and Brennan. She wasn't stupid though. She still stood closer to Brennan. "Stop!" she screamed. "Stop it! Just stop it! Hasn't there been enough fighting?"

"Devon," Brennan said, taking a step forward to help support her. She was wobbly on her feet.

"Reid, just stop. You've lost. You lost me," she said, trying to stay as strong as she could. "You've been following me in my dreams for months...and I want you to stop. I want you to stop following me. I'm not in your life. You're not in mine. You need to find a new life because we're over."

"Dev," Reid said, the life draining out of his eyes.

"No, Reid. We're done," she said. "I'm never letting you hurt me again. You've done enough damage."

"The papers," Brennan whispered.

Devon nodded. "I filed a restraining order. Someone will be serving you papers, and you'll have to appear in court."

"A restraining order?" Reid asked in a strangled voice. "But my med school applications."

"You should have thought about that," Devon whispered harshly, barely able to keep the tremble out of her voice, "before you ever laid your hands on me." She paused to let that sink in, and then she released a shuddering breath. "Low scores are the least of your problem. Good luck having your dad get you out of this one."

Devon felt herself sinking. Her vision blurred, wavered, straightened, and then blurred again. "Brennan," she said, her voice coming out slow, like her tongue was stuck to the roof of her mouth.

"Yeah, Belle?" he asked, pulling her in closer.

"You saved me."

"I'd do anything for you."

She smiled. Then, she felt her world tilt, and she lost consciousness.

CHAPTER 29
Filling in the Light

eep. Beep. Beep.

Devon's chest slowly rose and fell with the strange beeping noise. It clouded her already fuzzy thoughts, and it seemed to take over her consciousness. She tried to concentrate, but she found that tended to intensify the annoying sound. Instead, she thought about the placement of her body. Five fingers on the right hand. One. Two. Three. Four. Five. And five on the left hand. She could feel all ten of her toes, up to the balls of her feet, and across her arch to her heel.

Her face felt right but also wrong. It didn't hurt, but it didn't feel normal either. Her tongue felt solid, and her lips felt heavy. When she thought about her cheek, it only seemed to throb more, so she stopped. Her throat was dry, like she had swallowed cotton balls, and she started coughing at the thought.

Someone was at her side, taking her hand and slowly lifting her head off the pillow. She began to breathe easier. Devon remembered her eyes then, and they opened to the harsh lights. She blinked a few times, allowing her eyes to adjust, and then she squinted at her surroundings.

She was in a hospital. That much was obvious. White curtain, white bed, white floor. Sanitation heaven.

She saw that it was Brennan holding her hand. That made her smile despite her being in the hospital.

"Hey, Belle," he said, bringing her hand to his lips. "Good to see you're finally awake."

"I said no hospitals," she said immediately.

"I didn't hear you when you were unconscious," he said with a sad smile.

Devon giggled. "Fair point."

"How are you feeling?" he asked, taking a seat in the chair next to her.

"I've been better," she whispered.

"Are you in much pain? They gave you some painkillers, but I don't know if they have worn off," he asked, concerned.

"I'm doing okay." She squeezed his hand. "What happened?"

"You don't remember?" he asked with a frown.

"I remember, uh…Reid showed up. You guys got into a fight. I told him that we were over…and that's about it," she said, biting the side of her lip that wasn't swollen.

"That's about what happened. You passed out. When he pushed you into the wall, I guess it upset your already delicate condition. I scooped you up and drove you straight here. I was, uh…going to call the cops, but I was worried you might kill me when you woke up. I thought I'd leave that decision up to you…if that's what you want."

"No hospitals. No cops. No court."

"I know, but you've already broken two of those," Brennan said.

Devon narrowed her eyes. "No cops. Just because you keep breaking the rules doesn't mean I want to involve the police."

"I'll break every rule to keep you safe. The doctor said it was really good I brought you in," he said, pushing her hair back with one hand. "You've been out of it for a while."

"So…Reid just left?" she asked carefully. She was tired of being afraid of where he might turn up. She was beginning to see why the restraining order was a good idea.

Brennan shrugged and scratched the back of his head. He chuckled softly and looked away from her. "He was here earlier. They had to reset his nose. Seems he managed to break it in two places."

Devon giggled with him. "I wonder how that happened."

"I guess he was unlucky when he ran into my fist," he said. "Anyway, he tried to come see you. I hope you don't mind that I showed the restraining order to the nurses. He was escorted out of the building."

"Oh! The nurses escorted him out?" Devon asked.

"Uh…the cops escorted him out."

"Brennan! No cops!"

"I wasn't letting him anywhere near you. It's not like they arrested him…like they should have." He bent down and kissed her lips. "I'm just glad you're safe now. I don't care if you press charges. I just care that you're safe."

"I'm glad I'm safe, too," she said even though the injuries on her body told her that she didn't feel that safe.

Brennan leaned his forehead against her hand as he sighed softly. His lips found her hand, then her palm, and then the inside of her wrist. "You know what I'm going to do when you're feeling all better?"

"What?" she asked.

His lips traveled up to her elbow. "I'm going to kiss away every bruise and every scar and every headache. I'm going to kiss away every thought of heartache," he whispered. His kisses were now reaching her shoulder.

"You…you are?" she asked through gulps. When the beeps on the machine picked up speed, she tried not to blush.

"Yep. I'm going to kiss every inch of your beautiful skin, so when you look at it, all you see is me." He stopped his kisses and stared down into her eyes.

"All I see is you already," she responded huskily, trying not to let her mind stray to all the things she wanted to do to his body.

"I'll be a happy man every day that is true."

He bent forward and kissed her lips. Devon reached her arms up and wrapped them around his neck, anchoring them together.

Someone cleared her throat, and Brennan pulled back from the kiss. Devon blushed and looked over to see Hadley and Garrett standing together in the doorway.

"Hope we're not interrupting," Hadley said, planting her hands on her hips.

"Course not," Devon said. She looked back at Brennan. "I didn't know you called them."

Brennan shrugged. "I thought they'd want to know you were here."

"Of course we wanted to know you were here." Hadley tossed her oversized purse on the floor and rushed over to Devon's side. "You came to visit me when I was here. I couldn't imagine not visiting you."

"It's good to see you," Devon said with a smile.

"Do you guys mind giving us a minute?" Hadley asked, shooing them out of the room.

Brennan kissed Devon's forehead once more. "Want anything from the cafeteria?"

She smiled. Always thoughtful. "Jell-O."

He chuckled. "You're in the right place for that."

Hadley waited for Brennan to walk out of the room and close the door. "Oh my God, I can't believe what happened to you. How are you feeling? I'm so sorry I've been so completely self-absorbed. I had no idea any of this was going on. Don't kill Garrett or anything, but he told me what happened with you and Reid."

"He did?" Devon asked, her stomach twisting at someone else telling her story.

"Yeah, but don't hate him. He was worried about you, and he stayed up all night. When I woke up, he told me about it, and I was completely flipping out. I tried calling you, but you didn't answer. He said you weren't with Brennan, so I didn't even try him. I probably should have."

"I was, uh…worried that Reid might come after me at Brennan's, so I didn't want anyone to know where I was. Sorry, bad move on my part."

"No apologies," Hadley said, brushing off her apology. "I can't blame you for anything. Look at you."

"Ha! Yeah," Devon said with fake enthusiasm.

"Garrett also told me about what happened between you two," Hadley said softly. "He wanted to clear the slate. He said you were pissed at him and wouldn't forgive him. I don't blame you for that either, Dev. I'm sorry he did that though. The, uh…drugs really messed me up."

"What happened to you, Hadley?" Devon asked, wondering if Hadley would finally open up to her. "I never thought you would be someone to get caught up in drugs."

Hadley sighed heavily and tugged at her ponytail. "It started casually with some friends. It wasn't a big deal, but then, I was sneaking around everywhere and…it became a bigger deal than

I ever let on. Then, the stuff with Garrett not knowing and his parents on top of all the pressure at work…it just spiraled out of control." Hadley took a deep breath before continuing. "But I'm going to get better, Dev. That night with Garrett…I was paranoid, thinking he was cheating. I was angry all the time. When we got into our fight on the Fourth of July, I'd snorted some coke before the event. I was always too nervous around his parents. I shouldn't have gone off on him or his dad. I think my behavior pushed him over the edge."

"It doesn't matter, Hadley," Devon said, reaching out for her.

Devon hated that her best friend felt responsible at all for what had happened. Hadley had been selfish, but cocaine was addictive for a reason. It was hard to kick. Devon was just glad to see Hadley recovering.

"It does. My therapist said that I should try to right the wrongs in my life. I'm really sorry for not being there when you needed me…when you came to me for help. Even if you didn't ask for help, I should have known. And I'm sorry for Garrett's behavior. He and I have a lot to talk about and work out, but I really want to try with him, Dev."

"I know," Devon said.

"He said he wanted to talk to you for just a minute…that is, if you'll see him," Hadley said.

"Um…sure."

"All right. Let me go get him," Hadley said, standing. "I'm glad you're doing better, Dev."

"Thanks, Hadley."

When Hadley reached the door, she turned around and faced Devon with a devilish smile on her face. "I wish I had been there when Brennan beat the shit out of Reid."

Devon laughed and shook her head.

"I think I would have taken his balls if I knew what he had done to you," Hadley said.

"I believe you wholeheartedly, Hadley."

Hadley laughed and walked through the door.

A couple minutes later, Garrett shuffled into the room with a sheepish look on his face. "Hey, Devon," he said tentatively.

Devon sighed and looked out the window.

"I don't know if Hadley told you that I told her," he said awkwardly.

"She did."

"Oh, good," Garrett muttered. "I wanted her to know the truth about what I did because it was wrong of me under any circumstances. I shouldn't have kissed you. I shouldn't have... cheated on her."

Garrett cleared his throat when she didn't say anything. He started again. "I messed up, Devon. I was your friend, and I messed that up. I know that I'm part of the reason you're here. I'm not even going to ask for your forgiveness because if I were in your position, I think I'd have a hard time forgiving me."

Devon sighed and turned to look at him. He looked just like Hadley had said, like he hadn't slept all night. She wondered if he had been worried. Her heart softened some at the thought.

"So, while I don't expect you to forgive me, it doesn't mean I'm not going to try to be better. All I'm asking for is the chance to try to earn your trust again. I don't think it's fair to ask for more than that, but I've never been sorrier. I hate seeing you like this," he said, gesturing to the bed.

"Okay," she said softly. "It's okay. We'll, uh…get through it…get past it."

Garrett beamed like she had just handed him the keys to a brand-new sports car. "It's really good to hear that."

"Can I ask just one question?"

"Of course," he said hesitantly.

"Why would you answer my phone and tell Reid where I was?" She looked down at her hands to keep from crying again. She was tired of crying.

"I didn't mean for him to know where you were. I've replayed that phone call a million times in my head. I was so pissed that he was calling you. You're my friend, Dev. I didn't want to see you upset. I just told him to stop calling you, that you were working at Jenn's and that Hadley and I were taking care of you."

"Oh," she said. Hearing his explanation made it so easy to believe him. He looked too genuine to be lying. "I guess that's how he knew I was in Chicago."

"Yeah, only because I mentioned Hadley. I was stupid. I didn't think he'd be so determined to find you," Garrett said. "I hope I can make it up to you."

The door swung open then, and Brennan walked in, bringing a big smile to her face.

"They only had cherry. I hope that's all right," Brennan said, holding Jell-O out in front of him.

"Cherry is my favorite." She took the bowl when he handed it to her.

"I'm going to find Hadley," Garrett said, nodding his head toward the door. "I hope you feel better, Devon. I really do."

When their eyes met, unspoken words passed between them. She smiled slightly at him, and he returned the gesture.

"Thanks," Devon said just before Garrett walked out.

Brennan lounged and kicked his feet back in the uncomfortable hospital chair as Devon ate her Jell-O. As everything was with Brennan, their time together in the hospital was effortless. He occupied her time while she waited for the doctor to discharge her. He told her stories about following his dad around the hospital when he was growing up. She told him about her parents' music, how her mom and dad worked together to shape and flow the song, how they had tested them out on her when she was younger. That was before she had decided to take another turn with her life.

***

BEFORE SHE KNEW it, the doctor was there, checking her vitals and prescribing her more painkillers. Then, he sent her on her way. The medicine really worked, and she was laughing by the time they reached Brennan's Jetta.

"Let's get you back to bed. I think you could use another twenty hours of sleep." He shook his head as he helped her into the car, and then he shut the door.

When he sat down in the driver's seat, she rested her head on his shoulder.

"Sleep sounds nice," she said. "Will you sleep with me?"

He laughed. "Is that an invitation?"

"Open invitation."

"Oh man, I'm going to keep those painkillers around."

"You don't need them," she said, sliding her hand down the front of his shorts.

He rested his hand over hers and moved it to his thigh. "I'll take you up on that when you can think clearly again."

"I'm thinking very clear right now," she said through giggles.

Brennan shook his head and laced their fingers. "I'll believe that when you can walk unaided."

"Fine. Your loss."

"I'm not losing anything."

She smiled. "That's true."

"Your mom called while you were in the hospital."

"She did?" she asked, confused.

"On your cell. I saw it light up. Are you going to talk to her?"

Devon sighed and nodded her head. "Yeah, I am. But maybe after I've slept."

"That sounds like a good idea," he said, squeezing her hand.

Brennan drove them to his apartment and helped Devon up the stairs. As soon as they walked through the door, he picked her up and carried her into the bedroom. Sleep was pulling her under by then, and she let him help her into more comfortable clothes. They both crawled into bed, and he held her tight against his chest.

"Brennan," she whispered, feeling sleep drawing closer.

"Yeah?" he asked, kissing her shoulder.

"You're going to be here, right? You know, after this?" she asked.

"Belle, I'm going to be here for everything."

Brennan held Devon until she fell fast asleep.

Devon dreamed only of Brennan's face and the way he looked at her the first night they had spent together on the boat.

It was the first night she remembered what happiness felt like.

EPILOGUE

"I'm so proud of you," Brennan said.

Leaning down, he kissed Devon on the mouth. She returned his kiss full-on, wrapping her arms around his neck. He lifted her off her feet and spun her around until she threw her head back and started laughing. He buried his head into her shoulder and kissed her there.

When he finally put her back on her feet, Devon said, "I can't believe I did it."

"I can."

"Three months ago, I never would have gone through with this," she told him. "Gah! Three weeks ago, I wasn't sure I could do this."

"I knew you could do it. I'm glad you proved it to yourself though," he said, pressing his lips to hers again.

She closed her eyes and sighed. "Me, too. It feels pretty awesome."

Devon pulled out the little piece of paper that showed her permanent restraining order against Reid. They had just finished their hearing in court. Reid had showed his face. His daddy had gotten him a good lawyer, but when she brought out all the pictures of the physical damage that had been done to her body, the medical records, and the surveillance video from Jenn's, it was pretty clear what would happen.

Devon wasn't looking forward to the trial. But in the end, she had to think about everything he had done to her. This could ruin his life, but he had brought this upon himself. Reid was facing up to a year in prison if convicted of domestic battery. Devon expected he would get probation if his lawyer got what he wanted. Though, if Reid ever stepped foot near her again, he might end up in prison anyway. Devon was just tired of all the negativity. She wanted to be rid of Reid, and now, she was.

"Come on, let's get out of here," she said, slinging her arm around Brennan's waist.

Brennan guided her back to his car. She felt like a weight had been lifted off her shoulders. She had won. She had beat Reid. It wasn't even just that. She had proven to herself that she was strong. She had proven that she was better than her old life with

Reid. It felt good. She never knew how strong she was until it was all she had.

"Mind if we take a detour?" Brennan asked.

"I don't have anything to do today," she said, leaning her head back against the seat.

Life post-Reid was way better than she had ever thought it could be. She had to attribute a lot of that to Brennan, but she liked to give herself the credit, too. She knew though that without his help, it might have taken her longer to get her act together.

When she had spoken with her parents, they were mortified that she had endured so much at the hands of the man she had been dating. She thought they blamed themselves for pushing her and Mason together and then for not seeing what happened with Reid. But how could they blame themselves for what the men had done and what she had allowed to occur?

Her parents had tried to make up for it by offering to help her in any way they could. On their recommendation, she had started seeing a therapist in the city. Her mom was anxious to see her and take care of her. Before the conversation was even over, her mom had sent an email to Devon with a plane ticket home, so she could visit soon. Devon actually planned to use this ticket. Now that she could be honest, she was looking forward to spending time with her mom.

After everything with Reid, her mother was worried about where Devon would go and what she would do. Her mother didn't like the idea of Devon being back at Wash U with Reid, so Devon had finally told her parents that she had decided not to go back to school. She thought it would be best to at least take off the semester, so she could dedicate herself to recovery.

Her parents had offered to get her an apartment in Chicago since she had decided to stay, but Devon had declined. Hadley and Garrett had made it clear that she was welcome in their place for as long as she wanted. She didn't like being alone, so that worked out for her. Plus, it gave her the opportunity she needed to spend more time with her friend, like she had wanted to from the beginning, and then she could begin to rebuild that bond with Garrett.

Brennan had also told Devon that she could stay with him, but she had turned him down as well. As much as she liked Brennan, she couldn't let her life revolve entirely around a guy again. He had accepted her response with grace. It didn't really matter anyway since she spent so much time with him. The distance just helped ground her and give her space when she needed it.

"I can't believe school starts in a couple weeks, and I won't be going back," Devon said, staring out the window.

"You could still go back if you wanted," Brennan said.

He was always encouraging her to go back. She knew he wanted her to finish her degree, and when the time was right, she wanted to finish it. But now wasn't that time.

"I don't think so. I can't go back to that just yet. I need to get myself right first."

"I know. I just don't want you to think that you shouldn't go back..." He trailed off with an awkward pause.

She caught his meaning and turned to face him. "Do you think

I'm staying because of you?"

"I don't want that to be your reason."

"I want to be with you. I want to be in Chicago with you, but I'm not staying for you…if that makes sense. I know I need to finish college and get a job and all that. I just feel like I'll never really do any of that well enough if I'm not well enough mentally. That's why I'm staying. This is what I need," she tried to explain.

"Okay. Good," he said, smirking at her. "That's what I wanted to hear."

Devon relaxed back into the seat, feeling better now that she had explained herself. Therapy had helped with that. She found herself explaining everything to people. It was better than holing up inside of herself and being terrified of what she might say. At least now, she had a sense of control over what went on in her life. Brennan seemed to like it. He was her number one supporter. He always encouraged her to express her feelings and listened to her opinions.

"So, where are we going anyway?" she asked.

"You'll see." He smiled at her secretively.

Devon narrowed her eyes. "Is it a secret?"

"You could say that."

"Can I guess?" She bit her lip and tucked one foot underneath her.

"No," he said. "I'm not giving anything away. You'll like it…I think."

"I'll take your word for it," she said. She crossed her legs pretzel-style and stared out at the changing landscape.

Brennan pulled off of I-94 and started veering through the

streets. The area was nice, and Devon found herself admiring the beauty and simplicity of life in the suburbs. Her parents lived in the suburbs, and while this was nothing like southern Nashville, it had the same feeling.

"This area is beautiful. Where are we?" Devon asked as they crested a hill.

She sat up taller in her seat and stared out at the shore of Lake Michigan. It stretched for miles and miles past her line of sight. It was gorgeous and glorious in its magnitude.

"The North Shore. Evanston," he told her, driving down the hill.

"Wow," she breathed, transfixed on the passing scenery.

Brennan slowed to a stop in front of a large all-brick house on a plot that bordered the lake. "This is where I grew up," he said softly.

Devon's eyes left the house and landed back on Brennan. "This is…your dad's house?" she asked, feeling overwhelmed that he would bring her here.

"Yeah. It was. Mine now…I guess," he told her, pulling into the driveway.

After the car came to a stop, Devon opened the car door and slid out of the seat. Brennan popped the trunk and pulled out his guitar case. Devon smiled. She liked seeing him with that. He had been playing and singing to her a lot more when she was at his place. It relaxed her and brought her back to the first gig she had ever seen him perform. She had been so caught up in him and his music that she had left the venue. She hadn't trusted herself to be with him then. Her feelings were too strong even at that time.

They walked up to the front door, and Brennan just stood there with the key in his hand. He took a deep breath and slid the key into the slot. He turned the door and immediately disabled an alarm system. Devon cautiously stepped inside, feeling almost as if she were trespassing. But this was Brennan's home. He owned it. It belonged to him. It was somehow still a part of him.

He stood next to her, his muscles tensed, as he breathed in the emptiness that was once a home. She could tell this was hard for him. He had told her before that he only came up here to mow the lawn. She didn't know the last time he had been inside.

Devon reached out and placed her hand in his own. She squeezed gently, just letting him know she was there. She was there for him, just like he had always been there for her.

"I should have had someone come in here to clean beforehand," he said wistfully. It should have been the last thing on his mind, but the only thing he could concentrate on.

Devon didn't even notice that the house needed to be cleaned. She was too busy admiring the house itself with its massive high-vaulted ceilings, enormous fully furnished living room with a fireplace, and the twelve-person dining room table with antique china held in a nearby glass cabinet. The foyer opened to a spiral staircase, leading to a balcony upstairs. And that was just the view from the entranceway. Devon couldn't imagine what else lay beyond.

"It's beautiful, Brennan," she said, awestruck. She had been raised in a big house, but this was Brennan's house. It felt different.

"Thanks. My dad really cared about the place. He took good

care of it after my mom left. I guess I was in the fifth grade when that happened," he said with a shrug. "The house was too big for just the two of us. I think he wanted more kids, but he loved my mom too much to remarry."

"Is that why she thought he would leave her money?" she asked softly. She would have never asked that before, but now, she felt it was better just to get her questions out of the way.

Brennan faced her with a smile. "I think so. I'm glad he didn't leave her anything though. She didn't love him anymore. She didn't deserve it."

"No, probably not." Devon wrapped her arms around his middle and held on to him tightly. "I'm so sorry about your dad."

"Me, too, Belle."

He kissed the top of her head, and he let her hold him until they both had their emotions back under control.

"Come on, I'll give you a tour of the house, but first, I want to show you something."

He took her hand in his and walked them down a long hallway. Devon peeked into an open door on the left and saw a kitchen that was bigger than Brennan's apartment in the city. It had all dark cabinets, granite countertops, and stainless steel appliances. Devon gawked as she passed.

They entered into a sunroom framed with full-length glass windows. The entire room stretched out to the length of the house. It opened up onto an adjoining balcony that had wicker rocking chairs and a porch swing. The balcony had a set of stairs that led down to a covered rectangular pool. Beyond that was the entire expanse of Lake Michigan.

"Oh my God," she gasped.

"Pretty nice view, right?" he asked.

"Pretty nice?" she stuttered, turning to face him.

He was already staring at her.

Brennan dropped his guitar case on the porch, and then he bent down and kissed her, crushing her to him. His lips were hot on her. She threw her hand around his neck with abandon. All her thoughts stilled, and there was only the two of them. She was lost to the rest of the world, and for once, that was the right way to be.

They kissed like that until Devon pulled away. Breathless, her chest rose and fell heavily, and when he smiled, her insides ignited.

Grasping her hand again, he picked his guitar case back up, directed her down the set of stairs, around the pool, and down a large set of stairs to the shoreline. She kicked off her sandals before she sank her feet into the dark sand.

"Thanks for coming with me." He set his guitar case on the last step and then took a seat next to it.

Devon sat down on the step and stared out at the beautiful backdrop. "I wouldn't miss this for the world."

"I, uh…wanted to try something," he said, "if you'll humor me."

He reached for his guitar case, unlatched the lock, and pulled the guitar out of the container. It was the same one he had played on the night of his open mic performance. He had another one that he usually played at home, but she liked this one better. He picked at the strings and adjusted them until they were in tune. She watched his hands strum the guitar with precision. She had never thought she would be interested in a musician. She tended to steer clear of them, but as with everything else, Brennan was different.

Brennan started humming the final song that he had played at the show, "Moving Forward." She had heard it dozens of times over the last three weeks, and she knew all the words. Now, it made her heart happy rather than sad. He had known her pain even before she had allowed him in. That kind of chemistry and intuition astounded her.

He paused in the song, but he let his fingers continue to pick out the tune. "Will you do me a favor?

Devon nodded.

"Take the higher octave on the chorus?"

Devon stared at him. He wanted her to sing? She hadn't let herself sing anywhere, except the car and the shower, in years. She wasn't even sure if she still had a good voice. Music called to her but in lyric form only. She wasn't an artist.

She shook her head. "No, Brennan, I don't sing."

He smiled like he didn't believe her. "Humor me. No one else can hear you out here."

Devon looked around the shoreline. He was right. No one else was outside right now. The house was empty, practically deserted, and only the lake was before her. Still, she could hear herself.

"What if I sound terrible?" she whispered.

"Then, I'll make fun of you, and we can try again," he said with a laugh.

She rolled her eyes at him before she turned back to face the lake. She breathed in and out, letting the air calm her nerves. Her eyes closed just as he picked up the chorus once more. His smooth voice filled her ears softly, like he was waiting for her to harmonize with him. She could sense that he was about to stop, so she dug up the courage to join him.

Her voice was shaky at first. She didn't use it enough anymore. But she still sounded like herself, like she had when she used to sing for her parents, when they had told her she was going to be country music royalty one day. Brennan's song fit her voice better. They blended together with the music. They each felt every painful memory encapsulated in the words and sang them back to each other with more emotion together than they ever had separately. It was peaceful and healing. When the song ended, Devon opened her eyes and smiled.

"You were beautiful," he said, letting his hands rest on the guitar.

"Thank you. It's been so long since I've sang anything."

"Fooled me."

"I'm a fool for you," she said with a giggle, leaning forward to kiss his lips. Devon sighed, debating if she could go through with what she was thinking. Plucking up the courage, she asked, "Do you mind…if I try something? You know…since we're here."

Brennan smiled that gut-wrenching smile and nodded. "What did you have in mind?"

Devon reached into her purse and pulled out the notebook that she always carried with her, the one she never let anyone else see.

She flipped it open to a page near the back and left it resting on her lap. "You know that new song you've been strumming all week?"

He bit his lip like he was considering something, and then he started picking out a tune. "You mean this one?" he asked.

"That's the one."

"What about it? I've just been messing around."

Devon glanced down at her notebook and then back up at him, trying to draw on the courage he always gave her. "I wrote lyrics for it."

"You did?" he asked, surprised.

"Yeah. It seemed stuck in your head, but you weren't going anywhere with it. I could hear it, um…the words. I could hear the words you wanted to sing but weren't there yet. So, I wrote them down," she told him, looking up into his eyes. "I didn't think I would ever show you, but I think I could try…if you want."

"Of course I want to!" he said with an even bigger smile. "You're something amazing. You know that, right?"

Devon smiled hesitantly as he started the song from the beginning. The words flew out of her, like she had been waiting all her life to sing this song. She sang of knowing when to be strong, finding the strength buried within herself, and loving the person who showed it to her. She sang about Brennan and hope and acceptance. She poured her soul into the words until a tear fell down her cheek.

When she closed her song, Brennan set the guitar aside and held her in his arms.

"Devon, I don't know what to say."

"That's a first," she said with a chuckle.

"I've never had anyone do that before. It's like…you were in my head."

Devon sighed, planted a kiss on his lips, and then pulled back to stare into his eyes. "You know, my mama always told me that you are given a chance at greatness once in your lifetime. She found her greatness in my dad through music. She said, 'When it hits you, you won't know how you could have ever lived a day without. It's like the universe aligned itself perfectly, just for you.' I gave up hope on that a long time ago, I think."

"Belle…" he said softy, reaching for her.

"But I think I've known…well, especially after today," Devon said, "I think I found what my mama was talking about. You're my greatness."

The End

ACKNOWLEDGMENTS

For those people who helped me, you know who you are and you rock. I cried over this book, and when you cried with me, it made my heart happy. To everyone else who is crying and FEELS it, I love you too. And Joel, Hippo, and Goose

K.A. Linde is the USA Today bestselling author of the more than thirty novels. She has a Masters degree in political science from the University of Georgia, was the head campaign worker for the 2012 presidential campaign at the University of North Carolina at Chapel Hill, and served as the head coach of the Duke University dance team.

She loves reading fantasy novels, binge-watching Supernatural, traveling to far off destination, baking insane desserts, and dancing in her spare time.

She currently lives in Lubbock, Texas, with her husband and two super-adorable puppies.

You can reach her online at her website:
www.kalinde.com

Or Facebook, Instagram, and Twitter:
@authorkalinde

For exclusive content, free books,
and giveaways every month.
www.kalinde.com/subscribe